The Tarnished Rose

The Tarnished Rose

Robert Livingston

THE TARNISHED ROSE

iUniverse books may be ordered through booksellers or by contacting:

iUniverse
1663 Liberty Drive
Bloomington, IN 47403
www.iuniverse.com
844-349-9409

ISBN: 978-1-6632-1934-3 (sc)
ISBN: 978-1-6632-1935-0 (e)

Print information available on the last page.

iUniverse rev. date: 03/11/2021

Table of Contents - 1976

A Few Words

Most people with a bit of history running through their veins are very much enthralled with the "what if's of history." If, for example, Robert E. Lee had decided to avoid General Pickett's headlong charge into the face of booming Union cannons on Cemetery Ridge, might the South have carried the day? If the British, French and Spanish had elbowed their way into the Mexican War of 1848 as allies of our southern neighbor, would cartographers have redrawn the map of North America differently? If gold had not been discovered in a northern California streambed, how might the history of the West, and particularly the "Golden State," been altered?

Naturally, these "if's" of history cannot be answered easily or fully. They do, however, tempt and provoke. Certainly, this would have been true in the case of Iva Toguri, who found herself stranded in wartime Japan (1941-1945), and was later convicted of treason and sent to prison for her role as the infamous Tokyo Rose, a radio propagandist for the Japanese government.

The "if's" of history: If Iva Toguri had returned home before the Japanese attack on Pearl Harbor, would her life have been different? If she had not been forced to work for Radio Tokyo broadcasting to Allied troops in the Pacific, would things have turned out different? If she had not met two unscrupulous American reporters who wanted an interview with Tokyo Rose, might her life have taken a different road? The answer is, of course. But those "if's" didn't happen and Iva Toguri's life took a different turn.

In this story I have tried to envision a very plausible reinterpretation of her effect on average citizens in post-war America, who later judged her guilt or innocence in light of her alleged treasonable acts. The twists of history provided attempt to tease out the "what if's" of Iva Togri's life, and add, I hope, to the drama of the already unbelievable story of Tokyo Rose. I trust you will enjoy the story and an implied warning inherent in the narrative.

Robert Livingston
Northridge, California, 2018

Dedication

To my daughter, Rachel, and all the wonderful teachers who enlighten the young and help them to understand not only the lessons of the past, but the civilization they inherited, which is always in need of guidance and vigilance to protect our civil liberties and safeguard our freedoms. Our teachers are the first line of defense in this ceaseless struggle to remain a people governed by law and a judicial system based on fairness and justice. In the ramparts that are their classrooms, teachers are the necessary bulwarks against prejudice and bigotry, and in no small way indispensible to our way of life. Long may they wave these flags.

≈ *Chapter 1* ☞

THE PHONE CALL

San Francisco, 1976

THE PHONE IN THE CROWDED, smoke-filled newsroom rang and rang, a rasping sound, irritating and totally unwelcomed at this precise moment in Robert Samuels' life. Damn, he thought, not now.

The incessant ringing was finally getting to Samuels, the ace reporter of the *San Francisco Chronicle*, who carried celebrity status in the world of print news. He was trying desperately to finish what was known as a human-interest story in the news business before the dreaded afternoon deadline. Paying scant attention to the phone, Samuels' fingers raced across his old-fashioned Underwood typewriter pounding out a story about a bungled bank heist in the Mission District that led to the would-be robber finding himself locked in the bank's very secure vault with a middle-aged teller, who, of course, had to be nine months pregnant with her third child. Talk about a crazy situation.

Samuels' fingers continued the story:

> *Due perhaps to the excitement of the moment, nature decided to take a hand in human affairs and initiate birth contractions in the poor woman. Overwhelmed by all this and frustrated by his inability to scram for parts unknown before the police arrived, the unlucky criminal mastermind found himself considering the injustice of the whole affair. For the life of him, he couldn't figure out how the heavy vault door had closed. Now inexplicably to*

his confused mind, he found himself trapped in an impromptu emergency room in sight of stacks of luscious greenbacks just waiting to be plucked.

Still the phone's metallic ringing continued to the rap-tap-tap of Samuels' flying digits as he neared the finish of his story. Across the desk from him, sat his old buddy, Irish Mike McCormick, the *Chronicle's* best beat reporter for the *Sports Section*. He reached for the phone. With hands still rocketing across the keys, Samuels yelled, "Let the damn thing ring, Mike. I'm almost done."

Irish Mike backed off with a big smile and a knowing look, but not before snapping back, "Go Mr. P." This was the nickname Samuels received graciously and answered to happily after winning a Pulitzer Prize for stories about military chaplains in World War II.

Now if Samuels could just finish this story…

Thanks to an in-bank phone in the vault, the unlucky bank robber communicated his dire straits, really his companion's status, to those outside the vault, a few of whom were desperately trying with little success to override the vault's automatic locking system.

As fate would have it, a friendly, family physician was making a sizeable deposit. He was quickly pressed into service. Taking a phone in hand, he now coached the less than fearsome felon in how to assist the woman, even as she crouched in a serious effort to enlist gravity in the imminent delivery of her child. Thanks to keen medical coaching by phone and nature's own whims, a healthy baby boy plunked down on a bed of canvas bags containing crisp new bank notes. The robber found himself saying unexpectedly, *"Lady, good job."*

Once freed from their captivity and without bloodshed, the teller later spoke well of the robber, who had encouraged her, saying almost too calmly, *"You can do it, babe. Hold and push. Hold and push. Now push!"* Apparently, the brazen but inept bandit knew something about natural childbirth, perhaps as a compensation for his lack of "stick-up skills."

For her part, the bank employee subsequently told her boss, the FBI, and the SFPD that she would be a sympathetic witness on behalf of the robber and his failed heist in any eventual trial. Perhaps out of guilt for having foiled his robbery, the teller promised to name her newborn Robert, and to give him the nickname, Rob. The banker and the Feds were not completely overjoyed with her position. As to the SFPD, the officers simply took her words in stride. After all, this was San Francisco.

It was later revealed that the criminal genius was an out-of-work father of five, who had, it turned out, assisted his wife with the delivery of all of their kids. A novice robber, he might be, but as an experienced dad, he had been near perfect for the moment. As to the heist, he had been driven to desperation by a pile of bills and the news that his wife had lung cancer, and no immediate hope for a job.

As Samuels ended his story, he challenged his loyal readers to think about the bedeviled heist:

> *What should be done with this guy? Throw him in the brig or exercise civil restraint and help this poor joker to get back on his feet? Jail time or time with his family?*

Samuels was sure his sympathetic readers would vote for compassion and redemption. Hopefully, a job might even be found for this bonehead bandito. As to how the Court would respond that, of course, was another story. With a rush, Samuels pulled his story from the typewriter, and with a flourish yelled the immortal words often heard in the newsroom, *"Copy boy!"*

The *Bulldog* nightly edition would carry his joyful, funny, or sad story this Friday, January 19, 1976. His readers, loyal but often given to sharp critiques, would decide how to characterize it.

The Phone Call

Now freed of his deadline obligations, Samuels finally, if not reluctantly, reached for the phone, exclaiming to the assumed frustrated caller, "Samuels here." Silence greeted him and for a second Samuels thought the caller had hung up. As he waited for a response, he was happy his answering machine was out of order. He despised listening to messages, which were usually garbled and mushy, as if the caller were sitting in a bowl of *Ralston* right up to his ears. And he hated calling people back. Phone tag provided him with no joy. But for a reporter Ma Bell was a necessary conduit to the outside world, one he lived with reluctantly, and that was on his good days.

The news of a great city, the sinews of human courage, compassion, and concern, which were the stuff of his more positive stories, buzzed in his ear when the telephone lines crackled. Unfortunately, the darker side also availed itself of the newsroom in a river of unrelenting human depravity, lust, and greed. Inevitably, each manifestation of human culpability began with a ring. Over the years Samuels had learned how to live uneasily with both hemispheres of human behavior. As he waited for an answering voice, he wondered what happiness or anguish his caller, if he answered, would bring.

The silence finally ended. This caller, it was eventually determined, was not about to replace his receiver. He had much to say.

"Samuels?"

"Yes."

"The reporter, Robert Samuels?"

"One in the same."

"Stop your articles!"

"What articles? Who is this?"

"Stop writing about the bitch!"

"What are you talking about?"

"You're making her look like a saint."

"Perhaps you might explain yourself?"

"Iva, the innocent," the caller said very sarcastically.

"Is there a topic sentence here?"

"The bitch, Tokyo Rose."

"Iva Toguri Aquino?"

"Yeah. The Jap. The voice of the devil."

Samuels was used to crank calls. They came with the territory. If you were a reporter, you upset some folks. If you wrote the facts as you best understood them, some people really got angry, and in some cases, threatening. Those really upset ran the gambit from "pissed off" to zealots with a cause that brooked no contrary view. Some even threatened physical harm. You got used to it, but never completely.

Over the years, he had heard it all, at least until this call. But something in this man's strident voice was very unsettling.

"I think we're done here," Samuels said as calmly as possible, but with a sharp edge to his voice. Unless you can tell me what you want, there's no need to continue this conversation."

"No Nip name on the 1776 school site," the caller shouted out in absolute distain. "Nothing in your damn paper urging the adoption of that fucking woman's name. No more articles about her possible pardon. She doesn't deserve any honors, not after what she did. Understand?"

There it was, the caller's agenda, his cause. He didn't want the new high school in San Francisco, officially known as School Site 1776, to be named after this infamous woman, Iva Torgui Aquino. Most people believed she was a traitor to the American war effort against the Imperial Japanese forces during WWII. Nor did the general public want this hated woman to be pardoned by President Gerald Ford, as had been rumored, in the last days of his administration.

"She's a dirty Jap. No more sympathetic articles about her. Let her rot in hell."

Samuels had heard that accusation, that declaration of truth, that emotional indictment all too often during the past few weeks as his series on an almost forgotten sliver of American history played out in the *Chronicle*. Whether by phone or letters-to-the-editor, some of the unhappy anti-Tokyo Rose crowd was pushing back at him with an undercurrent of viciousness and hardly concealed anger.

"Look, my friend," Samuels said in a forced quiet tone, "the decision about school site 1776 will be made by the Board of Education and the pardon is a White House affair."

"Bullshit. Your series is giving 'aid and comfort' to the enemy. You're aiding and abetting the Pacific whore."

Aid and comfort to the enemy, thought Samuels, that was exactly what the government had accused Iva Toguri Aquino of some twenty years earlier. Aiding Tokyo. Denouncing America. A turncoat in the Pacific… Maybe this caller was a vet. Could he have fought in the Pacific theater? Had he been wounded on some battle-scarred island? Or did he see his Marine buddies mowed down on an inviting, bleached-white beach astride a lovely atoll surrounded by a beautiful, but dangerous coral reef? That, Samuels considered, might explain his hostility toward Aquino. What else could account for the anger and hatred of a nondescript Japanese-American woman who currently lived in Chicago well off the radar map working in her father's store?

"I'm just an impartial writer," Samuels said in his most neutral voice." "I'm not taking sides in this affair. Again, you need to take your concerns to the Board of Education."

"Fuck you, Mr. Impartial Writer. You know what those assholes want? I tell you. What do they call it? Oh, yeah, a person of color! Diversity, a white person won't do. They want a Jap, or a Chink, or a nigger, or a greasy bean pusher from below the border! Hell, a Jew would be even better than what these faggots are considering. Jesus, why can't they name the school after a white guy like Joe DiMaggio? Christ, who cares if he was from pasta-land! He could hit the shit out of a baseball."

"Thanks for mentioning Jews in your tirade," Samuels said flatly. "I was beginning to think I wouldn't make your Hit Parade."

"Screw you, Samuels."

"I think it's time to say adios."

That should have ended the conversation, if it could be described as that. The caller, however, went on non-stop as if he hadn't heard Samuels. As for Samuels, he found himself, truth be told, simply listening, wanting to know more about the strained voice on the line. Call it a reporter's instinct for a story. Samuels had it, many said, and he felt it now.

"I repeat for the last time. Take your grievance to the Board."

"You don't get it, Samuels," the agitated caller stated matter-of-factly. Those ass-kissers just want votes. They don't give a shit about what happened! They don't care about the guys?"

"What are you talking about?" Samuels asked as patiently as he could. "What happened? What guys?"

"Christ, man, you were in the Pacific aboard that destroyer. You saw the *meatballs* who tried to destroy your ship, fucking big-toothed Nips."

Samuels was sure now that whatever happened to set this guy off began long ago in the Pacific during the war. Without question, he reasoned, this guy was there. And he knew about Samuels and his numbing moment of truth when a kamikaze plane crashed into the *USS Aaron Ward* off of Okinawa in 1945. Bad day for his shipmates, over thirty of his fellow shipmates killed and so many wounded. But how could this guy know about that? The answer quickly came, not unexpectedly, or surprisingly in retrospect.

"I read your book --- *Miracle at RPS 16*. You hate the bastards, Samuels, as much as I do."

"You're wrong.," Samuels said perhaps too strongly. "I've gotten past that."

But had he? Samuels had told himself that he had. In his writings he conveyed that notion. Yet, in his darkest dreams when his protective and civilized shields were down, and Jap planes were crashing into the *Ward* in an attempt to immolate his buddies, the old angers and fears arose painfully, a constant reminder of the guys who died on the ship's blistered and torn deck. In the shelter of his own mind, Samuels knew that on some primeval level, he was kin to this caller. Perhaps that was why he couldn't just slam the receiver down.

"Look. I'm just a reporter. I write mainly stories about people, what happened to them, or how they dealt with a crazy situation. Sometimes the story tickles people's funny bone. Sometimes the story brings tears to their eyes."

"And sometimes your damn typewriter makes them fucking angry."

"Yes."

"You've made me angry."

"Why? I'm just writing about a woman who was, by a quirk of time and history, stranded in Japan after Pearl Harbor."

"B.S. Tell that to the Marines."

"You were a Marine?"

There was no answer. Samuels wasn't sure if the caller was still with him. Then...

"Leatherneck, yes."

"Okinawa?"

"No."

"Iwo?"

"No."

"Saipan?"

"No."

"Tarawa?"

"Yes."

Tarawa. The name struck a cord of revulsion in Samuels. That insanely little atoll, located approximately 2,500 miles southwest of Hawaii, turned into one of the bloodiest battle of the Pacific in 1943. Before it was over, the Marines suffered over 3,000 casualties. Of the 4,700 well dug-in Japanese defenders, only seventeen survived the carnage. Bloody Tarawa consisted of a series of coral inlets stretching through the ocean in a hook-like fashion. The largest of the inlets was called Betio. It measured less than 3-miles in length and was only a ½-mile in width. But it had an airstrip and the US Navy wanted it for its strategic value in preparation for the coming drive through the central Pacific toward the Philippines.

"You hit Betio?"

"Wrong."

"I don't …"

"Betio hit me. Damn Higgins boats came in at low tide. Our assault boat was torn apart on the razor sharp coral reef. We were stuck. We were sitting ducks for the fucking Jap machine gunners. We jumped into the water and tried to wade through waist-deep surf carrying full loads. The Jap gunners cut us down with merciless gunfire yards from the beach. The fucking ocean turned red."

"You were wounded?"

"Three times."

"Hospitalized?"

"Pearl."

"Serious?"

"Try walking around without legs. Serious enough for you, Mr. Reporter?"

"Yeah. I'm sorry."

"Save it. Just cut the fucking series."

"I can't do that. If I did that, the freaking phone would be ringing off the hook, some happy, some upset. I can't give the readers that power over what I write. Anyway, if I don't do it, someone else would be given the assignment. If you don't believe me, talk to the editor."

"Adams?"

"I'm impressed. Joe Adams believes in freedom of the press, and before you attack him, just remember he caught hell on Omaha Beach."

"You're leaving me no choice."

"Or what?"

"How about 32-minutes, big shot reporter?"

It took Samuels a short moment to understand the caller's threat, cloaked in the clock's ticking minutes. And then the horror of the past, which he had exiled into his repressed memories, launched an all out attack on his consciousness. First, he felt a sour taste in his mouth. Next came the smell of fear, ugly and sickening. Finally, the "sweats," unwanted perspiration clinging to his body. And then the supreme effort to put aside these torments and to do his job as the suicide planes dove on his ship, 32-minutes of unrelenting hell.

The caller, Samuels thought, was like a Jap Zero headed for his ship, the *USS Aaron Ward*, a destroyer patrolling off Okinawa in 1945, one of many ships stationed to alert the Navy of incoming bogies, the Jap kamikazes. A great sadness, tinged with bitterness, now claimed Samuels' mind and he was no longer in the *Chronicle's* newsroom.

◆◆◆◆◆

The Zero leaned to the left as it pulled out of a barrel roll, and then dived for the Pacific for a bow attack on the Ward. On and on it came, merely twenty feet above the waves, a menacing shape carrying a big, ugly bomb under its belly. Every gun able to fire on the Zero was in action, even as the ship maneuvered, zigzagging at high speed. Still, the Zero bore in as if following some invisible but deadly line of latitude. Bullets from the Ward tore into the plane, but still it flew on, apparently immune from the 20's spitting lethal lead. Standing on the Ward's bridge, Samuels felt the ship vibrate as it took evasive action. Unnervingly, he also felt that the Zero was coming directly at him, that somehow he alone was the target. Closer and closer it came through a canopy of anti-aircraft fire, thick and deadly. And then inconceivably, the impossible happened. Fifty yards from the ship, the Zero exploded and a rain of heated metallic junk rained on the Ward. The plane's propeller, still spinning at high revolutions, now free of its housing, careened into the ship's bridge wounding all there, including Samuels. The planes motor, white-hot and heavy, crashed into Mount #1 killing all in the 5-inch gun station in a blast of fire and death. The rest of the Zero, what was left of her, smacked into the portside of the Ward, embedding itself into the ship, a flaming wreckage with the pilot still in the cockpit.

Samuels forced himself from the *Ward's* mutilated deck and the bloody leg wound that would leave him forever with a hitch in his stride. He struggled, swimming upward through tortured memories, to reenter the present. And then he was back.

"Leave me no choice…" That's what the caller had said. Samuels didn't like the way the conversation was turning. It was bringing back unpleasant memories better left buried in the deepest recesses of his mind. He gestured to Mike McCormick to turn on a recording device that would tape the caller. Ordinarily, he would advise the party that their conversation was being taped, but not this time. The recorder turned on with a barely heard click and Samuels spoke.

"You always have a choice. Hell, read the *San Francisco Examiner,* and the *Oakland Tribune.* They're two fine Hearst right-wing rags that agree with you. They both want your so-called Jap bitch in jail, or, if possible, deported back to Nippon. And, yes, they're pissed off at Ford for considering a pardon."

"I'm more than pissed off."

"See a VA shrink."

"I have."

"Well?"

"The shrinks are full of bull."

"Try medication."

"I've had my fill of them."

"Well, damn it, try this. You're not the only one who lost a leg."

"Two."

"Okay, two. You have a right to be bitter. But you're alive. You're living."

"You call this living? A disability allowance from the VA each month; thanks a lot for nothing. And being locked to a wheelchair?"

"Better than the grave," Samuels suggested. "Get your ass into counseling."

"Up yours."

"Fine. The series goes on. Try not to read the *Chronicle*. I'm tired of your self-pity."

"Not if I can stop you."

Samuels blinked on that one. This was a direct threat. No question about it. He frantically motioned for Irish Mike to get on a party line, where he could listen in too.

"You threatening the paper?"

"Not the paper."

"What, then?"

"Guess. Mr. Writer."

"Me?"

"Give the man a Kewpie doll."

"Screw you."

"And Miss Principal."

"What?"

"You heard me. The little lady who will be the new school's principal."

Samuels' stomach flipped over. He felt an instant stab in his chest. The crank call had turned ominous. This was getting too personal. Directed against him alone would have been one thing. But the threat was not restricted to him. It now included the proposed new principal, his daughter, Rachel.

"You hear me, Samuels?"

"I hear you."

"And?"

"The presses roll."

"Bad choice."

"And stay away from my family."

"Too late."

"What?"

"Check your mail."

"I ..."

Click. The caller was gone. Samuels put down his receiver none too gently. Irish Mike looked at him with concern as did others close by in the busy newsroom. They saw the anxious look in his eyes, the obvious strain on his face. Something bad had transpired.

"Time to call security?" Irish Mike asked. Samuels slowly nodded but did nothing.

"You going to check your mail?" Irish Mike asked again. Again, Samuels nodded. Reluctantly, he turned to a pile of mail on his desk. Scanning through the envelopes, he looked for one he dreaded to find. It was there --- a standard white business envelope addressed to him. Of course, there was no return address. But there were two words written in heavy bold, black ink on the backside: THE WARRIOR.

Chapter 2

THE ASSIGNMENT

The Mysterious Letter

S AMUELS HELD THE ENVELOPE IN his trembling hands, which he was unable to conceal. He dreaded opening the letter. Looking at his ashen face, Irish Mike said, "You okay, partner?"

Samuels had learned long ago not to try fooling his colleague and occasional drinking buddy. The guy could see right through him.

"Scared to death, Mike."

"Want me to do the honors, old friend?"

Secretly, Samuels truly wanted Irish Mike to open the envelope and, hopefully, to tell him it was all a poor joke, no real threat, just our usual run-of-the-mill crank message. The offer tempted and was rejected.

"My job, Mike."

Evan as Samuels reached for a letter opener, his mind drifted back in time to a recent conversation he had with his daughter. Was it really only four weeks ago just before Christmas, when Rachel had told him about her problem and sought his advice?' In retrospect, their talk had been a precursor to what was now taking place.

"Dad, thanks for meeting me."

"You know I couldn't pass up an opportunity to have lunch with my daughter at O'Douls."

"I figured as much. That's why I picked this bistro."

The place was an old line restaurant once owned by the legendary Lefty O'Doul, a former major leaguer with the New York Yankees and for many years the baseball manager of the San Francisco Seals in the old "triple A" Pacific Coast League. O'Doul had retired from the majors with a .347 battling average and a gift of the Irish gab, plus a penchant for good corned beef and cold beer. Opening the restaurant in 1948 was a good match for O'Doul and his hungry patrons in a city that enjoyed good food and had nostalgia for past glories.

The place was adorned with memories of the good old days: photos of O'Doul with the legendary Babe Ruth, the Giants' great hitter, Willie Mays, and, of course, Joe and the other DiMaggio brothers. Resting peacefully in glass cases were relics of a beloved past, wooden baseball bats that had driven pitchers from the mound and leather gloves that had made impossible catches leaving hitters with blank stares and "what could have been" thoughts. Old baseballs, which were signed by the greats and dated for some marvelous past feat on the baseball diamond were everywhere. In short, if you loved baseball, you loved this place.

"Rachel, you have a serious look on your face. What's up?"

"It's that obvious?"

"Yes, but I'm your father. I recognize the signs. A little twitching, tight breathing, and a gracious offer to buy lunch."

"I may have to get rid of the last cue."

"Perhaps, but let's order first. I'm having the Philly steak sandwich with coleslaw and wedged fries, and, if you won't tell your mother, a large slice of apple pie."

"With a scoop of vanilla ice cream, Dad?"

"You know me well. What about you?"

"Chicken salad and tea and a small scoop of strawberry ice cream."

"A healthy selection, Rachel. Now what's going on?"

Samuels watch his daughter gather herself. Whatever the problem, it had obviously taken a toll on her. The lines troubling her forehead and the weariness under her eyes, suggested something serious. With all that, he mused, she was still a striking gal, long brown hair, striking blue eyes, and an attractive shape other women might die for, even as the male gender shared looks of appreciation with her mid-thirties package. Now, if she would just find the right guy.

"I met with the Superintendent last week."

"Andy Anderson?"

"The one and only. He wants me to leave Galileo High for a new school next fall."

"Leave your present position as an Assistant Principal?"

"Yes. To be the principal of the new school."

"School site 1776?"

"Yes, but how did you know?"

"Contacts."

Inside, Samuels was tickled. Rachel had moved up the ladder quickly after joining the school district a mere eight years ago. First, as a teacher, then as an administrator, she had dazzled her bosses with a competency and dedication to kids and their families and by her ability to get along with even the most sensitive teachers with a hardcore union bent. This promotion seemed overdue and richly deserved.

"You seem hesitant about accepting the Superintendent's offer."

"I am, Dad."

"Seems like a good move and a great professional challenge."

"Depends on the challenge."

Samuels studied his daughter. Dressed as she was in dark, navy-blue slacks and jacket, she was every inch the professional. She complemented her pants suit with sensible dark low-heeled shoes. She wore a white blouse just sensuous enough to reveal her femininity, yet still appropriate for work.

"Okay," Samuels said, "I'll bite. What's the problem?"

"It's all about a name."

"A name?" Samuels asked. "What are you talking about?"

"Here's the story, Dad. When I met with the Superintendent...."

"Sir, perhaps someone else would be better suited for this position."

"No, Rachel," the Superintendent said, "I've given a lot of thought to this and you're the one I want."

Rachel was meeting with the Superintendent, Andy Anderson, in his lavish office, at least compared to her crowded cubical at Galileo High in the Marina not far from Fisherman's Wharf. After urging her to sit and dismissing his secretary, he had gotten down to business. Rachel understood she was in the so-called "halls of power," where a word here or there could make or break a career. She knew this and understood she needed to tread carefully.

"Sir, I like my A.P. job at Galileo."

"And you've done a great job there, Rachel."

"I don't feel ready to be a high school principal."

"Trust me, you're ready."

"You've made up your mind, Sir?"

"Absolutely. The time for debate and discussion is over."

"I don't remember debating or discussing."

"I did it for you, Rachel," the Superintendent said laughing. You're exactly what I need. You're a bulldog who strives for perfection and doesn't like or put up with incompetence or the unprepared. Yet, you have excellent people skills. You've shown me an ability to work through a minefield of competing ethnic and racial groups at Galileo. You win people over to your view. People have confidence in you, as do I."

"Sir, why do I feel like the proverbial sacrifice to the gods?"

"Perhaps I'm coming on too strongly with the compliments. But they are well meant and true. As to being a sacrifice, that's not the case. As to a very difficult challenge, that is the case."

"And the challenge, Sir?"

"Daunting."

The Superintendent moved to his desk, which was extraordinarily bare except for one file. This he picked up and then approached Rachel.

"The District has an unusual and possibly an unseemly problem, which threatens to get out of hand. I need you to keep this from happening."

"Go on," Rachel said. "I'm listening."

"To quote the bard," he said, '*What's in a name?*'"

"A rose is a rose..."

"Quite right, Rachel, and closer to our problem than you might think."

"You are going to explain?" Rachel asked, perhaps in a manner a little too feisty.

"School Site 1776 needs a name and a principal."

Rachel had heard of 1776, the numerical name given to a yet unnamed high school, which would cater to mainly disadvantaged and low achieving students in mid-city when it opened in the fall semester. The rumor mill running overtime hinted at a problem, but little else. Apparently, Rachel was going to learn what the problem was first hand.

"Rachel, there are five competing names at this time which have been taken under consideration by the Board of Education. Ordinarily, this is not unusual. But this time, the situation is highly combustible. I'm going to need a principal to head off a political explosion and possibly something more. I'm considering you for the job."

"Sir …"

"As you know, the School Board is not longer elected at-large. Each member represents a distinct geographical and/or racial/ethnic constituency. Currently, the breakdown is as follows: one member represents the African-American community. Another represents our considerable Japanese population. The Hispanic clientele has an elected member on the Board. The Chinese folks also have a representative. In their case two because of their large numbers. And, of course, this is also true of the dwindling number of white families, which once were a concrete majority in the city. We've got seven Board Members, each representing diverse communities, each promoting a favorite."

"Democracy in action, Sir."

"Or anarchy and the possibility of violence beyond the heated rhetoric of the Boardroom."

"I don't understand."

"The Blacks want 1776 to be named *Martin Luther King High*."

"Good name."

The Chinese have put forth *Dr. Sun Yat-Sen*."

"The Chinese nationalist leader who wanted to replace the last vestige of the royal house of China, while driving out the western powers which had sliced the country into imperialistic enclaves. As I recall, he wanted to unify China under a democratic government?, isn't that so?"

"Correct. You do know your history."

"With a father who delves into history with passion, I had no choice."

"Of course. Well, going on, the Hispanic community has nominated *Cesar Chavez.*"

"Another terrific choice," Rachel said quietly.

"The Anglos want to pay tribute to the city's baseball history."

"Willie Mays?" Rachel asked.

"Joe DiMaggio."

"Naturally," Rachel said, "though Willie would be a great choice. "What about the Japanese?"

"That's the rub. They want to name the school after *Iva Toguri Aquino.*"

"Never heard of her. Who is she?"

"She's better known by her other name, Rachel."

"Which is?"

"Tokyo Rose."

Chapter 3

THE LETTER

BACK AT THE NEWSROOM...

"Mr. P!"

Irish Mike McCormick had raised his animated voice another two octaves to get Robert Samuels' attention. Still, there was no response from his colleague. Samuels sat statute-like before him holding the unopened envelope in a near death grip. He knew that Samuels got like this at times --- that is, to all appearances "zoning out." It wasn't that Samuels was rude or discourteous. Rather, as he described it, he would time-trip, sometimes into the past, occasionally into the future, but always in a reality tied to a current news story.

From Irish Mike's perspective, what Samuels did was weird. That Samuels could do this without at least a pint of a good Irish malt beer under his belt made it that more incredulous to his way of thinking... Yet, a buddy was a buddy, so he again sought Samuels' attention.

"Mr. P.! Your wife just called. The house is on fire. She wants to know what she should do? The fire department, according to her, won't respond because of the critical article you wrote about their overtime pay. Any comment?"

To that question, which would have garnered the attention of other mortals. Samuels remained mute. Irish Mike rubbed his pencil-thin mustache and twisted his rail-like body so that his squinting dark green eyes might look directly into Samuels' face. Christ, he muttered, "Mr. P is with the elves."

Around Samuels' desk had gathered a motley group of other

reporters and a few interns, who were learning the business. A husky water-hydrant of a man roared into the circle of news folks, who stood fascinated by Samuels' time-tripping journey on company time. A large Columbian cigar clung to a corner of the bullish intruder's mouth like a cannon projecting from a wooden man-of-war. Every puff seemed to suggest a cannon ball had been fired. Unable to keep his Sicilian passions under control, the smoker bellowed, "Does anyone still work here at the *Chronicle*? Or would you like me to put the paper out all by myself?"

"It's Mr. P, Boss," Irish Mike said in a low voice. "He's, well, you know what."

"What, again? I swear to God I'm going to dock his pay this time. Hell, I can't pay a man when his body takes up floor space, but his mind is wandering around elsewhere."

"But he does write well," Irish Mike reminded him, smiling as he did. "He's inspired by these interludes."

"Aren't we all," the Boss said in a tone laced with anguished acceptance of his reporter's penchant for going AWOL at times. "Well, just get him back, Mike."

"Boss, any suggestions or how to do that?"

"Tell the Sphinx his wife is being held hostage by two mentally-crazed escaped convicts and the police won't do anything because of the story he wrote about their overpriced pension plan."

"Won't work AA."

"Do you have call me that? You know I hate referring to people by initials."

In truth, Joe Abraham Adams, the Boss, loved his abbreviated calling card. But it was fun to act otherwise, even though everyone knew differently.

"All right, why won't my little ploy work?" AA asked Irish Mike.

"I've already been through the 'wife in trouble' bit. He's not biting."

Still playing to the crowd, AA said, "Damn, he's really into it today. That gimmick always worked in the past. Okay, well at least cut out the abbreviations"

"Boss, we've been through this a hundred times. I can't call you Abraham Adams. Takes too long Initials are easier and faster, right G.G.?"

"Right" said Gloria Gorham, chief writer of the *G.G. Gossip* column of the paper. Dressed in an obviously expensive black dress that belied her modest pay at the *Chronicle*, but not for her many books that exposed the hidden lives of celebrities, GG had been hovering close by Samuels' desk, witnessing first hand AA and Irish Mike getting into it about Mr. P.

"Does everyone in this newsroom have an abbreviated name?" AA asked out of curiosity and manifold impatience."

"Not everyone" said Oliver Pine, chief editorial writer and known to his friends as OP. "Irish Mike is just Irish Mike."

"God, am I running a zoo or a newspaper here?" AA asked, his words sort of sputtering out.

"A half-way house for recovering reporters, I think."

"Who said that?" AA yelled.

"I did," said Dolly 'Daisy' Davenport, the paper's entertainment editor."

"What'd you mean Dolly?"

"Be kind to DDD," volunteered Irish Mike. "Remember, she's a sensitive woman."

Indeed, she was. Her initials, it seemed, referred not only to her name, but also to her considerable bosom, which had brought her fame on the exotic stage long before she took up journalism. As she liked to say, her God-given endowment had paid her way through college.

Before the Boss could say, "not another one," Robert Samuels chose that precise moment to re-entered the newsroom.

"Hi, guys," he said with a half grin. "What's going on?" he asked, as if he didn't know. "Someone's birthday?"

"Mr. P, you're back," Irish Mike shouted. "Good trip down memory lane?"

"I zoned out again, didn't I?"

"You could say that," AA announced for all to hear.

""Any good, juicy stuff for my gossip column?" GG asked. "Lots of good stuff in memories."

Juicy stuff, thought Samuels, let's see: if two Asian ethnic groups get into a fight over a woman who never existed, would that be juicy enough? Actually, Samuels reasoned, it just might be. From what little he knew about Tokyo Rose, her life did sound a bit like a soap opera. Young girl goes to a strange land to help a family member. A nasty war breaks out. Young girl gets stranded in strange country. Young girl needs job to survive. She finds work on a radio talk show where she meets a younger guy and falls in love. War ends. While working for Radio Tokyo, girl gets involved with propaganda broadcasts. War ends. Girl come homes and goes to jail and loses guy. Juicy stuff, you bet. Was it a soap opera? You could bet the house on that.

"No GG, just a false alarm. I was thinking about my daughter and the threatening phone call I just received. Great kid, but no salacious gossip."

"Christ," said CW, the financial editor at the paper who byline was actually Charles Winston, III, "you really had us worried guy. We weren't sure if you were coming back to join us for the annual employee's party."

"Okay," said AA. "Now that that's cleared up and we're all on the same page, are you going to open that damn envelope I've heard about?"

Samuels had completely forgotten about the letter he was holding. Once more he looked hard at the cursive writing on the envelope spelling out his name and leaving an oblique return address on the backside, *THE WARRIOR*. With AA and his underlings watching, Samuels reluctantly opened the envelope. He was immediately taken aback by the letter's brevity, but not its import. To one and all, he read aloud.

> *Mr. Robert Samuels, Reporter*
> *Editorial Staff*
> *San Francisco Chronicle*
>
> *By now, we've talked by phone and accordingly you have denied my request to stop writing about Iva Toguri, whom I will refer to as Tokyo Rose, and never by her marriage name, Aquino.*
>
> *I knew you would reject my overtures to end the series. Am I not right? You would perceive me as just another crazed vet with a grudge. Right? Please understand, I don't want to*

harm anyone. I can't, however, abide by school site 1776 being named after her. No school should be honored so disgracefully.

*She was a **traitor**. She is guilty of **treason**. She was convicted. It would be an insult to all the guys who suffered in the Pacific for her **treachery** to be rewarded. You must stop writing your favorable articles about her. I can't let this **turncoat** be honored this way by the Board of Education. I won't let this happen.*

I don't want her made into a victimless celebrity. She was not a victim. She was Tokyo Rose As for your daughter, Rachel, who is designated to be the school's new Principal, she should refrain; she should resist doing anything to aid or comfort this woman. Tokyo Rose was the enemy.

This is your last warning.

THE WARRIOR

Samuels put the letter down on his desk. It was immediately snatched up by AA, who spoke for everyone when he said, "This one is for security. We're dealing with a guy who is certifiable. Hell, he's threatening the paper and your family, MR. P."

"I agree," Irish Mike said. "This guy is trouble."

"We need to know more about him," GG added.

"He's certainly not my cup of tea," DDD commented in her usual zesty manner. "Not my cup of tea at all."

"I can already see our coming editorial," OP explained. "*Mad Man Stalks the City.*"

"This joker needs a good insurance annuity for his mental state," CW chimed in with his best Dow-Jones voice.

As for Samuels, he was listening with only half an ear. His focus and thinking were about the letter itself. It had been typed on common bond paper such as that used in the school district, and most probably on an old manual typewriter with an ancient ribbon, since almost all the print was light, nearly faint depending on the letter. Here and there certain words had been typed and retyped in order to make them stand out, **traitor, treachery, turncoat, and treason**. Obviously, the typist wanted these words to catch the reader's attention. The letter "t" looked as if it had been pounded half a dozen times. It appeared to Samuels that the writer was venting his anger, almost as if by slamming this key he would be punishing Iva Toguri for her crimes. And he had made threats. No question about that. But there was something else. How did he know so much about Rachel and her appointment? Did he have a source inside the school district? Was he working with an accomplice? This must be the case, thought Samuels. After all, how much damage could a wheelchair-bound person do alone? But he wasn't operating alone. Samuels was sure of that. He knew too much.

Another thought tugged at Samuels. Compared to the ranting and raving, combined with the nasty language, the writer had used on the phone, the letter was reasonably sane, almost as if the *Warrior* were attempting to calm the waters he had already poured oil on, yet he was trying to avoid igniting his troubled sea of anguish. Certainly, Samuels picked up on the man's pain. No question, the guy had seen action. If he really were at Tarawa, he had experienced a horror beyond most people's understanding. As always, you had to be there to appreciate what some consider the most brutal three days of battle in Marine Corps history.

To a degree, Samuels empathized with the man. Yet, the *Warrior* had threatened the paper and, most of all, extended that threat to his daughter, Rachel. It was clear to Samuels that on some distant day yet unknown, he would meet this threat in a manner still underdetermined. Nothing else could have been clearer in Samuels' mind.

Galileo High School

Unaware of these events taking place at the *Chronicle,* Rachel Samuels was still musing over her decision to take on School Site 1776, even as she patrolled the quad during nutrition at Galileo High School. As she considered what she had said to the Superintendent, she watched the kaleidoscope of student activities around her. One group of nearby kids was frantically devouring tacos and downing soft drinks as they prepped for an obviously challenging test. Another group within earshot was discussing the upcoming football game against Lincoln High. In doing so, they described the other team in colorful terms that would never see the light of day in the school paper. More than a few students were stretched out on the no longer damp grass to enjoy the reluctant and transient San Francisco sunshine. There were, of course, young couples everywhere staring deeply into each other's eyes as only teens can. Ah, to be young again, the 37-year old Rachel thought, to be youthful again without serious responsibilities.

Her responsive note to the Superintendent had been succinct:

> *"Sir, as per your request, I have decided to accept your offer. I look forward to the fall semester and being the first principal of the new school regardless of its name. Sincerely, Rachel Samuels."*

◆ ◈ ◆

Rachel had agreed to sign on as requested by her boss, but not before speaking with her father. One question was troubling her: why would Tokyo Rose provoke the Chinese citizens in San Francisco to such a degree that violence might occur? His answer enlightened and frightened her.

"It all began in 1931, Rachel, when Japan invaded Manchuria, an area situated between Korea and China. By 1937 Japan's military forces had advanced up the Yangtze Valley and attacked Nanking, then the capital of China. Nanking was declared an "open city" by the Chinese government in order to avoid destructive aerial attacks and to reduce civilian casualties. Japanese bombers, however, paid little heed. Nanking was intentionally bombed in violation of all international treaties. Ugly stories emerged as Imperial Japanese forces entered the city: looting, raping of Chinese women, and mass killings of innocent non-combatants, including old people and children. The "Rape of Nanking," as it was called, was condemned by the League of Nations, but nothing could be done to stop it. In the post-war years, the Japanese government never formerly apologized for the atrocity, leaving both sides with bitter memories of the war."

"And this would be trouble if the school is named after Tokyo Rose?"

"People have long memories. Anything is possible."

"But if she is pardoned by President Ford?"

"Many in the Chinese community would take exception to such an action."

"And I would have my hands full as the new principal?"

Chapter 4

THE DREAM

W HILE ROBERT SAMUELS WAS READING the threatening letter at the *Chronicle*, and his daughter was accepting her new job as the principal of School Site 1776, in a rather shabby one-bedroom apartment on Howard Street in downtown San Francisco in what is referred to as the rough and tough tenderloin district, the *Warrior* was very much asleep and deeply into the recurring nightmare. It was always the same. And it always brought the same horror and terror to him. Time with the VA shrinks and a jar full of meds provided by the doctors never warded off the dream, which came at night. He came to hate the night and to despise sleep. Yet, paradoxically, it was the dream that now gave him purpose, a reason for being. The mad gods had chosen him to avenge the sins of Tokyo Rose. This he understood. This was his focus. This was his quest. He would be true to his fallen brothers. He was embarked upon a righteous cause. There would be no turning back.

But first there would be the dream…

He was in a LCVP crashing through the surf as it headed toward the coral reef surrounding Tarawa. He was scared. All the Marine training in the world and the Navy's continuous bombardment of the atoll couldn't shake the fear riveting through his body. He gritted his teeth and tried to force a smile that would not come. He tried to stop quivering all over. He didn't want to be seen shaking with fear. He had his pride.

It helped to know the other men, Marines all, were dealing with the same "shakes." He knew now, as did the others, that there were plenty of Japs on Tarawa who had survived the naval and air attacks. Lots of Japs were not dead.

Deadly bursts of gunfire all around him testified to that. Peering over the side of the Higgins boat, he saw another boat take a direct hit. One moment it was moving toward the beach, the next moment it was gone.

Then the LCVP struck the coral reef and embedded itself on it. The Navy kid steering the boat, who was a bit wild-eyed at this point, yelled, "That's it. You'll have to wade in from here." And so he had. Along with 15 other Marines, he had scurried over the side of the boat. He was about two hundred yards from the beach wading through three feet of water, when a hail of machine gun bullets whistled past, kicking up spray all around him.

He knew in that moment with absolute certainty he would never make it the damn beach. He was going to die before his 18th birthday.

He moved slowly through the water, an easy target for the Jap gunners to fire at as he came closer to the beach. Weighted down with his backpack, trenching equipment, and weapon, he must be, as he thought of himself, a pathetic sight.

He had never been this scared in his life. Eventually, he reached shallower water and noticed that bullets were hitting six inches to the left or six inches to the right. Spraying the water all around him, the lethal "pings" continued to miss him. Somehow, he reasoned, he seemed to be in an invisible bubble that the bullets could not penetrate. He was beginning to think he would make it. Beyond his fear, he felt anger at the Jap gunners and screamed at them, "You bastards, you are lousy shots."

Then the Jap snipers hiding in beached ships in the atoll opened up to his left and rear. He felt the bullets tear into his legs, the terrible pain, and then he collapsed into the shallow waters licking the beach. As he lay wounded, his mind crystallized on the radio show he had heard the night before --- the **Zero Hour,** *and the female announcer who said, the "Japanese soldiers would be ready for the invasion of Japanese-controlled islands." As he lay bleeding to death, he knew she had been right. And he hated her for making this prophecy.*

The *Warrior* awoke from his dream in a cold sweat and to the cries of his fellow wounded Marines. As always, he glanced at his body to make sure he was that he was alive. His gaze carried him to his missing limbs and he remembered he had made it off the beach to a hospital ship offshore. Most of him had made it, that is. Some medic he'd never seen had tied tourniquets on each leg above he knee before shooting him full of morphine. Stretcher-bearers later carried him to others who ferried him away from that hellish beach.

Years later the Warrior learned just what the public knew of Tarawa:

> *At home in the U.S., they could not believe it. Three days of hard fighting, over 1,000 dead and 2,000 wounded---to capture an island of less than three square miles. Newspaper photos of the corpses floating in the tide, or piled on the beach near wrecked and burning landing craft, made an indelible impression on an American public accustomed to viewing the war through the haze of censorship and inflated Allied claims of success.*

Finally awake, the *Warrior* would begin to shake and cry uncontrollably, and finally to scream inwardly at what had happened, and then, after wheeling into his bathroom, he would throw up his painful memories. After washing himself, he would head to the kitchen for a cup of coffee, a handful of pain pills, and a copy of the *Chronicle* that he had read earlier. He had outlined Samuels' story on Iva Toguri in red ink, and then he slashed an "X" across the photo of her that accompanied the article. It was all he could do at the moment.

He then tried to calm himself. He grabbed the phone and dialed a number he had committed to memory. He so needed to speak to his friend who knew so much about the controversy related to School Site 1776.

The *Warrior* needed his new friend. He had no other. This man understood his pain and appreciated his anger toward Iva Torgui. More than ever, he needed his new friend now that Samuels had turned down the ultimatum to stop writing about Tokyo Rose. His friend would know what to do.

He waited for the phone operator to answer. Finally, she did, saying, "San Francisco School Board. How may I direct your call?" He gave a name and waited for his friend to answer. He was no longer alone. He had a cause, which give meaning to his life. He had a friend. He was ready to act.

Chapter 5

THE SEMINAR

The Next Day – San Francisco State College

"Sorry, Bud, but you can't park here."

Robert Samuels was always an impatient man and today was no different. As usual, he was running late for his Tuesday evening college class, where he taught a seminar in "investigative reporting." And now this delay, caused by a young man in an EVENTS STAFF jacket, was holding him up, perturbing him even more than the long, frustrating day he had already put in at the *Chronicle*. First of all, he wasn't a "bud." He wasn't a beer. He preferred a glass of merlot. Nor was he a spring rose awaiting pruning. And lastly, as far as he knew, he wasn't on a friendly first name basis with this kid who was permitting himself to be so informal with an elder.

"You'll have to park elsewhere, Sir," the tall, blond-haired, blue-eyed, well-tanned, freckled-faced youngster said. "I know it's a bit of a walk from the next lot over, but you really can't stay here. This is for faculty only."

Bit of a walk, indeed, Samuels thought to himself. Hell, I'm not that old, mid-50's and in reasonable shape. Sure I'm a little overweight. Jan's cooking, of course, and the seductive availability of doughnuts in the pressroom, that was the problem. What more needed to be said? They were the culprits, not his lapsed exercised routine. Still in all, he could walk from the next lot, but he didn't want to, and certainly not at the urging of surfer-look alike, if not an actual wave pounder with police powers.

"Did you hear me, Sir?" Samuels' tormentor said in his most officious voice, as if he were rehearsing for an FBI position. "I repeat, Sir, you need to move your vehicle."

"Son, I am a member of the faculty."

"Sticker, Sir!"

"Sticker?"

"Faculty sticker, Sir. I don't see one on your windshield. All members of the faculty are provided with one to avoid misunderstandings.

Oh, God, thought Samuels. This aspiring Dick Tracy was right. In his haste not to be late for his weekly seminar, where his students expected him to be punctual, he had forgotten about the sinister sticker, which, unfortunately, was securely locked in the glove compartment of his car. Caught! The forces of righteousness had found him, a parking-lot sinner.

"You're right. No sticker, no laundry."

"Sir, we've been trained to avoid ethnic or racial slurs. Please affix your sticker, if you have one, to the windshield, or remove your vehicle now."

Dear God, Samuels muttered inwardly to himself. I'm dealing with Joe Friday. Hell, the next thing I'll hear is "dum-de-dum-dum." Christ, the way things were going, Frank Smith was liable to pop up and handcuff me for being insufficiently politically correct.

"Here it is," Samuels said as he planted the sticker on his windshield. "Are we okay now?"

"You're good, Sir. Sorry for any inconvenience."

"No problem, young man. Just doing your job, I imagine. I guess you're majoring in Criminology. Law enforcement? Training for the FBI? Or, better yet, the CIA? If not that, let me see, what about Army intelligence? Right?"

"Journalism."

"Really?"

"Finishing my M.A. this year."

"No kidding. Well, listen. If you're ever in Journalism 550, remind me of this incident. I'll pass you anyway," Samuels said, sounding a bit sarcastic, "if you're any good."

"I'll keep that in mind," the young man said with a big smile that seemed more at place on a surfboard. "I surely will."

As the rawboned kid left to protect his asphalt, white-striped empire, Samuels wondered aloud how he had come to this moment. "What was it? Three years ago? When he had visited an old friend at San Francisco State College."

"That's the proposal, Samuels. Are you on board?"

Samuels was sitting in Professor Jonas Morgan's office at State in the newly completed Media Center, which would be the heart of a television, radio, and journalism complex. Jonas, a graduate of Annapolis, and a navy man through and through, loved to speak in the jargon of midshipmen and was doing so now.

"What do you think, mate?"

"Only one class each semester?" Samuels asked.

"A seminar in investigative reporting."

"For M.A. students?"

"Quite so."

"No other obligations?"

"Just grades for the worthy ones. As to the others, throw them in the brig."

"We have a brig at State?"

"Metaphorically, yes. Threaten to fail the mutinous ones, who aren't up to our standards. And if that doesn't work, hit them with a broadside. Make them walk the plank."

"Dare I ask? The Journalism Department has a plank?"

"Indeed. Suggest that other majors await them. But whatever you do, clear the deck of flotsam and jetsam. We want a flotilla of outstanding journalists graduating from this department!"

"Clear the deck," Samuels said, "so to speak."

"That's the spirit, Professor Morgan said. "Full steam ahead."

"As to my pay...?

"As much as I can squeeze out of the budget and those piratical bean-pushers who plague my life."

"One last question, Sir, why me?"

Though a bear of a man in his early 60's, Morgan leaped out of his chair and hurried over to a bulging file cabinet, whose drawers refused to close because of three decades worth of "must keep" items packed in them. More quickly than one might imagine possible, he pulled out a stack of newspapers and raced back to his desk, a mighty smile on his beaming face.

"Look here, Samuels. This is why," he said, holding up one copy after another of the *San Francisco Chronicle*. "One highly researched story after another, all written by you, one investigative report after another, one clearly written expose after another, all so well researched, organized, and written that even the worst of the illiterates who inhabit our fair city could understand them. You're an 'Ace Reporter.' You're the man for this new seminar to navigate through any hostile waters. With you at the helm, our ship of state will prove victorious."

"Hostile waters?"

"The sharks in other departments, our competitors for scarce dollars. We must be vigilant to ward off their greedy hands by our excellence. More to the point, your excellence."

"If I give into your enticing pitch, you have to strike the word 'Ace' from the course catalog. I hate the term. Deal?"

"Deal. The word will be expunged, cast adrift never to bother you. Now just one thing."

"I'm listening."

"Go easy on the theory. Go heavy on them with application. I want these future journalists to know about the guns, but most of all, I want to use them. Give these students a real dose of investigative reporting. Get them out into the field. Find something they can sink their teeth into."

"Have them blast away?" Samuels asked as he got into the spirit of the moment. "Fire away with all guns."

"That's the stuff."

"Application, not seat time."

"Big time."

``I'll get back to you before the next watch," Samuels replied, unable to resist a bit of navy lingo. "One day to think about it."

"Excellent, Samuels, Professor Morgan said. "I'll keep the powder dry for you, shipmate."

And that's how Samuels found his way to San Francisco State and began his voyage through the shoals of education. Of course, he had asked his wife, Jan, for her take, which was immediate and positive. "Do it." When she saw he was still a little unsure, she reminded him of the bevy of beautiful young co-eds who would show up to breathlessly take a class from a first rate newsman, in truth a celebrity in his field, a winner of prestigious awards for his outstanding work in journalism. "They'll be flocking to your class. I don't know how your nervous system will handle such gushing admiration," she jokingly said before adding, "Perhaps I should attend all class meetings with you. I'll flash my ring and remind the gushers that you're definitely off limits."

"You wouldn't, would you?" Samuels asked half jokingly.

"Only if you started coming home very late."

Samuels had taken the job and was always home on time. He knew where his bread was buttered. As for his reputation as a visiting teacher, it had prospered. Students enjoyed the "hands-on-approach" to investigative reporting. He never had problems filling his seminar. And, fortunately, he had never had to ask a grad student to walk the plank.

As Samuels hurried to his class, he wondered if the class would take to the challenge he had in mind for them. After all, rather than dealing with a hot political story with the potential for smashing headlines, he was going to push them to reopen a story already 25-years old. Would they do it, he wondered? Would they care to spend tedious hours researching old courtroom documents, or interviewing possibly recalcitrant, if not hostile witnesses from the past? Would they assist him in investigating a myth? He concluded that he would have to be an excellent salesman. He already envisioned in his mind the quotes he would write on the board to win over his youthful charge. He would bet the house on "irony." The woman at the heart of their research, he would tell them, was Iva Toguri. But what would he tell these students?

She was geographically separated from her mother's death during her family's internment in a relocation camp. By the vagaries of history, she was imprisoned in a foreign land that during another time might have recognized her as one of its own. She lost a child during her enforced exile and found herself unwillingly divorced from her husband and, most significantly, suffered persecution from a nation whose values both she and her father had enthusiastically embraced.

If he needed a last pitch, he would be ready to arouse his students and to win their support with a provocative quote:

> *The American government wound up prosecuting a myth rather than a person.*

Having discharged his pitches, he would hold his breath and ask his new students, "Anybody interested?"

Chapter 6

THE RECRUITS

Loading the Deck

SAMUELS WAS STANDING BEFORE HIS new students. As planned, he directed their attention to the blackboard where he had written his quotations and discussed what he had in mind for the semester. Yet, no questions were voiced. He wondered if he were losing his touch.

"It all adds up to this. We are going to take a hard look at Iva Toguri, who was identified after V-J Day as Tokyo Rose. She was accused of 'aiding and giving comfort' to the enemy during WWII. We want to know though your research if she was something of an urban legend, a fictional person cobbled together from scraps of real history or, in truth, a master spy and traitor to her country? Understand that, incomprehensible as this might sound, there is considerable evidence that no such woman ever existed. Yet, there is also indisputable evidence that Imperial Japan used such a woman or women to broadcast propaganda throughout the Pacific war. Finally, as a matter of historical record, there is proof that only one woman confessed to being Tokyo Rose. That same woman was convicted of treason as a traitor, and is, of course, the focus of our attention."

Samuels let those tidbits of history sink in before going on. "Tokyo Rose was the most well-known of two female broadcasters during World War II. The other was a charming gal known as Axis Sally. We'll learn more about her later. She worked for Radio Berlin, which was the state-controlled Nazis mouthpiece. As to Tokyo Rose, she was vilified as an evil seductress, a spy who knew the location of American ships and installations, a temptress who inspired both lust and homesickness in G.I.'s, and urged them to desert their hopeless effort to defeat the Imperial Japanese war machine. Again, any questions?"

All teachers ask this question, Samuels thought. But deep inside their teaching soul, they secretly hoped none would be asked. Or, if asked, they would not be mundane queries about items already covered or things they could find in the class syllabus. It was always the first question, which, once asked, opened the dike permitting a flood tide of seemingly predictable intellectually moronic inquires. But just maybe, thought Samuels, this class will be different.

For a moment, it was very quiet in the classroom. But Samuels knew this momentary tranquility wouldn't last. It didn't.

"You're going to interview each of us in class before giving us our individual assignments concerning this woman?" Rita Howard asked in a husky voice. "Isn't that a bit unusual?"

"Yes, I guess it is," Samuels replied.

"But we're still going to have interviews?" Luis Lopez stated as much as he asked.

"Yes. For this particular project, yes."

"And we have only four weeks to research our topics?" Janet Lee inquired.

"Deadlines will have to be met," Samuels stated flatly. "We're working against the clock."

"Your newspaper's clock?" Philip Aquino asked in an aggressive tone. "So that you can meet your editor's schedule?"

"That's the deal. If you join this little excursion into the past, it's your deal, too."

"Our research goes into your stories," Tom Hayakawa commented rather than questioned."

"Your research, my byline," Samuels said straightforwardly. "It's like being an indentured servant, I suspect."

"Doesn't seem fair," Stan Mack said. "Looks like we're doing all the work, and you're getting all the credit," he added.

"We are doing all the work," Janet Lee piped in softly.

"There's that. But you will get exhaustive credit in the footnotes and my everlasting gratitude, plus a grade recognizing your contributions."

"Still," Rita Howard started to say before Samuels quickly cut her off.

"There is no still. I make the assignments, review your research and grade your application of theory with respect to your potential to be outstanding investigative reporters. After that I send you out into the world with a delightful and well-earned recommendation that any newspaper editor will find most inviting. And just maybe, if you're good enough, you'll get a job offer. When that happens, I'll expect an update from you acknowledging my efforts to develop your journalistic sniffing skills."

"Sniffing skills?" Tom Hayakawa asked.

"Absolutely," Samuels retorted. "A good journalist should be guided by three things in investigating a story: First, what does your head tell you? Second, what does your heart say? Third, what does your nose tell you?"

"This sounds like an Anatomy class, "Luis Lopez said with emphasis. "Head, heart, nose … Yuck."

"Yuck?" Samuels asked. "There's no 'yuck' in journalism. Get a grip, Mr. Lopez."

"I don't understand," Stan Mack said.

"Fair enough. I'll make it simple. The cognitive springs in your brain permit you to analyze within the scope of the subject-object boundaries of life. You (the subject) perceive something (object) and objectify it in order to figure out what's going on. Good start. Your heart goes where the mind fears to tread, that is, into the world of feelings, and emotions, where you may learn what's behind the actions, the observable behavior, stuff you can't see. Or at least you think you can tell. As to your lovely nose, think of your nasal passages as a laboratory where hunches are born, where fragmented pieces of information ever so slowly begin to make sense, where the human puzzle starts to take shape, where the hound dog in you finally sniffs out the truth. A good journalist makes good use of …"

"Her brain," Rita Howard said with cognitive pride.

"His heart," Luis Lopez sang out, his emotions tingling his few words.

"His nose," said Stan Mack, especially when things don't make sense."

"Exactly," Samuels said. "Exactly."

With that, the questions stopped. Samuels wondered to himself how many of the students would stay? Damn, he reminded himself, if we are to get a handle on Tokyo Rose, I need all of them at the oars, as we careen through uncharted waters.

"If you're not into this, I'll understand," Samuels said in his most reassuringly voice to his potential grad students. "You can check into Professor Morton's class, which, I should add, is inordinately loaded with tiny print in books overloaded in theory about how to write a good story as opposed to our effort that will be filled with an action-packed opportunity to invade the past and hound out the truth about the most infamous woman in American criminal history."

Samuels paused to give his charges an opportunity to digest his declaration of sincere sympathy before going on. "Obviously, I can't compete with Professor Morton's interest in hypotheticals combined with the theoretical, which are found in past cases presented. I assume pandemic language locked into a ponderous text totally lacking in any sense of the dramatic. However, the appeal to many to learn about investigative reporting by the seat of their pants in the classroom, I might add, as opposed to actual real-world experience, is something I wouldn't care to comment on, if you get my drift. Professor Morton is a fine lecturer in comparison to my halting use of the language, which is perhaps why I'm given to succinctness in what few words I use sparingly to get a few minor points across. Naturally, since this is a college grad course, I'm required to have a text for you, and, of course, for my masters who audit my puny efforts to claim your attention and interest for a long semester. For that reason, I downplay the dry, stale, even suffocating case studies in the few text readings I'll assign. Again, in all fairness to Professor Morton, I trust I haven't overstated the case for action in contrast to inertia."

Samuels' so-called disinterested commentary came to a close and he waited patiently for his students to respond. Rita Howard was the first to raise a voice. With a gleeful smile and a tongue-in-cheek voice, she said, "Mr. Samuels, I ... we, the class, certainly wouldn't want you to overstate your position."

"And?" Samuels asked with a hardly disguised smile on his face.

"Well, speaking for myself, I'm not into inertia."

"And the rest of you?"

"I'm for the action," chimed in Tom Hayakawa. "I'm not much for small print."

"My sentiments, too," Janet Lee said zestfully. "Bring on the field work. I'm all for drama."

"Count me in, Mr. Samuels," Philip Aquino blurted out. "I'm game."

"If we're in the footnotes, as you say, well okay," Stan Mack added. "Anyway, I'd be bored silly just reading about what other journalists did. I want to be in on the doing."

"Never let it be said that pervasive peer pressure got to me," Luis Lopez exclaimed. "I'm in. Let's get started."

Samuels was delighted with their positive responses. There would, hopefully, be no need for the brig or the plank.

"I appreciate your vote of confidence," Samuels said most diplomatically. "I think we have the makings of a top notched group, shipmates one and all. Now before we get into your interviews and assignments, one question. Does anyone know Ron Siegel?"

"I took Journalism 503 with him last semester," Janet Lee said. "He was a pretty good student as I recall. Why do you ask?"

"He's listed on my class roster but, of course, he's not here."

"I think he's got a job on campus," Luis Lopez added. "I've seen him around campus with the enforcement types."

"OK, I'll try to find out what happened to him," Samuels replied.

Naturally, at that precise moment, the classroom door burst opened and an-out-of-breath Ron Siegel lunged into the room, crying, "I'm sorry I'm late, Sir, but we had some major problems on campus."

Samuels could only stare at the young man standing before him in an EVENTS STAFF jacket.

"You," Samuels said all too loudly.

"Yes, Sir, it's me," the tanned Adonis replied.

"My parking lot persecutor!"

"I would word my duties somewhat differently, Sir."

"You're Ron Siegel?"

"I am."

"And you had major problems in the faculty parking lot?" he asked. "A shortage of stickers, no doubt?"

"No such luck."

"What, then, Mr. Siegel?"

"Drug users breaking into the vehicles and stealing anything of value. They pawn or sell what they find in order to feed their habit. We've been after these guys for weeks now."

"You exaggerate?" Samuels said still a little unwilling to give Siegel a pass too easily.

"No, Sir. In fact both of us were quite lucky today."

"We were?"

"Absolutely. We caught one fellow who was about to break into your car."

Samuels, of course, was caught off guard by Siegel's answer. The kid had saved him most probably a sizeable repair bill and the inconvenience of struggling with his insurance company. Truth be told, he owed the kid one. Still, he couldn't quite admit to all this without a little heartfelt wickedness.

"There is a God, Mr. Siegel," Samuels said to the young man. "It appears I have an opportunity to seek my revenge."

"Sir, I hope your God is compassionate."

"Not at the moment,"

For the other students watching this tennis match, they were unsure as to what was going on.

"Do you guys know each other?" Rita Howard asked.

"We do," Ron Siegel said. "Sort of."

"And we're going to know each other a lot better," Samuels remarked. "We have an entire semester to become best of friends. Right, bud?"

With that, Samuels, unable to contain himself, started laughing, even as a slight smile crossed Ron Siegel's face. As for the others, they just looked on wondering what they had really gotten themselves into?

Chapter 7

INTERVIEWS

The Inquisition

"TELL ME A LITTLE ABOUT yourself, Miss Lee."

"Do we need to be so formal?" she asked. "Please call me Janet."

"Of course. And I'm Robert."

"Oh, I couldn't call you by that, Mr. Samuels."

"Okay," Samuels said with a shy grin. Perhaps later."

"Yes, when I'm a working reporter."

Samuels was conducting his first interview. Janet Lee was his first victim, who he hoped would survive without any lasting scars. Miss Lee was a Chinese-American, petite with beautiful almond-shaped eyes. He noticed she was wearing an oversized sweater and a comfortable long shirt to ward off the cool San Francisco night.

"I was born in Shanghai. I came to the United States when I was five. My father was in the import-export business in China. He's still in the business in Oakland, mainly children's toys for the Christmas trade. I did well in school. Really, I had no choice. My family would have disowned me had I dishonored them with poor grades. I received a scholarship to CAL and my B.A. in English. From there, I matriculated to San Francisco State to study Journalism."

"Anything exciting at Berkeley?" Samuels asked.

"Exciting?"

"You know. Demonstrations? Afterall, you were at CAL."

"I did demonstrate against discrimination in the South. Is that what you're referring to?"

"Yes. Anything else?"

Miss Lee suddenly turned scarlet red as she lowered her head before answering in muted words. "I did participate in a bra-burning demonstration on behalf of women's liberation."

The response of the class was immediate. "That a way to go, lady." Though embarrassed, Miss Lee smiled.

"Well, I'm sure, Janet, no such effort will be needed in your looming research."

"My topic will be?"

"Actually, you have three topics, but they are all tied to one person, Iva Toguri, the Japanese-American who was accused of treason. We need to know her background, that is, the early years of her life. In addition, why did she go to Japan just a few months before Pearl Harbor was attacked? Finally, why did she get involved with the Zero Hour?"

"Zero Hour?"

"A radio show during World War II."

"Really?"

"Take my word for it, yes."

Next up was Philip Aquino. As his name suggested, he was born in the Philippines and grew up in a suburb just outside of Manila. His family enjoyed a rich place in the history of the country. His father had been with the Filipino Scouts, who waged a determined "hit and run war" with the Japanese until the archipelago was retaken by the Allies in 1945. His grandfather had sided with the guerrillas during the bitter nine-year Filipino Insurrection against American forces, who had kicked out the Spanish out of their colonial possession in 1898. It seemed the Filipinos didn't want to trade the yoke of Madrid for the imperialistic grip of the Stars and Stripes.

In the 1950's, Philip's family migrated to Southern California, finally settling in Eagle Rock just outside of Los Angeles. The family worked hard. His dad enjoyed gardening and made a living taking care of other people's lawns, shrubbery, and flowers. His mother cleaned houses on a regular basis, even as she raised five children, all of whom were encouraged to do well in school. Philip had done well, first at San Diego State College and now in San Francisco.

"Philip, what got you interested in journalism?" Samuels asked the thin, brown-toned, mid-20's student with stark, long black hair, who dressed in western garb: Levi pants and jacket, a wool checkered shirt, and deeply shined black boots."

"My history teacher in high school."

"Why was that?" Samuels asked.

"He got me interested in court cases like the Scopes Trial. He also prompted me to join the school paper, which I did."

"Never underestimate the influence of a good teacher."

"What will my topic be?"

"Philip, you're going to enter the world of romance, deceit, and bureaucratic frustrations."

"Sounds like a daytime serial on television."

"Like something out of Hollywood, Philip?"

"Yes."

"Even more so; we need you to research one Felipe d'Aquino, a young man who befriended Iva Toguri. Also, you need to determine if our State Department acted injudiciously with regard to her passport problems. Lastly, dig into her first trial, which was held in Japan. Figure out what happened."

"d'Aquino?"

"A Portuguese citizen who was trapped in wartime Japan."

"Not Filipino?"

"From the land of Henry the Navigator. Portugal."

"If you say so."

"I do."

"But lots of romance and intrigue, Mr. Samuels?"

"Enough for a lifetime."

Samuels next turned his attention to Rita Howard. From what little he knew about her, she was an all-American girl from Pittsburgh, the only child of a God-fearing middle class family. Her father was a pharmacist, who worked for the old Owl Drug Store Company. Her mother was a high school English teacher. Given her short stature, Rita learned early to push hard with her studies or through a tight crowd to be front and center in order to see what was going on or to pursue her ambitions. One might described her as a fullback in skirts, but much cuter. With her wholesome, lovely mid-western complexion, she was an animated, always on the go, teenager before receiving a scholarship to the University of Pittsburgh, where she was a language major, digesting both Spanish and Latin. As a strong practicing Catholic, she believed deeply that miracles were possible. She also had an adventurous spirit. After Pitt, she migrated to the Bay Area, finally settling down in Marin County just north of "Frisco." There she followed her mother's trail and went into teaching. She taught Spanish in the local Catholic High School for girls only. It appeared that she was an outstanding teacher from the word go.

"Rita, what brought you from the cloistered classroom to State?"

"I always had a passion for writing. I guess it's always been my secret desire to write for a great newspaper."

"Any one incident that prompted you in that direction?"

"The Civil Rights movement and those brave reporters who covered the story in the South."

"Indeed."

"And what topics will I cover, Mr. Samuels?"

"You get to trace the dastardly activities of two reporters in post-war Japan, Clark Lee and Harry Brundidge."

"Dastardly?"

"For the lack of a better word, yes."

"Anything else?"

"The evolution of Iva Toguri from a celebrity to a criminal in Tokyo. Okay with that, Rita?"

"I'm good. But I do have a question."

"Shoot."

"You seem to know a great deal about Iva Toguri already. Won't are research just be redundant?"

"Good observation. It's true, I do know a lot about the woman but only the broad outlines of her life. I need you folks to put flesh on her bones, to tease out who she really was beyond the news stories that stereotyped her as a villain in front of a microphone. In short, I know enough to get you started."

Even as Robert Samuels was assigning topics to his grad students, **in** another part of town fate was, as always, intervening in the human drama. In her apartment in the Marina, Rachel Samuels, the newly appointed principal of the still unnamed school site 1776, was checking through her mail after a long day at work planning for the new school. Beyond the usual monthly bills from PG&E and ATT and a slew of advertisements and charitable requests, there was one envelope that stood out due to the return address, which simply read *THE WARRIOR*. Her father had spoken to her earlier about a phone call and letter from a potentially dangerous man so it was with trepidation that she nervously opened the envelope. Fumbling with the letter as she unfolded it, and sat down at her kitchen table, she finally read it. As she did, she spoke quietly to the the stalwarts in her kitchen, the refrig and the stove, saying aloud, "I may need something stronger than a glass of wine today."

Miss Rachel Samuels,

I've already written to your father but to no avail. He is determined, as is the Chronicle, to publish a series of articles about Iva Toguri, better known as Tokyo Rose. I cannot let this happen.

Within a few months the first students will arrive at your new school and the School may be named, if the Japanese-American population has its way, for this traitor to our country. I cannot let this happen.

The school board, I'm afraid, will only be too willing to support that nomination, especially if the rumored presidential pardon of Toguri takes place out of some misguided effort to appease the Asian community. I will not let this happen.

As I told your father, I don't want to hurt anyone. But I cannot abide by the school being named after this treasonous woman. You must convince your father to desist. If you love him, you must do this soon. I cannot give you another warning. I will not be responsible for what happens if this warning goes unheeded.

The letter was simply signed *THE WARRIOR*.

Rachel put the letter down and, as calmly as she could, poured herself a large glass of white wine, a Riesling from the cool coastal climate of Northern California. She reached for the phone and then remembered her father was at his seminar. No matter. She would call him in the morning. There was no need, she thought, to worry her mother by calling at this time. It would be better to speak directly to her father.

***

Unaware of what was taking place, Robert Samuels continued giving out assignments.

"Stan, I think that covers it."

"You want to know about this guy, Walter Winchell?"

"That's right."

"And about Iva Toguri's second trial?"

"Yes, the one held in San Francisco."

"And the judge's decision?"

"Most definitely."

Stan Mack. Samuels had been unsure about him when the interview began due to the young man's confrontational tone.

"Please don't refer to me as an African-American, Mr. Samuels. I wasn't born in Africa. I've never been there. I have no desire to go there. I'm from the 'projects' in Bayview just north of Hunter's Point, you know, the land of guns and gangs."

"My mistake, Mr. Mack."

"Another thing, I don't like being referred to as a Black. As you can clearly see, I'm pretty light-skinned due to a Hawaiian mother and a mulatto father. Calling me "Black" is an insult."

"Again, that would never be my intention. "Anything else?"

"I detest the term Negro. It lacks push, juice, presence."

"I assume you have the same distain for the term "Colored?"

"Immense distain."

"Not much left," Samuels said.

"How about Mac?"

"I can handle that," Samuels said. "Short for Mack, I guess."

"My dad drove big trucks, the "Big Macks," when he was in the Army in Korea."

Stan Mack was a tough guy. He had attended City College of San Francisco after graduating from Poly High School with less than a stellar academic record. Through hard work and damn persistence, he had done well enough to matriculate to State, where sprinter speed on the track team and improved grades had led him to graduate school. While a history major, he was pushing hard to be a journalist. To Samuels, he seemed to have a chip on his shoulder that needed venting through the inky world of the press-room. The trick was to write good prose without getting splattered with ink. He hoped Mac was up to it.

Luis Lopez was up next, a Hispanic kid whose parents had footed it from a dusty village south of Mexico City to the Rio Grande and then north to Texas. Eventually, the family migrated to California before settling into East Los Angeles. Their journey had been made in the shadows of Immigration Officers, who were constantly looking for those without "papers." Luis parents were just that, "undocumented." In time the family was graced with six kids, all born in the USA. Luis' father got hooked up with a small repair shop, Gonzalez Handyman Repairs and in time, acquired the skills of carpentry, plumbing, and electrical work. All this was done in the absence of a Green Card. His mother, between kids, worked for Motel 6 cleaning up the debris of temporary guests.

At Gardena High School, Luis got interested in social issues, especially as they related to Hispanics. He joined La Raza and was a student volunteer working on behalf of the grape pickers of the Central Valley. It was in Fresno that he met Cesar Chavez, a charismatic labor organizer. From that moment on, Luis wanted to fight on the side of the "little guy," not with rocks and insults, but with the written word. Chavez had encouraged him to go into journalism, which he did with a twist. He would also major in labor relations.

""Well, Luis, what do you think?" Samuels asked the serious young man before him. "Can you do this?"

"You want to know about Iva Toguri's jail time following her second trial??

"Right."

"And what's happening that may lead to a pardon by President Ford?"

"Very much so."

"Done."

Tom Hayakawa and Ron Siegel received their topics next. Samuels had saved the "fill-in" topics for them with the hope that all **"loose ends"** might be tied together due to their research.

For Tom, a Japanese-American and native of Santa Clara by way of the Manzanar relocation camp in California, where he was born in 1944, the road to San Francisco State had been rather straightforward. After being released from the internment camp his parents had resettled in the lovely town. They started a flourishing nursery business and pushed their children hard to do well in school. While in high school, Tom worked for the *Nisei Gazette*, a local paper catering to the Japanese community. His love affair with journalism began at that point.

"I want to know about Fred Korematsu," Samuels said without any preamble. "And another fellow, Wayne Mortimer Collins."

"That's it?" Tom asked. "Just two guys?"

"It's plenty. Take my word for it."

"You're the instructor."

"That I am."

Now it was Ron Siegel's turn. Ten minutes later, the handsome gendarme, mouth a gap, asked, "Do these topics come under the heading of 'vengeance is mine'?"

"Research," Samuels replied with a satisfied look on his face.

"Ernest Besig, who the heck was he?"

"A lumber strike in Northern California. Humboldt County to be exact. And a general strike in San Francisco in 1935. That's it."

"And all this has to do with Iva Toguri?" the young man asked with a mixture of defiance and incredulity on his face.

"Without question, Mr. Siegel," Samuels said pointedly. "You're OK with this?"

"Sure, but remind me to be more cautious next time I ask a faculty to move his vehicle."

"I will."

Of course, the other grad student had no idea what was transpiring between Samuels and the local sheriff. The just wanted to get going. Rita voiced their impatience. "When do we start, Mr. Samuels?"

"Now."

Later, after his students left for parts known but to them, Samuels scanned a list of assignments, scribbled earlier in the day, now residing with his aspiring journalists. One by one, he checked off each name.

Janet Lee

1. What was Iva's family background?
2. Why did she go to Japan six months before Pearl Harbor?
3. How did she get involved with the Zero Hour?

Philip Aquino

1. Who was Felipe d'Acquino?
2. What were Iva's passport problems?
3. What happened during Iva's first trial in Japan?

Rita Howard

1. Who were Clark Lee and Harry Brundidge?
2. How did Iva go from celebrity status to criminal in 1945?

Stan Mack

1. Who was Walter Winchell?
2. What happened in Iva's second trial in San Francisco?

Luis Lopez

    1. How did Iva cope with jail time?

    2. Why was President Ford considering a pardon for Iva?

Tom Hayakawa

    1. Who was Fred Korematsu?

    2. Who was Wayne Mortimer Collins?

    3.

Ron Siegel

    1. Who was Ernest Besig?

———————————— ✦ ✦ ✦ ————————————

In Navy parlance, Samuels thought to himself, the crew, as yet untested, were at their battle stations. Beyond the horizon incoming bogies, as yet unseen, were headed their way with intent to maul and destroy. How would his young shipmates acquit themselves, Samuels asked himself? And how would he captain this crew in the unsteady seas ahead?

Chapter 8

THE MAN

San Francisco – Evening

T HE MAN APPEARED TO SIT comfortably in the thick, burnished, black leather chair, which clung to the dark-toned, reddish traditional high-low carpet pile covering the study's floor. Though the Man's legs were propped up on a matching Ottoman in an apparently relaxed fashion, he was anything but in his private book-lined retreat. Occasionally, he would put down the book he was reading to stir the quiet flames in the fireplace, or to add another small log. Seated again, he would sip his brandy when it suited him before returning to his reading. He did enjoy the brandy's warmth and its ingrained disposition suggesting all was well in the world.

Of course, the Man knew that all was not well and this accounted for his discomfort.

He was in his mid-60s, still fit, and with a hairline that refused to acknowledge his advancing years. Most people would describe him as burly, but not fat, merely big, but not ungainly, and unusually quiet spoken. He lived alone in his Pacific Heights home in one of the more affluent neighborhoods in San Francisco. In this room lined with mainly biographies and history books, he found what pleasure life still afforded him. Where space permitted, pictures of his deceased wife adorned mantle places, along with his two sons, each lost in Vietnam. Alone in this room where the past never died, he was a lonely soul. But it had not always been this way.

Upon returning from a hitch in post-war Japan, the Man entered college, married, started a family, and went into business. Thanks to an inheritance from his parents, he opened a liquor store in the Mission District. Why liquor? "Why not?" was his usual answer to the curious. The truth was a little more personal. He simply liked the business, the product, and the customers. He liked unpacking the bottles of wine and whiskey, whether the cheap stuff or the high cost premium versions. He enjoyed lining the shelves with glistening glass, labels front and always dusted. He even enjoyed stringing wire in front of the bottles to secure them in case of an earthquake. He took to the simplicity of the business.

"I'll have a fifth of rye," the customer would declare.

"*Old Turkey?*"

"You know your ryes."

"I do."

In any event, the Man's business prospered, and, eventually, he ran a string of five stores throughout the city. He had a knack for making money in the industry. He was very creative in the tight retail industry that seemed stuck in the 1930's.

For his very cost-conscious customers, he merely slapped on a label with a likeness of *Peter the Great* and Russian-looking script, and magically an authentic imported bottle of vodka appeared. His customers never knew about a small distillery in Napa County that produced the drink of the Czars and other desired spirits. What made all this possible was the high quality he expected and strong price discount he demanded. The same was true of gin and scotch. A gallant-looking label complete with "royal arms," was sufficient to claim the genuine gin of the Brits. The Irish and the Highlanders also found their way to his malt whiskey. All he needed, he once said, was a clean printing press and some excellent artists to produce and help sell a passable product.

As the Man liked to say to his closest associates, "I import the world without the inconvenience of an excise tax."

He had hoped to leave the business to his sons, but the Vietnam Conflict intervened. Mitch and Mike, his two identical twins, had done most everything together, Boy Scouts, high school football and baseball, honor classes, and even double dating, which they always found amusing. Then came the draft, the Mekong Delta, and words of "regret" from the President. Still together, their names shared a common concrete place on the Vietnam Wall. All this was too much for his wife and the breast cancer that attacked her with unseemly anger. Within one year, he had lost his entire family. With them, the light in his eyes dimmed and blinked shut against the harshness of this world.

The Man was accustomed to family death now, but he hated the terrible pain it summoned when the past crept into his mind. It had started with his older brother, Nick, a gung-ho Marine, who died on Iwo Jima after a Jap mortar landed on his squad. One moment he was John Wayne, the next moment he was flesh and bone, broken and scattered from this world. He had seen his mother and father cry when they learned of his brother's death. And so he sobbed, too, through the anger of his clenched fists and broken heart. What else could he do? He could not kill those who hd destroyed his brother. The war was over. But in his anguish, he wanted to with a passion he hardly understood. Someone, he thought, needed to pay. Someday, he believed, someone would.

The Man's personal losses were almost too much to bear. He was depressed to the point where suicidal thoughts screamed for his attention. For a time, he really didn't want to live. How could he carry on? What joy would be in his life? Since he was a "vet," he sought help from the local VA Hospital. Over a period of time, grief therapy and anti-depressant pills pulled him back from the abyss, and his life went on, alone and lonely.

At the urging of old friends, the Man poured himself into his business, but he now found it unrewarding. Others could run the stores for him and did. The profits flowed in regardless of his involvement. And then it had happened...

He was having dinner with an old competitor, Harry Greenberg, who owned *Martell's Liquors*. Harry had two suggestions between bites of his New York steak. "Look, why don't you sell out to me? I'll make you a ridiculous offer. You'll be a very wealthy man."

"I've got plenty now."

"You'll have more."

"So?"

"Travel," Harry had said.

"Alone?"

"Take a cruise. Meet someone."

"Any other suggestions?"

Harry had another suggestion and it surprised the man. "As a matter of fact, yes."

"Well?"

"Sell out to me and run for political office."

"You've had too much to drink, Harry."

"Hear me out. You come from a conservative part of town. There's an open school board position. Why not run for the school board?"

"Harry…"

"You'd be perfect. That school board crap would occupy your mind much of your time; it would give you something to do. Hell, you might even do some good for jerk-off kids in the city."

"Harry, I don't know the first thing about education."

"Permit me to correct you, dear friend. You're perfect for the Board. You've run a business, haven't you?"

"Still do. Score one for you."

"You've met a payroll every two weeks?"

"Of course."

"You've met every competitive challenge, including those I engineered, did you not?"

"A matter of record, Harry."

By the time they had dessert, Harry convinced the Man to run. It did seem like a way to use his time. Harry promised to line up big donors and to get able people to run his campaign. All he had to do was make a few speeches at some scheduled town hall meetings. Just act normal, he was told, and be the charming person you are.

And so the Man ran, half-heartedly at first and then with quiet determination. His campaign pledges were few, but always direct, and always contrary to what his political advisers advised.

"You can't say that," one experienced consultant said.

"Why not?"

"You'll lose votes."

"But it's what I believe."

"What you believe can get you killed in this business."

The Man's competitive juices were aroused and he stuck to his guns. He would say what he wanted to say. If he won, okay. If he was defeated, that really didn't matter. He had lost so much already. What would another loss matter?

"Running the schools is akin to running a business," he told the voters. "Expenses must not exceed income. Salaries must be fair, but not so generous that red ink flows. Benefits are okay as long as the district doesn't go into hock to pay them. Tenure and seniority are fine if complacency and incompetency doesn't result from too much security."

As for families in his district, the Man said with equal zeal, "Parents, if your kids attend school, pay attention, and make sure they do their homework. Good things will happen if you do this. That's it. The school owes your kids an opportunity for an education. Nothing more. We won't put up with stupidity and behavior that detracts from others. If you can't handle that, find another school district."

To his complete surprise, he won by a landslide. Harry couldn't have been happier. "I told you, buddy, you would win, didn't I?"

"You did. But now what?"

"Do your things, whatever that is and consider my new company's bids from time to time."

"New company?"

"*Jones and Jones, Construction, Inc.* I'm a consultant for them."

"Consultant?"

"I help them win bids to build new classrooms," Harry said without a falter. "We also repave the asphalt so the little ones will have a nice place to play. If the district needs a new cafeteria, we can do that, too."

"I see."

"I knew you would."

In time he came to like the job and to win the grudging respect of his more liberal colleagues on the Board who wanted to remake the world in the classroom. The Man kept them honest, however. As long as the tax revenue paid for their earthly ideals, he went along. He even gave his support to *Jones and Jones* when the numbers made sense.

The Man was still alone, but a little less lonely.

After two years on the Board and a successful reelection, events conspired to jolt the Man with painful memories, which eventually led him down a road from which there was no apparent turning back.

The school board, driven by increased enrollment, pushed through a bond issue to build a new school. Until a name was chosen for the school, it was simply identified as *School Site 1776* to honor the 200th anniversary of the Declaration of Independence. At the same time, the board requested possible names from the community. Among the many suggestions, the Japanese community suggested Iva Toguri if, they pointed out, she received a full Presidential pardon for her alleged role as Tokyo Rose.

The Man found this situation unacceptable. No traitor's name, he declared to the high heavens, would grace the new school, certainly not while the death of his brother on Iwo Jima still lived in his heart. As time went on, he felt increasing anger, such as he had never known before. The anger was a living thing that over-whelmed his sensitivities and pushed aside his desire to forgive and forget. His sense of proportion and perspective were shunted away by the need to square things. Revenge replaced compassion. He was losing his essential humanity. He knew this and he accepted what was happening. He needed to vent his anger.

He vowed he would find a way to stop the outrage.

Chapter 9

THE SOCIAL WORKER

The Lady Social Worker

"GOD, HOW THESE DAMN YEARS flew by," the *Warrior* said aloud to the four walls in the seedy, small studio apartment that was his home and self-inflicted prison for the past seven years. He recalled that overly solicitous, very middle-aged social worker, Mrs. Rose Franklin, from the VA Hospital who had found the room for him. It was his luck to have the" Jewish-mother" of all time supervising his case.

"It will be perfect," she said. "It's on the bottom floor with easy access for you and just large enough to meet your needs."

"Access?" he questioned. "You mean my wheelchair will go through the front door without jamming me?"

"Of course," she said, trying hard to remain upbeat. "Entry into the bathroom won't be a problem either."

"Thanks," he said bitterly. "It's good to know I can take a piss when I need to, Mrs. Franklin."

The social worker refused to bite at his caustic words, or the use of "Mrs.," indicating that he really was irked. "You can take your 'piss,' as you say, and a shower or bath. The tub opens compliments of the VA."

"How nice," he remarked. "I'll be the cleanest person in town."

Again, refusing to be pushed by his words, she said, "The room does have a large picture window looking out on the street."

"So I can watch people scurrying about?" he asked with a touch of anger in his voice. "I'll be able to see the whole world passing by while I sit locked in this room in this contraption, won't I?"

"You have to live somewhere," she said flatly. "And you can wheel your contraption, as you call it, outdoors. You're not stuck in here."

"To enjoy the south of Market Street sights?"

"You didn't want," she reminded him, "the other areas of town I suggested, did you?"

Mrs. Franklin, he admitted to himself, was right. He had rejected a similar studio apartment in the Sunset area not too far from the Great Highway adjacent to the Pacific Ocean. He ducked taking a place near Golden Gate Park in the proximity of the "Panhandle," where only a decade ago the "peace movement" broke out between puffs of pot and cries of *"We Shall Overcome."* Nor did he take a shine to the outer-Richmond whose old Russian-Jewish population was dying out only to make room for the Chinese and Japanese who were moving out of their traditional high-density area north of Market Street for the relative quiet and space of the neighborhoods. The Merced Lake area with its high tower apartment houses and surrounding duplexes, plus the *Stones Town Shopping Mall*, constituted a suburb within the city. Not his style, he had told her.

But that wasn't his real reason for ducking the area. He knew that. She probably did, too.

He didn't want to be near the "normal people." He didn't want to see a band of kids playing in the street, screaming and yelling with the energy and vigor of the young who were still innocent of the shadows cast in a world of misery and pain that he knew far too well. Nor did he want to see the youthful women, with the wind blowing through their hair and sunlight splashing on them, pushing their newborns in perambulators on bright, shining days. He didn't want to see couples walking hand-in-hand, whether old or young, enjoying both a stroll and speaking the language of love. He didn't want to see shiny new cars being washed and polished on Saturday by robust men making them still shinier. On Sunday, he didn't want to smell a multitude of BBQ's hard at work roasting pork ribs, half-chickens, or the ubiquitous American favorite, the burger and hot dog. He didn't want to see all the things he desperately desired.

"You're right, Mrs. Franklin. I turned down the other locations."

"And you know why, don't you?" she asked with an edge in her voice.

"You tell me."

"You were looking for a foxhole. And now you've found one. How nice. Once I've gone, you're going to climb into it and hide for the rest of your life," she stated without equivocation. "It's safer here in your rent-a-bunker than joining the world. That's about it, isn't it?"

"You can be bitchy at times."

"One of my better qualities when dealing with the likes of you. Since I'm bitchy, I'll continue. I wouldn't want to sully my reputation. From your chair, you can observe the bustle and hustle of industrial traffic and people shuffling to work, each in a hurry, all of them disregarding your presence. Add some drug dealers and addicts, plus the down and out, and you've found paradise, a place where the dispirited can decry the joy of others. Here you're going to be inconspicuous, just another vet who had trouble adjusting two wars late!"

"Enough," he shouted.

"Quite right," she said, her voice bristling with hardly concealed therapeutic contempt. "You lost your legs, and you're wading knee deep in self-pity. You've spent almost fifteen years in and out of VA hospitals or halfway houses. It's time for you to settle down," she said with a smile, half cheerful, half-mocking. "It's time to get a life."

Get a life, he thought. What the hell is she talking about? How could she know how I feel? She's just another VA bureaucrat working her way through her caseload, one GI at a time. Yet, though he thought it, he knew that wasn't exactly true. She had been on his back for three years now, always positive and cheerful regardless of his generally "ticked-off" disposition. She had always matched him in the brutal verbal combat that marked their relationship. She never let him enjoy the self-pity, which he believed he richly deserved and wanted desperately to keep at all costs. She, he thought, had no right to invade his pity-party.

Still, he had to admire her. Every week she stuck her head into the lion's mouth. Every week he slapped around her good intentions. Every visitation he turned into a confrontation. Every smile he met with a smirk. But, still he had to admire her. She took every rejection and objection he meted out and came back for more.

"You call this a life? I'll be chained to this damn room, to this wheelchair, to lonely meals and television repeats, and *Time Magazine* telling me all about the world. I'll sit here chain-smoking my way to oblivion munching on painkillers. That's a life?"

"It's the life you've chosen. If you don't like it, change it."

"You sure know how to twist the knife," he said through clenched jaws.

"I do," she said. "I've had lots of experience with fellows like you."

"It shows," he said sarcastically.

"Good. I'll show you sympathy, but not pity," she retorted. "I know all about you. You lied about your age and joined the Marines when you were not yet 18. You were just a kid not yet out of high school. A year later you landed on Tarawa."

"And some Jap bastard took away my legs," he cried out.

"The same bastard you would have killed?" she asked.

"It was war."

"It was, wasn't it?" she queried. "Anyway, you were lucky. You were shoved onto a hospital ship and the good doctors saved your life."

"By cutting off my legs," he screamed.

"You spent considerable time in physical therapy and not enough time dealing with your head," said, as if she hadn't heard him. "You refused to live with your parents, or any relatives, and for far too long you've been a walking "poor me case' popping pills and drinking far too heavily."

"Walking case?" he yelled. "I don't think so."

"And smoking too much. And there's no need to raise your voice. My hearing is still pretty good."

In time, he settled into his bunker. True to her word, Mrs. Franklin visited him once a week to see how he was doing. She pushed and prodded him to shop at the local *Safeway*, where he loaded up with fatty food, booze, and cigarettes much to her dismay. She did made sure a nice Mexican lady, who needed a few extra dollars, came by every two weeks to clean his apartment, especially the accumulated dirty dishes and numerous unwashed pots and pans. It was almost as if, out of his anger and contempt for any assistance, he purposely kept a "rat's nest" to show them, all those VA doctors and psychologists, and, of course, his social worker.

Nevertheless, she made sure his monthly disability check arrived on time, and that he paid his utility bills and rent without fail. Given her scrutiny, his visits with VA doctors were scheduled and kept. She would drive the VA van that permitted wheelchair access. While he sat rock-like, quiet as an Egyptian mummy, she would rattle off a bewildering onslaught of commentaries on everything from the lousy weather to those idiots in Washington. Concerning him, she was very insistent and persistent. She never seemed to give up.

"You're drinking too much."

"I am."

"You're smoking too much."

"True."

"You're gaining weight."

"Yes."

"You're watching too much television."

"So?"

"You're still feeling sorry for yourself."

"My privilege."

After a while, he fought with her less and less. Mrs. Franklin made her comments. He listened and supplied succinct answers to endure her visits. She was a constant reminder of all he had lost and his failure to transcend the pain that afflicted him.

During the year, and soon years, they went through a simple ritual. On his birthday, she would arrive with a present and a small cake. He learned to say "thank you," and nothing more. She would give him her special social worker "look" and sigh before leaving with a quiet, "Happy Birthday." At Thanksgiving, she would invite him to join her family, which he always refused to do. Like clockwork, the day following the national holiday, she would show up with a "care package," leftover turkey, stuffing, yams, cranberry sauce, and apple pie. He was convinced she made extra food in order to do this. He would accept the offering, often muttering almost too quietly to hear, "Thank you." After she left, he actually ate her offerings over the next few days. Grudgingly, he had to admit, she was a good cook. He also turned down entreaties to be with her family at Christmas. The joys of Christmas were not his. The was no real "peace and goodwill in his world." The holidays were a barren time for him. Predictably, however, she would leave him with a nicely wrapped present. Almost always, she got him a shirt, or socks, or a sweater. No matter how many pounds he put on, she always got the right size. He often wondered how she pulled off that neat trick?

He knew Mrs. Franklin was taking a special interest in him. She put up with his negative attitudes and social refusals, even his discourteous behavior, which was his first line of defense against her affection for him. Against all her assaults of friendship and assistance, he ringed himself with high walls and manned them with anger, contempt, and sorrow in order to keep out the barbarian hordes he most feared, the outside world of love and friendship, and most of all, the existential meaning that made life bearable in the face of grief and pain. Her constant battering at the gates required an enormous effort on his part to withstand her attacks. At times, and certainly lately, cracks had appeared in his armor.

"And how are you today?" she would ask.

"Okay."

"Sorry you missed Christmas with us."

"You had a nice dinner?" he asked.

"Ham and yam, as my husband likes to say."

"Sounds great."

"Perhaps you join us next time," she stated warmly. "That would be so good for all of us."

"Next year," he said with a shrug. "A real dinner."

"Are you putting an old lady on?" she asked with a surprised tone in her voice. "That wouldn't be nice."

"Christmas is a long time from now," he muttered. "A lot can happen between now and then."

"For the better, I hope," she said. "Now that would be nice."

For better, thought the Warrior? Was what he was planning leading to a better world for a legless man? Too many questions, he reasoned. Easier to simply focus on the plan to protect the sanctity of School Site 1776 against the traitor.

In a perverse way, Mrs. Franklin's absolute refusal to cease and desist from the battleground provided him with a reason to survive another day, another week until her next visit. The struggle itself animated his life. He came to look forward to her visits and the ensuing combat. He always wondered why she continued to throw herself into the struggle? What was it with this woman? Why, like some crazed prizefighter, did she continue to get off the canvas? Why couldn't she just wait out the count, 7, 8, 9, 10? Why did she keep coming back for more punishment? No matter how hard he hit her with right crosses, stomach punches, or an uppercut on the smacker, she wouldn't give up. What the hell was wrong with her? Hadn't she ever heard of a glass jaw? Why didn't the man in stripes just call the fight?

Secrets

Deep within himself though, he kept a secret securely squared away from his consciousness, for to acknowledge it would destroy the prison he had locked himself into before throwing away the key. He could not completely remain aloof from the stirrings in his unconscious. At night, especially after her visits, he would awake from his "killing dream" in a cold sweat, trembling and crying like a baby. But his tears were not for his lost legs he understood on some level. Rather, he cried for the love he rejected, for the friendship he recoiled against, for the understanding and compassion he so desired and refused to accept. His salty tears unmasked his deepest feelings then, which contrived to cast away his last defenses against the helping hand this good woman offered him.

Deep down, he really did care for her, and he wanted to enjoy her affection, and, if she would permit, allow him to love her as only a son could. It was, he knew, a bitter world in which to be alone, and more bitter yet to be cast away in a sea of loneliness and despair, and yet, still locked into his anger and pain, he had not found the courage to accept her, to simply say, "Yes, I'll be happy to come to Christmas dinner. What can I bring?" He didn't have the courage to hear what he knew would be her answer. "Just bring yourself." He doubted he ever would find the courage to find such happiness. The terrible anger in him still choked his reason and strangled the few shreds of humanity he still clung to in some last effort to know, if only for a brief moment, some peace with the world.

Of course, he never knew her secret and the reason why she felt compelled to lock horns with him in an unending dance of push and shove. Her sleep was also troubled by "bloody Tarawa," and the terrible telegram from the War Department so long ago about a younger brother.

Chapter 10

THE MEETING

The PX

"I'LL HAVE A DOUBLE CHEESEBURGER, Joe, and French fries, and a strawberry milk shake," the *Warrior* said to the elderly volunteer taking orders in the PX at the VA hospital. "And let's not be stingy with the fries."

"With onions?" asked the Medicare soda jerk.

"Pile them on."

"Swiss or cheddar?"

"Cheddar."

"Pickles?"

"And lettuce."

"Mustard?"

"The hot stuff."

It was an innocent little game that the *Warrior* played with Joe. Every time Mrs. Franklin brought him in for an appointment, he wheeled himself into the PX for lunch and made the same order much to the dismay of his social worker. He and Joe then went through what they called their "burger bit" before turning to the milk shake.

"One or two scoops?" Joe would ask knowing full well what the answer would be.

"Two."

"Reduced fat milk or the real thing?"

"Right from the cow."

They knew Mrs. Franklin was hearing every word and what she thought. In this they took great delight. Joe especially liked to tease her. The Warrior simply liked getting under her skin.

"Fries… Stringy or wedged?"

"Shoestrings."

"Salted or unsalted."

"Heavily salted."

Joe always completed the ritual, asking, "Would the lady like something? Perhaps a tuna sandwich and tea?" This was, of course, what Mrs. Franklin always ordered. Naturally, she was aware of what was going on and occasionally tried to upset the boys, as she referred to them.

"Egg salad, today and a Coke."

"No tuna salad?" Joe would ask. "No tea?"

"Add a slice of apple pie," she would say without a pause, "and see if my friend would like some."

On this particular visit to the PX, the Warrior had another reason for visiting the hospital for his monthly meeting with the Dr. Thomas Malone, his psychologist. Unlike his apartment, the PX was air-conditioned.

A freak April heat wave had descended on San Francisco four days earlier and was projected to last another 72-hours. Unusually high triple digit temperatures roasted the city more accustomed to foggy mornings and evenings and cool, ocean driven breezes during the day. In a town where the yearly mean temperature hovered around 56 degrees, air-conditioning was generally limited to high-rise towers in the financial district, department stores, and movie theatres. For the most part, units in the city's many apartment houses and hotels, duplexes, and single-family homes depended on fitted window A/C units and ceiling fans to endure the infrequent bursts of heat. This particular heat wave had caused a run on portable box fans, adding to the *PG&E's* already overloaded generating system.

Thousands sought relief at Ocean Beach and the cooling Japanese current that ran along the coast. The three-mile long parking lot along the Great Highway was full, something which had not happened in anyone's memory. As for the beach, which usually catered only to the most hardy, it now resembled *Coney Island*. Over 250,000 bathers and waders were squatting on the sand or plunging into the roller-coaster waves. Lifeguards were brought in to watch over the multitude and, if necessary, to rescue them from the vicious riptide off shore. Others, certainly the more adventurous folks, packed picnic baskets and drove across the Golden Gate Bridge until they reached the turnoff to "the special beach" a few miles north of the great span along Highway 101. There they parked and, gathering blankets, ice chests, and picnic baskets, carefully walked down a steep path to *Stimson Beach*, once home to a thriving nudist colony for the sun lovers. It was also where rebellious teens sought a secretive place to smoke "pot," while condemning the adult world for every over thirty abuse imaginable. Both groups shared the beach with dog fanciers who enjoyed a brisk walk with their tail-wagging buddies.

Those who didn't clamor for salt water were truly inventive. Thousands purchased movie tickets, especially if there was a long, two-film bill with lots of previews at the *Coronet*, the *Alexandria*, or the *Bridge*. Feasting on salty and heavily buttered popcorn and gushing down large soft drinks, they enjoyed the pumped in cold air. They resisted the temptation to critique the films. They remained happily indifferent to the quality of the screenplay and plot line as long as the central A/C units worked. Hollywood never had it so good.

Many, who had absolutely no interest in purchasing a new washer and dryer, or a refrigerator, spent hours looking at K*enmore* appliances at *Sears* where cool air was to be found. The television section of the store also drew large crowds. People stared at test patterns as if they could discern some hidden code in the flip-flopping 20-inch screens. At the two *Emporiums*, many made early, pre-season Christmas purchases as a way to thank the store for its refrigerated air. Husbands, who really found no joy in shopping, accompanied their wives to the supermarket, and were unusually patient as they strolled the wide aisles of the store. It was noted that many spent considerable time at the frozen food section commenting on the variety of frozen meats, packaged, pre-cooked items, and juices in cigar-shaped containers. For a few days, they even surprised their spouses with their devoted attention to the fresh fruit and vegetable section

As for the kids, they piled into local swimming pools where weary parents struggled to remove their children's prune-like bodies after hours of watery delight. In Golden Gate Park, visitors and residents waited for the mid-day sprinkler system to turn on, and then the more daring of them danced in the watery paradise. The fire department, ostensibly to test the water system, opened up a few hydrants much to the delight of the kids all over the city.

The highways to Reno and Lake Tahoe were crowded with expatriates shunning the city for the higher elevations and cooler climes of the Sierra Nevada Mountains and, of course, the lure of smoke-filled but air-conditioned casinos. Gambling had its virtues, so it seemed, as long as the electricity flowed and the air was cooled. Sin, so to speak, was cool.

Such were the circumstances that brought the Warrior to a fateful meeting in the air-conditioned PX. How had it begun?

Chance Meeting

Mrs. Franklin, having finished her meal, sauntered off to check on something, leaving the Warrior alone in the crowded PX to eat his greasy, very fattening lunch. His solitary confinement proved temporary.

"Anyone sitting at this table?" the well dressed in his mid-50's man asked. "Not much room today," he added.

"No."

"No, you don't mind?" the Man asked, "or no you've rather not have company?"

"No, the seat's empty."

"Sure is hot today."

"It will be hotter tomorrow."

"Never seen anything like it," the stranger said. "You?"

"Not since yesterday."

"Right," the man said with a charming smile. "You a Korean war vet?" he asked.

"WWII? You?"

"Post-war Japan. Occupational duty, really."

"Nice way to serve."

"Yeah."

For a moment it was quiet. Then the man asked, "European theater?"

"Pacific."

"Iwo?"

"Tarawa."

The stranger swallowed hard and put down his root beer float. He looked closely at the Warrior and for a moment he saw other faces.

"Marines?" he asked.

"The Corps."

"Wounded?"

"Slightly," the Warrior said dismissively.

"I didn't mean to pry."

"What, then?"

"I lost two sons in Vietnam."

Now it was the Warrior's turn to swallow hard and to look closely at this stranger.

"I lost my two legs on Tarawa."

"War can be cruel," the Man said.

"Life is cruel."

For the first time, the man noticed the wheelchair and the soft, Scottish blanket that covered the *Warrior's* lap. He also picked up the bitterness in the Warrior's words, a feeling he felt kin to since the day he lost his boys.

"You work?" he asked.

"Full disability. You?"

"Retired."

"Before…?"

"Liquor business."

"Profitable?"

"Very."

"I probably added to your bottom line," the *Warrior* said. "Still adding."

"Not too much, I hope," the man said.

"Just enough to pass the day."

"Jesus."

"You sound like my social worker."

The two men continued to talk about many things. The more they conversed, the greater was the impromptu bond that quietly settled on them.

"You had an appointment today?" the Man asked.

"Monthly visit with the shrink. You?"

"Monthly with my therapist."

"Mental or physical?"

The stranger pointed to his head before asking, "You live in the city?"

"Below Market, off Folsom."

"Tough neighborhood."

"Meets my needs."

"Family?" the Man asked.

"No. You?"

"No longer."

"By yourself?"

"Most of the time, yes."

They agreed to meet again the in two weeks at the PX.

"By the way," the Man said, "my name is Williams, Thomas Williams. Yours'?"

"Simms, Michael Simms."

"Good to meet you, Michael," he said extending his hand.

"Same," the Warrior said, as he shook hands.

Later, when Mrs. Franklin caught up to them, they said nothing of their conversation or their arrangement to meet again. For her part, she was delighted her charge was talking to someone other than hospital staff.

"I see you've made a friend," she said.

"Yes."

"People need friends, don't you agree?" she asked the Man.

"Indeed."

"I must say," she added, "you look familiar. Do I know you?"

"Perhaps we've seen each other in the elevator. I come here often."

"Maybe."

"That's probably it."

"You're probably right."

A week later, she remembered where she had seen the Man. He had been on local public television, KCET, chairing a meeting of the Board of Education.

Over the ensuing months, the two men saw a lot of each other. Their friendship prospered. They related to each other like two lost brothers. Each had a need met by the other. Lost legs could not be replaced, nor could two sons. This they both understood and accepted. But they would no longer be alone. This they desired and appreciated. Mrs. Franklin observed the bonding and prayed it would continue. What modern medicine and excellent psychiatric therapy had been unable to achieve, a chance meeting was making possible.

Intervening, fate was playing out a yet unfinished story. Where the Warrior desired but denied the motherly love of a social worker, he now seemed to be accepting a booze-selling father figure. How strange is the fickleness of life.

The two men talked about many things, certainly the war, and, of course, Vietnam, but never without lamenting or exhorting the Giants and the 49ers. The White House inhabitants, both LBJ and Nixon, did not escape their critical eyes, nor did the social issues of the day, whether it was abortion, female emancipation, or the alarming divorce rate. They even talked about the liquor business.

And one day, they discussed school business before the Board of Education touching on a new high school nearing construction, School Site 1776, and questions and problems related to naming the campus. In doing so, they reached a mutual conclusion. The new school could not, and must not be named after Iva Toguri. From that moment, they pledged themselves to use any means to stop this potential stain upon the nation's honor. Self-anointed, they would stand at the gates and man the ramparts. They would hold against the intruder.

In tandem, they adopted new code names for the purpose of necessary communication. Thomas Williams, booze dealer and current Board member, would be the *Friend*. His counterpart, a former leatherneck and embittered cripple, would be the *Warrior*. The enemy would be, as she always had been, *Tokyo Rose*.

Both men now had something to live for, which gave meaning to their lives beyond four walls and the mundane. They would protect the honored dead and the grievously maimed. They would stand side by side in this endeavor, which they sealed with a handshake on July 4th, the most spirited, patriotic day of the year.

It was also the birth date of Iva Toguri.

Chapter 11 ❦

STRANDED

Gerald Ford's Decision

MARCH 1976 BROUGHT AMERICA a torrent of political news as the two major political parties geared up for the Presidential primaries and the November election. For the Republicans, the current occupant of the White House, Gerald Ford, was seeking his party's nomination against the strident attacks of two energetic men with strong conservative credentials. Out of California rode the former governor of the state and one-time movie actor, Ronald Reagan. From Minnesota, Harold E. Stassen, was his state's perennial candidate for the "top job." The Democrats were engaged in their own three-ring primary battle with a host of candidates, all claiming the liberal mantel of the party. The four major ones were Jerry Brown, Governor of California, George Wallace, former governor of Alabama, Morris Udall, a member of the House of Representatives from Arizona, and Jimmy Carter, a little known former governor of Georgia.

By March, Ford, though burdened with a weak job economy and his very unfavorable pardon of Richard Nixon, was maintaining a slim, but widening lead over his challengers. Within the Democratic Party, Carter, posturing himself as an "outsider and reformer," was forging ahead of his rivals as he sought to be the first elected president from the South since Zachery Taylor in 1848. Already some of the gambling "pros" in Las Vegas were predicting a Carter-Ford race in November with Carter eking out a close election victory.

At the water coolers in offices and around the kitchen tables of American homes, politics was the developing topic of conversation. Everyone, of course, had an opinion, sometimes more than one, and on occasion, even opinions that were in direct contradiction with those held 24-hours earlier. The "great American pastime" was in full swing and not just on the baseball diamond. The messy job of running a democracy was once more being played out as the public was again asked to choose its next president. Some referred to the campaigns as the "silly season," when unrealistic promises were made, and accusations, short on evidence, were leveled.

"I'll end the wasteful spending in Washington," cried the outsider, whether representing the donkey or the elephant.

"Americans need jobs, not greater corporate profits," the *Left* argued. "The average working man needs protection."

"Lower taxes and reduce regulations," countered the *Right*. "Don't get in the way of free enterprise."

"My opponent does not understand the suffering of the unemployed," fumed one candidate seeking the Oval Office. "I do."

"Jobs are coming back," the current President argued. "We've turned the corner."

"Pardoning former President Nixon was a disgrace," the outside party candidate cried. "He deserved to go to jail."

"The pardoning power was used to end our great American nightmare, and constitutional crisis," the ruling party retorted. "Our country must get past Watergate."

At this moment in March, however, Janet Lee had other things on her mind besides political debates. This was the night, after the arduous and challenging effort of intensive research, that she would share her findings with her grad school colleagues and her teacher, Robert Samuels. Though a bit nervous as she shuffled her notes and prepared to speak, she willed herself to do an excellent job. Coining an old saying she had once heard, she was determined to "knock their socks off." With a heave of her chest, she began.

IVA

"Today I will talk about Iva Ikuko Toguri's background. She was born on July 4, 1916, on Independence Day in what is now called South Central Los Angeles. She was the second of four children born to Jun (her father) and Fumi (her mother) Toguri, Japanese immigrants who settled in California where in time they opened a small import business. Since they were the first generation of Japanese-American immigrants, they were called I*ssei*. Their children, American-born and the second generation were known as *Nisei*. When two Nisei married, by way of explanation, a third generation was established with the birth of grandchildren. They were referred to as *Sansei*."

Catching her breath and wondering if she was boring her fellow students out of their minds, Janet Lee continued.

"You should know three things about the family. First, everyone worked very hard to run the family business. Second, Iva's mother was crippled by diabetes. Third, her father wanted to Americanize his children. To that end, he made them speak in English. Except for a few words and phrases, Iva never learned to speak Japanese while in America. In their home, her father combined American food dishes with traditional Japanese fare. And lastly, he celebrated American customs and traditions rather than those of Japan. His effort to emphasize being an American would, believe it or not, one day come back to haunt his only daughter and lead her down a road ending with criminal charges of treason."

"How could that be?" an impatient Rita Howard interrupted. "I don't see the connection."

"You will, I trust," Robert Samuels said. "I'm sure Janet will pull all of this together."

"Yes, of course," Janet said somewhat defensively, but no longer timidly. As I was saying ...

"Iva's youthful background was typically American. She was raised as a Methodist and, though small in stature, played competitive tennis. She was also in the Girl Scouts. She was quite good at the piano as the result many lessons and lots of hard practice. She went to the movies whenever possible. I'm told she had a crush on Jimmy Stewart. He was a famous actor before my time. I guess a lot of girls had crushes on him.

As did others, she listened to the radio shows of her day. Her favorites were *The Shadow* and *Orphan Annie*. This second show would play a pivotal role, believe it or not, in the government's case against her as a traitor."

"A radio show," announced Luis Lopez, "no way."

"Unfortunately, yes," Janet replied to her skeptical friend. "Just hold your horses," she said, wondering why that phrase had popped into her head."

"Horses held," Samuels firmly stated.

"After graduating from Compton High School, she attended UCLA, where, according to my research, she was well liked by her fellow students and considered a loyal American. During her college days, she looked after her sick mother, worked part time in the family store, and majored in Zoology. In 1941, she graduated with a Bachelor's Degree in this field. At that time, she planned to enter a medical school and become a doctor. This was her dream, her American dream. Her parents supported her in this endeavor. As to her politics, she was a registered Republican, who voted for Wendell Wilkie, and against FDR in the 1940 presidential election. Ironically, by most standards, she was a GOP conservative in her political convictions. Believe me, you didn't get more American than that."

"GOP? Asked Stan Mack. "What does that mean?"

"Grand Old Party," answered Samuels. "It was a title coveted, perhaps even earned, by the new Republican Party after our Civil War."

"The one that supposedly freed the slaves," Stan said with mockery in his voice.

"The very one," Samuels answered quietly, refusing to be baited by his youthful firebrand. "The very one." Turning to Janet, he said, "Please continue."

"Shortly before she graduated from UCLA, her family received a letter from Aunt Shizu, her mother's sister, who lived in Japan. The aunt was ill and requested assistance. That is, she wanted her sister to come and live with her for a time. Naturally, this was impossible due to Fumi's own illness. Since all her brothers were working in the family business, it was decided to send Iva to Japan. She would leave for Japan on July 5, 1941, one day after her 25th birthday, on the *Arabia Maru*."

Pushing aside her written notes, Janet said, "Iva was supposed to spend six months in Japan before returning home. She would end up spending over four years in the land of her ancestors." She waited for that point to sink in before saying, "You should know that she took 28-pieces of luggage with her."

"I don't believe it," said Tom Hayakawa. "Twenty-eight, what a clothes horse."

"She'd never make it on American Airlines, I agree," Janet quickly responded. "In Iva's case, however, appearances are not what they seem." Many of the cases contained presents for her aunt and extended family. And many of them contained American canned food for Iva. She was simply not used to the traditional Japanese rice and fish diet of her relatives. She wasn't sure she could eat rice three times a day. She certainly knew she couldn't even use wooden chopsticks. She was a knife and fork gal. She had enough food for almost a year if what a relative told her is true. She was definitely not a clothes horse, whatever that is."

"Do continue, Janet," Samuels encouraged.

"Iva left for Japan in haste and without a passport. The State Department, it appears, couldn't (or wouldn't) issue one on short notice. She was given, however, a <u>Certificate of Identification</u> by the Immigration and Naturalization Service that did just that; it identified her as Iva Ikuko Toguri. In theory this document was sufficient to get her to and from Japan. And most importantly, this document was sufficient to prove that she was an American citizen. That was at least what she was told. Occurring as it did in the midst of a tense international crisis, this document would later cause bureaucratic problems with respect to Iva's lack of a passport. Indeed, it would prove fatal to her."

"What international crisis?" Ron Siegel, still sporting his EVENTS STAFF jacket, asked."

"The looming war with Japan," Philip Aquino said quickly. "You know, all the stuff that led to Pearl Harbor."

"That's my next point," Janet said. "To do that let's go back to July 25, 1940, about a year before Iva sailed for Japan."

"On that date, the White House banned the export of all items that could be used to pursue Japan's war in China. The banned exports included petroleum products, scrap metal, and aviation gas. This severe embargo was a last effort by the Roosevelt administration to stop Japan's aggression in South East Asia and China. This was in direct defiance of Japan's desire to create a 'New Order' in Asia under her leadership in what was called the Co-Prosperity Sphere.

"All this must be seen in the context of the day. Europe was already at war and the Nazi regime was conquering all of Europe and large portions of North Africa. German tanks were threatening the Suez Canal and England's lifeline to India. Russia in particular was reeling from a three-prong attack on her western border with Berlin's aim to destroy three great cities, Leningrad in the north, Moscow in the east, and Stalingrad in the south. England was choking from a dual assault. In the air, Germany's bombers were dropping a cascade of bombs on civilian targets in an attempt to destroy British cities and morale. At sea, Third Reich submarines were sinking ships vital to the island's survival. In the midst of this, Japan joined with Italy and Germany to form the Axis Alliance.

"By mid-1941, as Iva was preparing for her journey to Japan, things were really heating up. By November 26th. to be more accurate, relations with Japan were close to boiling over even as Iva was assisting her aunt in Japan. On that day, our State Department sent an uncompromising response to Japan demanding the withdrawal of all her troops from both South East Asia and China. If rejected, war would be inevitable. On December 1, 1941, the rejection was announced by Japan. It should be noted that the Pearl Harbor attack force was already at sea.

"In November 1941, Iva applied for a passport to return to America before war broke out. She had become increasingly nervous about her own welfare. What would happen to her, she wondered, if hostilities occurred while she was in Japan? She was already unhappy with her situation in Japan. She had found the Japanese a secluded and provincial people who distrusted foreigners, especially Americans. In letters to her family, she alluded to this: 'I felt like a perfect stranger, and the Japanese considered me very queer.'"

In another letter, she expanded on her situation and pleaded with her family to appreciate their new country.

I have gotten used to many of the things over here, and I think that in a few more months, I will be able to say that I don't mind living in Japan. It has been very hard and discouraging at times but from now on it will be all right I'm sure... but for the rest of you, no matter how bad things get and how much you have to take in the form of racial criticisms, and no matter how hard you have to work, by all means remain in the country you learn to appreciate more after you leave it.

This letter was dated October 13, 1941.

"She sure doesn't sound like a traitor to me," Rita Howard announced for all to hear. "She sounds like a real patriot."

"Keep that thought in mind," Janet added.

"What happened next?" Philip Aquino asked.

"Yeah, what happened to her after Pearl Harbor?" Tom Hayakawa added, "Did the Japanese consider her an enemy?"

Inwardly, Robert Samuels was delighted with Janet's presentation and the mounting interest in Iva's story.

"Iva's attempt to return to the United States proved fruitless. Her application for a passport hit a brick wall. The American Consulate in Japan concluded that there was no evidence that she was an American citizen her <u>Certificate of Identification</u> notwithstanding. She was refused a passport. Unknown to her, she was caught up in a larger net. As tensions increased between Japan and America, the State Department was increasingly suspicious of all requests for passports coming from Japanese Nisei. The genesis of this policy was tied to the Great Depression when thousands of Japanese-Americans returned to Japan for jobs in the 1930's. Now, as war approached, they wanted to return to the United States. With tensions running high, our government was concerned with possible spies and saboteurs entering the country. The government was experiencing a very real fear of subversion. Increasingly, as war seemed inevitable, national security took precedence over individual needs." World events, so to speak, were conspiring against Iva.

"By telegraph, she pleaded with her father to help her. This he did and most successfully, or so it seemed for a moment. On December 2, 1941, she was to board the *Tatsuto Maru* and return to the United States. Unfortunately, a last minute bureaucratic snafu caused her to miss her boat. Ironically, even if she had taken passage, she wouldn't have reached California. Five days into its journey, the *Tatsuto Maru* received a message in mid-ocean to return to her home harbor. Unofficially, Japan was already at war with America. The ship could not be in an American port when the bombs fell. Along with over 10,000 other fellow foreigners, or internees from all over the world, she was stranded in Japan when the Pearl Harbor attack occurred."

In his studio apartment, The *Warrior* also felt stranded, tied to his wheelchair and interned in his one room prison. He was speaking to the Friend by phone.

"I'm almost ready," he told the Friend. "I prepared to do the first stage of our plan."

"Excellent."

"Next week at the college."

"Very good."

"You'll provide the transportation?"

"As agreed."

"The radio and television people?" the *Warrior* asked.

"They'll be notified."

"Finally, we can challenge Samuels."

"And Iva Toguri?"

"Yes."

After a short break for the restrooms, coffee and candy machines, and an opportunity to stretch their limbs, the graduate class reconvened to hear more about Janet Lee's research.

"The first problem she faced after Pearl Harbor was one of status. The Japanese authorities wanted her to renounce her American citizenship and to register as a Japanese citizen. She refused to do so. Ironically, this decision worked against her in the long run. If she had become a Japanese citizen, as offered, and even under duress, she couldn't have been tried for treason, since only citizens of the United States can be tried for that crime. A second irony also impacted her. Many Nisei, who did accept Japanese citizenship and worked hard to prove their loyalty to Japan, were still treated as second-class citizens. Essentially, she was in a no win situation.

"She registered to be interned with other foreign nationals, but the authorities refused. Their reasons given were scurrilous at best. She was a woman. She was of Japanese extraction. It would cost too much to feed and house her. She could, if she chose to remain an American citizen, work in order to survive. Apparently, the authorities, especially the Kempeital, the secret police, were determined to make life hard for her. To a degree, this was partially her fault. Since Pearl Harbor, she had openly voiced pro-American views. This was particularly true following the Doolittle Raid on Tokyo, the amazing 30-seconds over Tokyo attack that proved America could bring the war to the Japanese mainland. She whooped and hollered during the attack, even as she dove for cover. As one could imagine, this didn't sit well with the authorities.

"Another challenge for her concerned her aunt and uncle, who bore the brunt of complaints from neighbors for harboring an assumed enemy agent under their roof. Along with her extended family, Iva was continuously harassed, sometimes even by the children. They called her Horyo, which meant POW, or prisoner of war. Others simply threw stones at her. Eventually, in order to relieve the stress on her sick aunt and her uncle, she struck out on her own. In doing so, more problems confronted her. Though Japanese by ancestry, she was almost completely illiterate and ignorant of the language. To deal with this, she took language classes. To pay for the lessons, she provided piano lessons to children.

"Once she was somewhat fluent in Japanese, she found a first job as a typist, transcribing English language news broadcasts for the Domei News Agency in Tokyo. While there, she learned that her family in America was listed for removal, by force if necessary, from Los Angeles and the West Coast. Her parents would spend most of the war in a relocation camp, even as she was trapped in a belligerent country. She learned they were being sent to the Gila River Relocation Camp in a rural part of Arizona. Far from America, she could only fear for their well-being. She was especially concerned for her sick mother. The notion of a relocation camp brought to mind the European concentration camps and the dreadful things happening in them."

"What?" yelled Stan Mack, "She's in Japan trying to be loyal to the US, while her family was being packed into a concentration camp."

"Relocation camp," Samuels corrected him.

"Some hell of a difference," the young man shot back at him.

"No gas chambers," Stan.

"Still an oppressive camp," Luis Lopez stated matter-of-factly. "Anyway, isn't there a basic contradiction here?" he asked.

"Absolutely," said Rita Howard. "From what I understand, the camps were guarded by armed military police and barbed wire fences," she continued. "How do we square that with Iva trying to remain loyal to America?"

"Maybe we can't," Samuels said, "at least not completely."

"What are you getting at?" Ron Siegel asked.

"Just this, Ron," Samuels replied. "Sometimes we have to live with unholy, if not painful contradictions. Isn't that right, Stan?"

"What?" Ron bellowed.

"Contradictions, Ron. You know, like Negro soldiers fighting the evil racial policies of Nazi Germany in Europe, while in the American Southern state governments enforced blatant discriminatory practices against a distinct minority."

"Yeah, one hell of a contradiction."

"What happened next?" Tom Hayakawa asked. "At her job, I mean."

"It was a Domei that she finally found a friend," Janet said. "I'll let Philip tell you about that."

Janet sat down and an unassuming Philip Aquino picked up where she had left off.

"While Iva was at the news agency, she met Felipe d'Aquino, who was a Portuguese national living in Tokyo. A few years younger than Iva, they became close friends, and in time, it seems, lovers. Eventually, they would marry in the waning days of the war. He shared with her his pro-American sentiments and provided moral and financial support when she most needed it. For example, she was in the hospital for over six weeks for a combination of illnesses, including malnutrition, pellagra, and beriberi. The malnutrition was a direct result of the authorities denying her a ration card for food. The hospital costs were beyond her means. This forced her to borrow money from Felipe and her landlady. Once better, she looked for a second job. As events would have it, she found one at Radio Tokyo, which was also known as NHK --- Nippon Huso Kyokai Radio Tokyo. Again, she was a typist, this time typing up English language scripts drafted by Japanese authorities for broadcasts to the Allied troops throughout the Pacific. It just so happened that Felipe also worked for Radio Tokyo."

"What a story," exclaimed Rita Howard, but I must confess my ignorance. What is pellagra?"

"I had to look that up," Felipe said. "It turns out it's a disease characterized by digestive disturbances, skin eruptions, and nervous disorders."

"God, I sorry I asked," Rita said.

"What causes it?" asked Tom Hayakawa.

"It's caused by a niacin deficiency in the diet," Philip said with exposed pride in his voice. "I did my homework."

"Dare I ask what niacin is?" asked Rita.

"Dare all you want," responded Philip. "It is a vitamin of the vitamin B complex occurring especially in liver, yeast, beans, and grains. If you eat these things, it prevents or cures pellagra."

"Really?" Ron Siegel. "I never knew that," he added. "Okay, I'll confess my lack of medical knowledge. What's beriberi?"

"Speaking as a novice, I can answer that, too," Philip said with a smile. "It's a disease affecting the nervous system, muscles, and the heart. It's caused by a deficiency of vitamin B, or thiamine. It seems to occur mainly in Asia and is treated mainly by administering vitamin B, or by improving the general diet. Now, before you ask, thiamine is a vitamin necessary for normal carbohydrate metabolism. It is found in lean pork, dry beans, peas, and liver."

"This discussion is sounding more and more like a pre-med class," Samuels said with a beguiling smile. "But that's good. An investigative reporter needs to know as much as possible. For example, we know why Iva was ill. Without a ration card and with limited money, her diet suffered. Partially, because of this, Felipe d'Aquino provided financial assistance to her, which, in turn deepened their relationship. Determined to pay back the loan to Felipe, she hunted for another job, and this led to Radio Tokyo, and that, as some say, is history. Before we close for the night, any last words Janet?"

"Early on I could see that I had an immense topic, one that I needed some help with. Graciously, Mr. Samuels permitted Philip to join me in researching the *Zero Hour* and a conspiracy beyond our wildest imagination. That's my round about way of saying you'll see a team effort next week."

As his grad students were about to leave, Samuels, ever the reporter on top of the next newspaper scoop had a premature "senior moment," which he shared with the class.

"Who knows what time the presidential debate is tomorrow?"

Chapter 12

CONFRONTATION

The Incident at San Francisco State

TWO DAYS LATER A WHITE paneled Ford van left Howard Street in the south of the Market Street area of San Francisco and headed toward I-280 along 4th Street. The two men in the front seat were dressed warmly out of respect for the cool, brisk breeze flowing across the city in the late afternoon. The driver had on a woolen cap and sunglasses, though there was little glare from the setting sun, and a heavy leather long coat. The passenger, a college-age young man, wore a USF (University of San Francisco) team jacket that announced he was a member of the school's basketball team. Their other passenger in the larger van area, where he sat fastened to floor grips, had on a CCSF jacket (City College of San Francisco) with leather sleeves and red, cotton panels. No one spoke. No one needed to. Their drive had been well rehearsed. They knew exactly where they were going and how to get to their destination.

The van took I-280 for a few miles before exiting for Park Merced, an outlying area of the southwest section of the city. From there the van moved through thickening traffic toward 19th and Holloway Avenue, where it slowed before finding a truck entrance onto the sprawling college campus before them.

The van arrived at San Francisco State at precisely 6:30 P.M. as planned. All was going according to schedule.

The vehicle stopped abruptly in front of the new campus Media

Building. The young man in the front seat quickly exited the van. As he did so, the van's side door slipped open. The passenger was unfastened from the floor grips and wheeled slowly down two wide planks brought along for just that purpose.

The Warrior had arrived at his destination. It was now 6:40, twenty minutes before Robert Samuels would meet with his seminar students.

The young man in the USF jacket pushed the wheelchair toward the Media Building, even as his buddy drove away. For all intents and purposes, he appeared to be a fellow college student assisting a handicapped person to his class. The young man wore a heavy canvas backpack on his back. A noticeable sagging of the backpack indicated it was carrying something heavier than just books and binders.

The wheelchair stopped in front of Samuel's first floor classroom door next to a very large 30 inch painted pipe screwed to the wall. The pipe carried a very large string of electrical wiring needed by the television and radio studios on the floor above. A few undergrad students were gathered in the immediate area, but for the most part, they paid little attention to the young man quietly pushing the wheelchair. Students were accustomed to seeing such sights. What they saw next, they were not accustomed to seeing.

The young man opened his backpack and quickly pulled out a length of extremely strong chain, which he then weaved through the wheelchair and around the pipe before securely bringing the ends together with an enormous padlock. King Kong would have hated these chains. A moment later, the young man pulled out two pairs of handcuffs of the type used by law enforcement. He handcuffed each of the Warrior's hands to the chain. Before leaving, he pulled out a folded cardboard sign, which he placed on the *Warrior's* lap. The whole exercise took no more than two minutes.

The astonished students in the area gazed open-mouthed at the *Warrior* and his sign, which simply said, **"SCHOOL SITE 1776. DO NOT NAME IT AFTER A TRAITOR."** Astonishment gave way to perplexed looks. "What the heck is going on?" one student asked. Another yelled, "What's school site 1776?" Still another person asked, "Why is that man chained and handcuffed? What's going on?"

A moment later they heard the wail of police sirens, and large trucks–like vehicles screeching to a stop outside the building. In a matter of a few minutes, the city's finest, dressed in full riot gear, pounded into the building just as Samuels and his students arrived. A moment later the fire department arrived. The television networks, especially station KRON, Channel 4, were right behind them, cameras, newscaster, and strong-armed guys carrying portable lights. Not to be forgotten was a junior reporter from the *Chronicle* and a wizened old guy from the *Examiner*. A three-ring circus was descending on San Francisco State.

Upon seeing Samuels, the *Warrior* realized that everything was going according to the plan just as the Friend had said it would. Their first step in their showdown with Tokyo Rose was at hand.

Miles away in his home, the Friend turned on his television set and sat down to watch the fruits of his recent endeavors. On the screen, a charming reporter with a voice resonating in investigatory glee from station *KRON* said, "In a moment we will take you to San Francisco State College where a World War II vet is staging a demonstration on behalf of patriotic Americans, and especially 'Gold Star mothers' who lost a son in the war. A note sent to the station 30-minutes ago indicates that the demonstrator is opposed to naming a new public school after an acknowledged traitor to the United States, a woman known as Tokyo Rose. We now take you to San Francisco State."

The Friend smiled. All was going well. Weeks ago, he had hired two men to drive a rented van to the college with the Warrior aboard. The younger man had been instructed on what to do once on campus. A chain and two pairs of professional handcuffs had been provided. The pipe had been checked for its sturdiness, as well as its importance to the Media Building. The police and television people had been alerted. Beyond that, an attorney sympathetic to their cause had been retained in the event the Warrior was arrested and bail had to be set. Money for these purposes had been set aside. All was in place. The confrontation would happen as planned.

Robert Samuels took in the scene in one cursory glance. His reporter's instincts flashed into awareness. His complement of students hadn't a clue yet as to what was transpiring. But he did. As he walked up to the *Warrior* and the police, who were testing the strength of the chain and handcuffs, his students grouped around him in a tight semi-circle and under the intense glow of the television cameras.

"We meet at last," he said straightforwardly to the *Warrior*.

"I told you we would," the chained man answered in a voice devoid of any real emotion.

"I guess it was inevitable," Samuels said.

"Yes."

A hefty Irish policeman interrupted the conversation, asking, "Do you know this man?"

"I know about him," Samuels replied.

"What the hell does that mean?"

"He's a vet, a Marine who served in WWII. He was severely wounded at Tarawa in 1943. That's correct isn't it, Michael Simms."

"You know my name, the *Warrior* said with a mixture of curiosity and pride. "I guess you are a good reporter."

"It wasn't too hard. After all, how many veterans of Tarawa, who lost both legs, are running around in San Francisco? A check with the VA Department found you almost immediately after the letters to me, and my daughter. No big deal."

"Smart guy, well get this. I wanted you to find out about me, and you did. Now you know I'm the real thing."

"I never thought you weren't, and I know why you're here. So let's get it over with."

"As one vet to another?" the Warrior asked.

"Yes."

The burly police officer said, "Gentlemen, perhaps you would like to enlighten me as to what's going on before I bring in the 'jaws of life' to cut this damn chain and these handcuffs that are probably missing from the Department?"

"It's quite simple, Officer. Mr. Michael Simms would like to make a statement to the television and print press. Right, Michael?"

"That's it," he said nodding his head.

"I would suggest," Samuels said, "that everyone back off and give Mr. Simms an opportunity to speak. When he's done, the chain and handcuffs can be cut."

With that, the police, always cognizant of lousy press and even worse TV coverage, moved away from the *Warrior*, even as the television cameras purred. There was no need for a physical confrontation with a crippled GI if it could be avoided. A young female reporter with sweeping brown hair and a figure to compete with Helen of Troy, pranced over to the Warrior, microphone in hand.

"Mr. Simms, I'm Marie Preston, roving reporter for *KRON*. What is it you would like to say?"

"This is about School Site 1776, which will open in the fall."

"All this is about a school?" she interrupted.

"Not the school per se."

"What then?" she asked impatiently.

"The school board wants the community to provide possible names," he said with rising emotion."

"Well, what's wrong with that?" she asked.

"One of the submitted names might be Iva Toguri," he said with just a hint of anger in his voice.

"Who?"

"Tokyo Rose."

"Who?"

"Jesus, don't they teach you anything in school?" he asked no longer trying to keep his emotions in check. "The bitch propagandist for the Japs during the war who may be pardoned by that jerk, President Ford."

"I remind you, Mr. Simms, we are on live television."

"So what!" he said. "Toguri was convicted for giving 'comfort and aid' to the enemy with her radio broadcasts during the war. She joined with the enemy against our country. A jury found her guilty. She was sent to jail. And now the idiots on the School Board want to name a school after her just because the local Japanese community wants a Nip name on a school. Because of that evil woman, a lot of guys lost their lives. I was lucky. I only lost my two legs on Tarawa. That wicked person told the Jap-bastards we were going to attack."

The *Warrior* had lost it. He was throwing around incorrect

information and unsupportable charges. The madness of anger and hatred had taken over his mind. The emotions he felt were true. The words he used were open to debate. Again, as before when he had first read the letter from the Warrior, Samuels felt a certain kinship with the guy. Each had experienced battle. Each had seen buddies die. Each knew the pain of loss.

"What do you hope to accomplish here today, Mr. Simms?" the reporter asked.

"I want everybody to know what's happening and to stop this tragedy from occurring," he said with barely controlled fury. "The guys who died shouldn't be dishonored this way. Iva Toguri was a traitor. She admitted to being Tokyo Rose. She confessed to making propaganda broadcasts to our troops. She shouldn't be honored this way, or any way."

"Why did you pick this particular location to voice your views?"

"Ask him," the *Warrior* said, pointing at Robert Samuels. "He's got all the answers."

"Is that correct?" the reporter asked as she placed the microphone before Samuels.

"All the answers, no," Samuels said.

"What can you tell us?"

"A few weeks ago, Mr. Simms called me at the *Chronicle* to voice his displeasure with my series on Iva Toguri. He wanted the paper to drop the story, or there would be trouble."

"And?"

"The *Chronicle*," Samuels continued, doesn't give anyone the right to censor what goes in the paper. We continued with the story. Several more episodes will be coming out over the next few months."

"Is it true that President Ford is considering a pardon?"

"That seems to be the case."

"Would you favor that?"

"I haven't made up my mind. My seminar students are researching the history of this affair and assisting me in the *Chronicle* series."

"So?"

"In time, I hope to take a definitive position."

"Are you leaning in any direction?"

"Yes."

"Toward?"

"Getting all the facts. Figuring out what happened. Getting at the truth, whatever it might be."

"How do you feel about Mr. Simms?"

"I appreciate his pain and his sacrifice. All of us should. He was just a kid when we sent him into the hell that was Tarawa."

"Tarawa?"

Samuels found himself sympathizing with the *Warrior.* What the hell were they teaching in the schools?

"Do you think the police should arrest him?"

"No. He should go home, and the rest of us should just go about our business, whatever that is. For me, that means meeting with my seminar class."

The reporter turned away from Samuels and the cameras panned back to show the two antagonists, the Warrior and the Journalist. As it did, the police cut the chain and handcuffs and carefully removed the crippled Marine from the building. A wink from the Irish cop indicated to Samuels that no charges would be filed. None. Inconvenience there was, but no real crime.

As the Warrior was led away, he yelled in a shrill voice, "This is just the beginning, Samuels. Just the start!"

* * *

In his home, the *Friend* turned off his RCA and sat back thinking, it went well. We got our message out. No one was hurt. Samuels was put on the spot. The Gold Star mothers were alerted. The Japanese-American community was challenged. The Board of Education was put in the spotlight. Yes, things had gone well. In time, the second stage of our plan will be implemented. He decided to enjoy a glass of wine to celebrate the moment.

* * *

In another home, Superintendent of Schools, Andy Anderson, sat dumbfounded on his living-room sofa. The image of the Warrior and the words of Robert Samuels still assaulted his brain. Jesus, he thought to himself, if I didn't have enough problems running this school district, now this. The Board is sure going to love this hornet's nest. God, if I could, I'd name the school after Mickey Mouse. Though he was usually a one beer-a-week man at most, he decided he needed something stronger and now. He reached into a cabinet and brought out an unopened bottle of Scotch, thinking it was time to put this to good use. With that, he poured himself a double Scotch without water.

Not far from the Superintendent's residence, Matthew Nogata was still amazed at what he had heard on *KRON*. As the elected president of the local Japanese-American Cultural Society (JACS), he had led the charge to consider Iva Taguri's name for School Site 1776 if she were indeed vindicated by a hoped for presidential pardon. Now the situation had taken a quite unexpected turn. No matter how outrageous the comments of Michael Simms, a few timid members of the Board of Education would be influenced by the inflammatory statements, and fearful of upsetting other ethnic groups in the city. In particular, he worried about the Chinese-American community. What would their response be? Would this situation animate the Chinese to be more forceful in putting forth Dr. Sun Yat-Sin as their candidate? Probably. Things were going to get ugly, he thought. "God," he said aloud, "Where's the Sake?"

Larry Chin turned to his wife and said, "Honey, cut the juice." This was shorthand for pull the plug on the television. Usually this was done when the kids were wearing out both the set and their bottoms watching intellectually numbing television fare. Today, however, it applied only to the news.

"Do you believe what that crippled guy said?" he asked his wife.

"He's a sick man," she said. "Those were terrible things he said about the Japanese."

"Not the Japanese, about that person, Tokyo Rose. The one he called a traitor."

"He didn't bring up those other things. The terrible ones," the wife said. "The ones we want to forget."

"Nanking! Manchuria! Treatment of POW's!"

"I'm glad he didn't mention them."

"I agree, but maybe this will help with our nominee, Dr. Sun Yat-Sin. We'll see."

His wife nodded and said, "Would you like your tea now?"

"Yes. Perhaps you would put a little something extra in it."

"That newscast really got to you," she said with a tired half-laugh.

***

Returning home later in the evening, Rachel Samuels listened to the late news as she was preparing for bed. What she saw blew her mind. So that's what you look like, *Mr. Warrior*, she thought. And you have a name, Michael Simms. You're no longer just a shadow threatening "whatever" in the night. You're flesh and blood, and up to mischief. That's okay as long as you leave my dad alone. You fuss with him, and I make you wish you never left Tarawa. If you think you're crippled now, just wait.

Having fumed and vented, Rachel went to bed a daughter guarding her father's backside but not before a half-glass of Chablis.

***

Robert Samuels was standing before his class, still digesting what had happened. The confrontation had been painful for him. It was hard for him to oppose the *Warrior*. They had been on the same side in the war against an enemy who fought to the death. They had each seen the ugliness and despair of war and the terrible violence of men and machines clashing. Somehow it seemed wrong that so many years later they were antagonists.

"Well, that was certainly unexpected," he said.

"Unexpected hardly describes it," Rita Howard said firmly. "What was all of that about?"

"Simple," said Samuels, "Simms doesn't want School Site 1776 named after Iva Taguri, a traitor in his mind."

"But she wasn't," Philip Aqunio blurted out.

"You're that sure?" Samuels asked. "We're just beginning to learn about her involvement in the Zero Hour. That is your topic for tonight, isn't it? Okay, let's get to it. Okay with you, Janet?"

"Of course, and I think you'll find that Philip has evidence to support his claim."

Chapter 13

ZERO HOUR

The Other Man

"Iva Toguri's life changed when she met a tall, suave, and very handsome man at Radio Tokyo in 1943, and it wasn't Felipe d'Aqino, her future husband," Philip Aquino said with a half-smile. "This chance meeting would be pivotal. Iva's life would never be the same. The road to sinister celebrity status as a traitor to America began with this engaging, sophisticated, and quite charming fellow, who was born in Poona, India in 1903, August 26th to be exact. Would you like to hear more?"

"With an introduction like that," Rita Howard said with delight, "how could we not want more?"

"On with it," directed Tom Hayakawa. "We've taken the bait."

"We're hooked," cried Luis Lopez, "hook, line, and sinker."

"Reel us in," Ron Siegel said jokingly, as he continued with the spontaneous fishing metaphor.

"Let's have a little filet of Iva," muttered Stan Mack.

"My God," cried Samuels, "I feel like I'm at the *Boston Fish Market*."

Unable to resist the temptation, Janet Lee added, "I always knew there was something fishy about this class."

"Perhaps I shouldn't have asked the question," Philip said grinning. "But since I did, I'll take this *Field and Stream* humor as your desire to get on with the story."

"Call it tension-reduction," Rita said. "We needed a laugh after meeting up with that guy, Simms."

"Indeed we did," Samuels added, "but now its time for Philip to continue before the clock slices and dices us into fish sticks for *Long John Silver's* plate. Right, Philip?"

"Did you say plate or palate?" Ron asked in his most officious manner. "Just for the record, you understand."

"Will this never end?" Samuels said with mock seriousness. "Philip, pay no attention to J. Edgar Hoover. Continue your presentation."

"To repeat, the man Iva met was tall, dignified, and mustachioed. He was also an officer in the British army in charge a rifle company in Malaya. His name was Charles Hughes Cousens.

"With the fall of Singapore, Cousens became a POW. Within a year, he was conscripted by Japanese authorities and sent to Tokyo. He was intimidated, that is, threatened with his life if he didn't manage an English-language radio program for Radio Tokyo. The Army in particular wanted a professional-style shortwave propaganda show broadcasting throughout the Pacific to lower the morale of Allied troops. He had been picked for this job due to his extensive pre-war radio experience in Australia where he had a celebrated news show, the *Radio Newspaper of the Air*. To assist him, two other prisoners were assigned to his charge, Lieutenant Norman Reyes, a Filipino, and Captain Wallace Ince of the US Army. The two men had worked together on an Allied propaganda programs before the fall of Manila.

"The three men were assigned to create a radio show that had credibility in order to attract and hold a suspicious audience composed mainly of English-speaking military forces in the Pacific. The show would be called the **Zero Hour**. It was named after the famous fighter plane used extensively by the Japanese air and naval forces. To do so, they would read scripts, laced with propaganda, which had been prepared by their captors. The result, however, was an awkward 15-minute broadcast featuring some jazz recordings interspersed with news from home, whether America, Australia, or Britain. The heavy-handed scripts focused on disasters on the home front and charges that wives and girlfriends were cheating on their husbands and boyfriends.

"Early on, the three men made a fateful decision. Led by Cousen, they agreed to a covert effort to undermine the propagandistic aspects of the show. They would do this, if it were to be done at all, right under the nose of their Japanese supervisors. The trick was to gain control of the show. To do this, they complained to their handlers about the botched English grammar and syntax permeating the scripts written by Japanese officers with a poor understanding of the English language and Western culture. As a group, they requested the authority to write their own scripts. Major Shigetsugo Tsuneishi, a career Army man, who had no experience in broadcasting or propaganda, agreed.

Cousens and his two co-conspirators then implemented a plan to sabotage and undermine their own broadcasts with double-entendres, on air flubs, muffed readings, and sarcastic comments, along with clever parodies beyond the comprehension of the Japanese. To do all this, they needed a typist whom they could take into their inner circle. At the same time, the Japanese wanted a woman disc jockey on the show. This top-down recommendation came to the three men as an order. The conspirators knew only one person they could trust, a young Japanese-American woman in the typing pool, Iva Toguri.

"Wow," Rita said, "what a story."

"Unbelievable," chimed in Stan.

"Right under the noses of the Japanese, you say?" Tom remarked.

"The story only gets better," Janet added, "doesn't it, Philip?"

"You bet. To continue: The conspirators had grown to know Iva over a period of three months. At a terrible risk, if caught, she had smuggled food to the men as well as medicine and vitamins. All this she had purchased on the black market. To pay for these items, she used her own meager wages. Apparently the haggard look of Cousen, Ince, and Reyes, all POW's who had barely survived the brutal treatment of the dreadful marches and prisoner-of-war camps, touched Iva. She was sympathetic. To a degree, she seems to have adopted them as "her POW's." At first, the three men were suspicious of her assistance. Was she a plant? Was she a spy for the Japanese? Could they really trust her? Eventually, they put their many suspicions aside and accepted her into their plot. What they did was to take a 'leap of faith.' Unknowingly to them, Iva would have to make the same leap.

"At first, Iva resisted their offer. She complained that she didn't know the first thing about radio or radio announcing or anything about scripts or records.' Cousens, of course, refused to be put off by her resistance. She was exactly what he wanted. He viewed her lack of radio experience as a plus. As he later testified after the war at Iva's trial for treason;

Her lack of radio savvy, combined with her masculine style and deep, aggressive voice would definitely preclude any possibility of her creating the homesick feeling which the Japanese Army were forever trying to foster.

"Before agreeing to work on the show, Iva made four demands. First, she would not make any propagandistic comments. On that point, she stood hard as a rock. Second, in no way would she betray her country. She would do nothing to aid or comfort the enemy, nor detract from her own country's war effort. Third, her involvement would be strictly tied to entertainment and news. She was willing to be a disc jockey, but not a quisling. Fourth, the scripts written by Cousens wouldn't violate the before mentioned concerns."

"The conspirators agreed to her demands?"

"Yes. She was a feisty one, Janet." More than you can imagine."

"You will continue."

"Had Iva not joined the program, Mr. Samuels, her life would have been at great risk. As Cousens pointed out in a deposition after the war:

The Japanese had discarded every semblance of civilized behavior, if you can apply the words to war. You did what you were told, or you died. In this respect she had no choice if she wanted to live.

"Once on the show and privy to the full conspiracy, Iva jumped into the effort with both feet. Slowly, as she was trained by Cousens, she grew more confident in her broadcasting abilities. He became her unofficial voice coach. He slowed down her delivery and helped her to sound jolly when reading her scripts. He also instructed her in how to mispronounce words without appearing to do so.

"She was a fast learner. For example, she referred to her radio listeners in mock contempt as 'honorable boneheads,' the adjective came out "onable." At other times, she lampooned Japanese misapprehensions of English, asking her audience, 'You are liking, please?' As she deepened in involvement in the conspiracy, she openly warned her listeners that the show contained 'dangerous and wicked propaganda, so beware.' To the Japanese supervisors, this all sounded like a joke, not a threat to their efforts.

"And then came her first crisis. The Japanese supervisors demanded that all on-air talent have a name. She could not remain anonymous. This being the case, she adopted the name **ANN** from the abbreviation for announcer. In time, Cousens expanded the name to **Orphan Ann**. It would be her alias for the duration of the war. The name alluded to the comic strip, *Little Orphan Annie*. In addition, it also referred to a term used by the Australian military to describe their forces cut off from their home bases and allies, that is, they were *Orphans of the Pacific*.

"A second crisis involved the other, mainly Japanese women working at Radio Tokyo as broadcasters. They were flabbergasted that Cousens picked a person with a poor voice for radio. Some thought she sounded like a cow. Her voice, they complained, came across as rough, certainly not alluring, sexy, or feminine. They lobbied against her, but to no avail. As noted already, her weaknesses were the very strengths Cousens was looking for."

At this point, Philip, more than happy to do so, sat down and Janet continued with the presentation.

+•❖•❖•+

"The Zero Hour was on the air daily at 6:00 P.M. sharp. The show was expanded from the original 25-minutes to 75-minutes. Iva's portion of the show never amounted to more than 20-minutes. During her segment, she played popular jazz music and classical music provided by Cousens. Usually, he chose British selections that he deemed very boring, certainly ones that wouldn't make the GI's homesick. Her choices included Benny Goodman, Glenn Miller, and Artie Shaw, and such popular hits as *Speak to Me My Love*, *In a Little Gypsy Tea Room*, and *Love's Old Sweet Song*." These musical selections were upbeat to avoid creating what she called a 'homesicky' feeling among Allied troops. In the end, through her efforts, she conspired with Cousen to achieve the same end.

"She also read messages from POW's. The theme song for her segment was *Strike Up the Band*, the fight song for her alma mater, UCLA. Finally, she included news and music in a most interesting way. For example, she warned the Allies of an impending aerial attack as follows:

> *Hi boys, this is your old friend, Orphan Annie. I got some swell records from the States. You'd better listen to them while you can, because late tonight our fliers are coming over to Bomb the 43rd group when you are asleep, so while you are still alive, you'd better listen.*

"She also warned her listeners to be aware of propaganda.

> *Hello there, Enemies! This is Ann of Radio Tokyo, and we're just going to begin our regular program of music, news, and the Zero Hour for our friends --- I mean our enemies in Australia and the South Pacific. So be on guard, and mind the children don't hear! All set? Here's the first blow to your morale --- the Boston Pops playing Strike Up the Band.*

"Her warnings to our military forces paid off. After the war, one Army officer's view was often quoted in her defense. 'Almost without fail, the Jap bombers would come over. She (Tokyo Rose and/or Iva) was a better air raid system than our own.'

"In time, Allied forces came to reinterpret what she was saying, as in the following statement. *'Your number one enemy actually meant your number one friend, their best enemy, their best friend.'* Lines like this fooled the Japanese censors who thought she was saying the Marine's greatest enemy. The Japanese authorities perceived the Zero Hour as a success following reports from Portugal and Sweden that American forces were listening raptly to the broadcasts throughout the Pacific.

"How did Cousen and his fellow conspirators pull all this off? The most basic reason is that they exploited cultural differences between the captives and the captors in Tokyo. They convinced their overseers that humor made it difficult for the target audience to dismiss the Zero Hour as mere propaganda. In short, humor would make the show more popular.

"On one occasion, her covert efforts became too overt as when she played the *Star Spangled Banner* after the Marines landed on Saipan. For this, she was severely reproached. Her already modest pay, $7.00 per month, or 150 Yen, was reduced.

"Eventually, she broadcasted 340 times over 21-months. She was 29-years old when the war ended and Radio Tokyo ceased broadcasting."

"When did she take on the name Tokyo Rose?" Luis Lopez asked. "Wasn't that the person she confessed to being?"

"Good question, Luis," Janet said. "And this is where things get a bit sticky."

"Sticky?" Samuels asked.

"Complicated," she replied.

"Ah, sticky and complicated," Samuels said in a teasing manner.

"And debatable," added Philip.

"Though the Japanese knew the Zero Hour was popular, they were perplexed by one fact. The GI's had another name for the program. They referred to it as *Tokyo Rose*. No one, it seems, at Radio Tokyo knew to which program the name Tokyo Rose applied. More to the point, there was no one at Radio Tokyo that went by that name. The name existed merely in the minds of the Allied troops in the Pacific.

"There was one other possibility, however. On Sundays, a Japanese woman with a low-pitched, very seductive voice broadcasted. She was known to have spread much information about impending air attacks and hanky-panky taking place at home with their loved ones and defense workers with pockets full of money. For many troops, this mysterious person became the stereotype Tokyo Rose of legend. Two things stand out about this Sunday show. First, according to Cousens, since no one at Radio Tokyo was involved to his knowledge, he assumed another woman was broadcasting from another location in Japan. This assumption was never proven.

"A second point is most interesting. On December 11, 1941, only a few days after Pearl Harbor, an American submarine picked up and

102

recorded a Japanese female radio announcer known as Foumy Sarsho, who also went by another byline: Madam Tojo. She was broadcasting from Radio Tokyo. As recorded, she said, 'Where is the US fleet? I'll tell you where it is, boys. It's laying at the bottom of Pearl Harbor.'

"Within a short time, the tag name Tokyo Rose was applied to this woman and any woman who broadcasted to the Allies. In any event, this broadcast occurred two years before Iva joined Radio Tokyo. To top this off, Iva was hired one month after *Yank Magazine*, a publication of the military, had an article about Tokyo Rose on August 20, 1943.

"All this adds up to one significant point. Iva was not the first Tokyo Rose, if indeed one actually existed. Other women were already broadcasting before she joined Radio Tokyo. Finally, none of the other female broadcasters had Iva's music-hall comedic style of delivery. A classic example illustrates this.

Greetings everybody! This is your Number One Enemy, your favorite playmate, Orphan Ann on Radio Tokyo --- the little sunbeam whose throat you'd like to cut! Get ready again for a vicious assault on your morale, 75-minutes of music and news for our friends --- I mean our enemies --- in the South Pacific.

"Well, was there a Tokyo Rose or not?" Rita Howard asked. "I won't be able to sleep tonight without knowing."

"I'm with Rita," Tom Hayakawa snapped. "Did a Tokyo Rose exist?"

"Let me put it this way," Philip said. "Shortly before the Japanese surrendered, the US Office of War Information concluded that there was no Tokyo Rose, that the name was strictly a GI invention. This report pointed out that government monitors listening twenty-four hours a day never heard the words Tokyo Rose over a Japanese-controlled Far Eastern radio. As the report stated, the name could be applied to a dozen or more women broadcasters, but to no single one." "Then Iva wasn't Tokyo Rose," Stan Mack said.

"Not according to this report," Janet responded.

"What about other reports or investigations? Rita Howard asked. "Did they reach the same conclusion."

"Iva was arrested after the war," Janet said, "and investigated by the Eight Army's legal section. Army researchers," she continued, "after a very exhaustive investigation, concluded:

There was no evidence that Iva Toguri ever broadcasted greetings to units by names or location, or predicted military movements or attacks indicating access to secret military information and plans, etc. as the Tokyo Rose of rumor and legend was reported to have done.

"That seems to be the ball game," Stan Mack said. "She wasn't Tokyo Rose," he said with finality.

"But she confessed to being Tokyo Rose," Luis Lopez retorted. "How can she not be Tokyo Rose if she confessed to being Tokyo Rose?"

"That is the question, isn't it, Janet?" Samuels asked. "How can you be someone who doesn't exist according to both Japanese and American authorities but only in the minds of Allied forces in the Pacific?"

"There must be an answer," Janet replied. "Perhaps Rita will solve this puzzle for us. She's covering the two reporters who gained the confession from Iva."

"What about that?" Samuels asked. "Will you be able to solve this puzzle?"

"In part, yes."

""Now that's what I call clarification," Tom Hayakawa said.

"No Mississippi mud," Ron Siegel proclaimed. "Just solid facts."

"Well, while you're all trying to figure this out, would anyone like to know what happened to Cousens and his motley gang as the war came to an end?" Philip asked everyone.

"Speaking on behalf of the class, I would," Samuels said. Janet, if you will."

"In June, 1944, Major Cousens suffered a heart attack and was forced to leave the Zero Hour. He was 41-years old. He was hospitalized for the remainder of the war. He could no longer carry on his private war with Japan. At the time, Iva had already left the Domei news agency in order to take a full-time job with the Danish legation, where she hired on as a typist. She had left the news agency due to criticism of her obvious pro-American views. She then tried to resign from the Zero Hour. The officials at Radio Tokyo refused to let her go. She was ordered to work with a successor to Cousens' position, most probably a person with a greater willingness to use the program for propaganda purposes. Iva was aware of this possibility. To make up for her lack of script writing skills, she used his old scripts or revised them as necessary. Seemingly, things were back to square one. Things were not, however, as they seemed."

"How did she do that?" asked Rita Howard. "I mean, Cousens had been her mentor, and now she was on her own."

"It's difficult to know," Janet responded, 'but she did provide a partial answer after the war.' According to her, 'she used more or less a standard pattern using again old scripts as the basis for the script.' She used most of his phrases as best she could, because she had no experience in radio work at all, especially scriptwriting. As she said, 'I hadn't any idea what to do with the script and I used his scripts almost word for word.'

"In April, 1945, she married Felipe d'Aquino. Somewhat fearlessly, she started playing hooky from her job. For weeks on end, she would not show up for work. During this period, other women substituted for her. In May 1945, Denmark broke off relations with Japan and she lost her job with the legation. In August, some three months later, American B-29's dropped two atomic bombs on Japan and the war was over. Almost four years after she arrived in Japan Iva looked forward to returning to the United States with her new husband.

The fates decreed it was not to be.

"After V-J Day, Major Cousens was arrested and brought back to Sidney, Australia. He was tried for treason in New South Wales, where treason was a capital offense punishable by death. The slim evidence against him came from two Japanese men who had worked with him at Radio Tokyo. The jury found the testimony against him open to question, and the case was dropped. He was stripped of his commission, January 22, 1947, but he was not court marshaled. He returned to radio news reporting and later did so on television.

"As for his colleagues: Captain Wallace Ince was taken off the program for insubordination. Lieutenant Norman Reyes was declared a "friendly alien" following Japan's annexation of the Philippines. Little else is known about them during this period, at least based on our research. It appears each returned to their own country without the questions that haunted both Cousens and eventually Iva."

"Now that's a story," Samuels said, "and like all good stories, the outcome is still in doubt."

"In other words," Stan Mack said, "there are still more questions to be asked about Tokyo Rose."

"Exactly, Stan, and we'll do so next week.

Iva Toguri Prison Photo
https://www.docsteach.org/documents/document/iva-toguri-mug-shots

Cesar Chavez
https://www.spokanepublicradio.org/post/september-programs-7

Dr. Sun Yat-sen
https://en.m.wikipedia.org/wiki/Sun_Yat-sen

Iva Arrested in Tokyo
https://marteau7927.wordpress.com/2011/11/29/tokyo-rose/

Iva at Radio Tokyo
https://marteau7927.wordpress.com/2011/11/29/tokyo-rose/

Iva in Jail in Japan
https://www.politico.com/story/2017/01/
president-ford-pardons-tokyo-rose-jan-19-1977-233646

Meeting Reporters
https://commons.m.wikimedia.org/wiki/
File:Correspondents_interview_%22Tokyo_Rose.%22_Iva_Toguri,_American-
born_Japanese._-_NARA_-_520994.tif

Iva in Tokyo
https://www.docsteach.org/documents/document/iva-toguri-mug-shots

Iva in San Francisco

https://usselmore.com/pacific_war/tokyo_rose/files/card_image_673.png

Joe DiMaggio

https://www.nydailynews.com/opinion/huskies-favre-pale-dimaggio-
56-game-hit-streak-greatest-feat-sports-article-1.474415

Tarawa Dead

https://www.nationalww2museum.org/war/articles/photo-finish-battle-tarawa

Tokyo Rose Movie Poster
https://movieposters.ha.com/itm/movie-posters/war/tokyo-rose-paramount-
1945-folded-very-fine-one-sheet-27-x-41-war/a/162011-53484.s

Chapter 14

DUPLICITY

Mel's Drive-In

GEORGE LUNA KNEW THE GEARY Street location well. As a high school student at George Washington, he had frequented the drive-in on a regular Friday night basis after watching his beloved *Eagles* trounce the opposition on the gridiron. Flushed with victory, he would roar down Geary, if speeding down the street at 30 mph could be considered roaring, to *Mel's Drive-In* with a boatload of friends in his old '47 Chevy sedan. In those days, he had a knack for getting the last drive-in space almost as if it were assigned to him.

As he drove, he also recalled with gastric joy the Mel's menu of yesteryear, so dear to his heart when hr would order a cheeseburger. Long before *McDonalds* touted its *Big Mac* and thrust it upon an unsuspecting public, Mel's provided a burger that would bring tears to the *Golden Arches*, a half-pound of Texas steer, even though it was from herds munching on grassy knolls in Northern California. The meat, regardless of how you ordered it, was always broiled medium and to perfection. Large slices of tomato and a generous two-slices of cheddar cheese complemented an offering fit for kings. Relish, mayo, and leafy lettuce completed the teen meal-of-choice. Burger and shake, plus French fries like *Ronald McDonald* could only dream of making, not cookie-cutter, cut and counted, but rather unmeasured, uncounted, and unsurpassed.

As he pulled into a parking spot, the last spot, Luna wondered if his dining colleague was reminiscing, too.

***

The Reverend Harrison Fork

The Reverend Harrison Fork was running late. But then again, he was always running behind schedule. He once told his mainly hard working African-American congregation that the "pearly gates" would be closing as he arrived a tad late and with the Almighty checking his *Timex*. It wasn't that he intentionally chose to be tardy. No, he was habitually late because he crowded too many things into his daily schedule: visiting the ill, counseling the couple contemplating marriage or considering divorce, gathering fruit, vegetables, and meat for the church's food bank, and, if he still had a breath left, preparing his sermons. How, he wondered, had God created the universe in seven days? He must have had assistance, a bevy of angels at his disposal. You would think the "old guy" might spare one. He really felt that the Divine had shortsighted his Creation in pushing a 24-hour day.

As he neared Mel's, Fork remembered a great day in 1967 when the well-known director, Stanley Kramer, stopped by his church in the Fillmore. The man was going to film a movie with Spencer Tracy and Katharine Hepburn called *Guess, Who's Coming to Dinner*, and he needed a few authentic extras who were African-American for a scene at Mel's. Fork, the director thought, might supply them, especially if a small donation were made to the congregation, which was, of course, welcomed and made. In the resulting film, Tracy and Hepburn pulled into Mel's, where Tracy ordered Oregon Boysenberry ice cream and then had a scripted minor traffic altercation with a black man. The film, though it dealt with testy social issues, was, of course, a hit. If only the real world, Fork thought, were as accommodating when it came to the issue of race. But then again, he thought, perhaps Tracy and his leading lady were God's angels. Perhaps the silver screen was just another avenue in acting out some grand plan beyond our comprehension. If so, God was truly the eternal scriptwriter.

Dealing

Though *Mel's* was full and noisy with the rattle of dishes, waitresses taking orders, and talkative customers trying to be heard over each other, Luna and the Minister were deep in conversation.

"God, I love this food," Luna said.

"I won't tell your mother," Fork replied. "You call yourself Mexican, and you devour Yankee concoctions. Such blasphemy should not be tolerated."

"And I won't confess to your family," Luna pronounced, quickly taking up the charge. "What's a nice Southern boy from Georgia doing at a burger joint, and not a rib house?"

"He's enjoying, George, what the Lord has provided."

The two men were about the same age, each moving quietly into his mid 50's. Luna, short and stout, with dark, combed-back hair, and a brown skin-tone that not even *Sea and Ski* could match, was a compact man, both physically and mentally. He had made money in the construction industry, mostly through his company, *Taco and Burrito Electric Repairs*. For the uninitiated, it sounded like he repaired only Mexican restaurants. Others in the industry knew better. His contracts with the school district in particular had made him reasonably comfortable. His numerous critics cried foul arguing that "affirmative action polices," not skilled work, accounted for his success. George just laughed off the jibes considering them "sour grapes."

Rev. Fork had survived the Georgia of *Jim Crow* before traveling first to Los Angeles after attending Moorhead College in Atlanta, and then to San Francisco, where he was known for his spellbinding Sunday sermons, and his uncompromising stance against racism in all its ugly forms. As a contemporary of Martin Luther King, he wanted "justice to flow like a great river." Unlike Luna, he was tall, on the thin side with salt and pepper hair and a voice strong in its desire to bring the *Word* to those who would listen, and even to those less responsive.

"We need to discuss the problem," Fork said.

"School Site 1776?"

"Is there any other problem?"

"I guess not, Harrison," Luna said with emphasis. "I mean, how can our crazy drop-out rate, school violence, and teen drug usage compare with naming a school?"

"It can't and shouldn't, but it does, unfortunately."

"Silly business. Seven members of the Board and five potential names for the school," Luna said as he salted the last of his French fries.

"We're only concerned with two at this time," Harrison said. "Your nominee, Cesar Chavez, and mine, Dr. King."

"A couple of pretty good organizers."

"Please clarify, George."

"Well, my guy tramped through the Central Valley organizing the grape pickers, and creating a union, United Agricultural Workers against all odds."

"And mine?"

"Fork, King tramped through the same soil seeking salvation for our souls in the name of fairness and righteousness."

"Two good men," the Minister mused.

"No question about that. Too bad the School Site 1776 can't be called *Chavez-King High*," Luna declared. "That would settle everything."

"Perhaps, but shouldn't it be *King-Chavez High*?"

"Sir, I'll give you this. You're always pushing. But we both know the Whites, who still have three votes on the Board, want Joe DiMaggio, but that won't happen," George said. "No way a minority-packed Board will vote for the Italian slugger in a city where almost all the streets and schools were named after dead white guys."

"True. But which minority nominee will win out?" Fork asked with an edge to his voice.

"Let me put it this way, old friend. The winner won't be Asian if we have our way."

"The Chinese want Dr. Sun Yat-sen, the Chinese revolutionary and nationalist, who ousted the old imperial monarchy, and the Japanese will definitely put forth Iva Toguri if President Ford pardons her for treasonable offenses against the country," Fork reminded his colleague." "Our hope, George, is that the two Asian communities will cancel each other out, leaving the field to our nominees. Then each of us can compete for the White vote after the Italian slugger strikes out."

"There's a good chance of that happening, isn't there, Harrison, given the loose rhetoric passing between the two Asian communities? If recent tuffs are a harbinger of what's to come, they're going to leave each other muffed."

"Did you prepare and practice that ditty?" Luna asked.

Nodding, Fork said, "Some."

"I knew it. Anyway, there's an excellent possibility, one we might, of course, quietly encourage, if not ensure, that they will be at each other's throats."

"You're speaking metaphorically, are you not?" Fork asked. "We wouldn't want hard rhetoric to turn into something more."

"Shrugging, Luna said, "Yeah."

The two men paused for a moment. It wasn't that they had reached an impasse. Far from it… They each understood that extraordinary efforts were sometimes needed to accomplish a worthy goal. But one had to be careful; harsh words often turned into hard violence. And more to the point, they understood that riding a tiger's back was not always the easiest thing to do. The tiger, growling and baring its teeth, generally always had something to say.

The Minister broke the silence. "The loose cannon, as I see it, is Thomas Williams," Fork reminded Luna. "It's difficult to get a handle on him. No question that he harbors low-keyed anti-Asian attitudes."

"Because of losing two sons in Vietnam?" Luna asked.

"That's it, I'm sure," Fork said. "But I think there's something more, some-thing we don't know about. Perhaps we should dig more thoroughly into his background?"

"But generally, he puts aside his biases in Board discussions. Christ, he's more interested in District solvency than anything else."

"Ah, George, let's not take the Lord's name in vein."

"I got excited."

"Apology accepted. As to Williams, he's a bean-counter," Fork said.

" We'll get his vote if we commit to his new budgetary reforms and bond issue campaign. There are many ways to heaven."

"Don't you mean 'skin the cat?'"

"Indeed."

"One last thing dear friend. You recall our, what should I call it, confidential deal reached last week?" Luna asked.

"Of course, but I prefer to call it a meeting of the minds."

"If I win ... If Chavez is School Site 1776's new name, Luna said, I'll vote for your candidate the next time around."

"The new elementary school if the proposed bond issue passes?"

"That's it," Luna said.

"And if King wins," Fork, shared, "I support your candidate next."

"Deal," Luna said.

"Deal," the Minister said.

Golden Flower Restaurant

Harrison Fork and George Luna weren't the only ones wrestling with School Site 1776. Earlier in the week, two other members of the Board sat down at the *Golden Flower Restaurant* on Geary Street and 18th Avenue out in the Richmond District. Larry Chin and Matthew Nogata were there for a quiet meal and serious talk. The restaurant, while quite capable of cooking authentic Mandarin dishes that catered to a traditional Chinese palate, was also known for a menu cognizant of American tastes, including: shrimp with lobster sauce, sweet and sour chicken, BBQ pork with sweet peas, pineapple fried rice, and chicken fried soft noodles

"Enjoying your meal, Larry?"

"Of course, not Japanese fare, but I'm into cultural diversity, whether political or gastronomic."

"You chose wisely: pork fried rice, lemon chicken, and egg flower soup."

"All delicious, Matthew."

"Then you must have a bowl of green tea ice cream to complete your meal."

"If you insist."

Around the two men customers were entering, others were leaving, and the waiters, constantly moving, cleaned tables and reset them. In the kitchen the cooks presumably cooked.

"Well here we are," said Larry Chin, a retired mechanical engineer, who had spent a lifetime with Pacific Gas and Electric making sure homes were heated and businesses had clean burning energy. "Time for us to dance."

"If I didn't know you better, Larry, I would consider your overture either a prelude to a date, or a becalming effort to get me to drop my defenses."

"You're not my type, Matthew,"

"Must be the other," Matthew said with a nod.

The two Asian men were Board members serving their second terms. They had arrived on the scene together, each representing a distinct ethnic/racial group. Larry Chin was the chief economist for the Chinese Chamber of Commerce in San Francisco, and a leading advocate on behalf of naming School Site 1776 after Dr. Sun Yat-sen. His colleague, Matthew Nogata, was President of the Japanese-American Cultural Center and the outspoken supporter of Iva Toguri pending a potential presidential pardon. It would be fair to say that the men respected each other, even liked each other, but on this school naming issue they were miles apart.

"Matthew, the hard facts are these. There's no way the Chinese community will support a *Japanese* woman in naming the school, no matter how many pardons she receives. Too many bitter memories."

"Japanese-America, Larry. Iva was born in the good old USA."

"Still Japanese."

"She even attended your old school in Westwood," She's a Bruin through and through. She's got the 'eight-clap cheer' down. And besides her UCLA pedigree, she's got red, white, and blue in her veins."

"It's not her veins, Matthew, "it's her ancestry. She's Japanese. That's the way my community sees her, and I can't change that perception."

"Her parents emigrated from Nippon long before the recent troubles. You know that, Larry."

"As did your folks, Matthew, "but your, how should I say this, your former country attacked mine, didn't it? Larry asked. "Bombed and raped Nanking as I recall."

"My former country under the influence of militarists was infatuated with an Imperial Empire," and unfortunately against your former homeland."

"The Japanese government never formerly apologized to the Chinese people, Matthew. In their schools, the history textbooks white-washed the attacks on Korea, Manchuria, China, and, of course, Pearl Harbor. And you know that."

"I do, and I do not approve. Japan should take a lesson from the new Germany. Painful as it has been, the Germans have tried to come to grips with the ugliness of Nazi Regime. They have acknowledged and apologized for the atrocities. Japan is reluctant to do so."

"Where do we go from here?" Matthew asked.

"We cut a deal."

"Deal? What kind of deal?"

"You vote for Dr. Sun Yat-sen," Larry said.

"You call that a deal?" Matthew asked, almost spilling his teacup.

"I vote for your candidate next time around."

"Even if its Toguri?" Matthew asked.

"As long as she receives a pardon."

"How can you pull that off with your Chinese voters?"

"Good faith. By voting for my guy, you're showing consideration for the sensitivities of my constituents. The Chinese in my district will appreciate that and they'll reciprocate the next time around."

"I can trust you, Larry?:

"We must trust each other."

"If I do this, some of the more frantic folks might just run a Samurai sword through me. I don't want to hear Banzai in my sleep."

"Matthew, we'll push the idea of an Asian-first vote in both communities, which isn't far from the truth. We'll talk about honor and fidelity. We'll call upon all our ancestors to help us in this campaign to put Asians first."

"Sounds like we're playing a race card, Larry."

"How can it be avoided? Race is the frosting on this cake called the School Board politics. It's served with every Board meeting. Each of us represents distinct areas of the city, each with distinct racial and ethnic groups. Race is always on the table."

Again, the two men were quiet as they contemplated what had been said, and what remained to be discussed. An impasse had been reached. Each one understood this.

"Strategy, Larry. How do we break away enough minority and white votes to win, to elect an Asian?"

"We need four votes. Simple arithmetic. We need two more votes.

"Can we get the Minister's vote?

"Easier than George Luna's vote, Matthew. He's bursting with new born power because of the rising political clout of Hispanics."

"Larry, why would the Minister vote with us?"

"We'll play the two of them against each other, pointing out to Mr. Fork that relative to the Hispanics, the blacks are losing political strength. He needs, we'll point out, some Asian friends."

"Raw politics, Larry."

"Like the sushi fish you enjoy, Matthew."

"What about our Anglo friends?"

"Admittedly a challenge. I'd like Thomas Williams' vote, but Christ, he's got a hard-on for Asians. Hell, we all know that, even though he keeps his feelings pretty much under wraps. He'll probably vote with Luna. He likes Luna."

"Didn't Williams steer a contract to his buddy, Harry Greenberg, who just happened to sub-contract the electrical work to Luna's company?" Matthew asked, already knowing the answer.

"That he did,"

"What's left?"

"The ladies," Larry said. "We work on the Jewish lady. Forget the Italian. She loves DiMaggio."

"Adds up. Two Asians, one Black, and a Jewess," Matthew said. Who ever said that being on the School Board was boring?"

The Italian Chop House Restaurant

Three days later, the two ladies in question were enjoying a martini at *Joe DiMaggio's Italian Chop House Restaurant* on Union Street near Stockton in North Beach. Though the restaurant was known for its steaks and seafood, the ladies were enjoying Happy Hour with their favorite appetizer, a garlic and cheese pizza, which consisted of a super thin crust of flatbread with a block of brie cheese and one of garlic, both of which you mash and spread out on the bread. For those who loved it, this appetizer melted in their mouths. Surrounded by original photographs of "Joe," and resting comfortably on leather-tufted chairs in a room with dark wood, the setting was cozy and appropriate for private conversations.

This particular day, the ladies had much to discuss.

"Those men on the Board just drive me crazy," Mrs. Ruth Cohen said with a voice dripping criticism. "They're always plotting and conniving."

"And pushing for our vote for the new school," her fellow Board member, Mrs. Lucy Patrissi replied.

"You sound like you've had your full of them, Lucy."

"I have. It's because they're so full of themselves, so sure they can wrangle a vote out of us, making racial guilt a ploy to garner our support."

"I'm so tired of their less than obvious tactic."

"Not that it will do them any good, Ruth."

"You don't include, Thomas Williams with all those men, do you?"

"No. I guess I don't, Ruth. He never plays race politics, but he is one queer duck. I always have the feeling that he's a one man-conspiracy, that beneath his cool exterior hot lava flows, and I don't mean his libido. Something is really bugging that guy. But you're right, he's certainly not full of himself, at least outwardly."

"And he does keep good books, Lucy. "I can't remember a more spendthrift Board member. He does pinch the pennies and keep us solvent. I'll give him that. But the others …"

The ladies considered them. Ruth, dressed in her trademark green pants suits with a matching lacy, very feminine blouse, and trademark

2-inch heels, had problems with the other Board members, all of whom, except for Thomas Williams, had been pushing her hard for her vote recently. Lucy, true to her Sicilian background, wore a long, black skirt and matching blouse with a string of white pearls, simple and stunning. She too had been prodded for a favorable vote. Both ladies were in their mid-forties and uncommitted to their male counterparts. Each now represented an affluent, mainly white neighborhood of San Francisco. For Lucy, the Sunset area was her domain. For Ruth, the Richmond District.

"Enough critiquing, Lucy said. "Let's get down to brass knuckles."

"Sure, but what the hell does that mean?"

"I haven't the slightest idea, but it does sound good. You know, like something out of a good detective story, something Sam Spade would say at just the right movement."

"Okay, you bum," Mrs. Cohen said in her deepest voice, "this is your last chance. Time to get down to brass knuckles. I want the Maltese Falcon. Where is it, you creep?"

"Gads, I don't think Dashiel Hammett would buy your impromptu version, Ruth," Lucy said with a big grin. "And Bogart, poor man would forget his lines if you were in the scene."

"I quite agree, but maybe Peter Lorre might find me interesting."

The two women giggled, sipped their martinis, and then zeroed in on the subject at hand that had drawn them to this meeting.

"Well," said Lucy, "I can't vote for the other choices. I'm Italian in case you haven't noticed. Joe gets my vote."

"I expected as much."

"Your vote, Ruth?"

"I'm torn…"

"You haven't decided, have you?"

"Too many good candidates."

"Including Tokyo Rose?'

"I find myself fascinated with her life," Ruth said. "If she's pardoned, I might…"

"You'd vote for her?"

"I'll certainly consider her."

"Why, Ruth?

"Blame it on my mom."

"Your mother?"

"What can I say? You try growing up with a social worker mom, who tells you about her VA patients at the dinner table. Never their names, of course, just the story. And she's so partial toward the mental cases and the grievously wounded, especially if they were in the Pacific Theater. I think it has something to do with my uncle who died out there."

"Still, I don't see …"

"I guess, Lucy, I just see this woman, Toguri as a kind of female Marine, trapped behind enemy lines, and trying to survive. At least, that's what I'm picking up in the *Chronicle* by that reporter, Samuels."

"I admit it's quite a series, Ruth."

"My mother," has started a Toguri scrapbook. 'Cut and paste' seems her new motto."

"Forgive me, Ruth, if I change the topic a tad."

"You're forgiven, I think."

"Ruth, what would it take for you to vote for Joe?"

"The Queen's jewels might be a starter."

"Anything more?"

"Am I being bribed?"

"Such a nasty word," Lucy said. "Approached sounds so much nicer."

"As I said earlier, I'm undecided."

"Or just holding out for more, Ruth?"

"Lucy!"

"Just kidding, I think."

"I wonder how all this will turn out?" Mrs. Cohen said somewhat philosophically.

"Only time, a few bribes, and history know that answer," Lucy said more realistically.

The waiter arrived at that moment with their bill, which Mrs. Cohen chose to pay. After all, it was her turn. She did so with her VISA card. As always, she signed her full, hyphenated name as many newly emancipated women were doing: *Ruth Franklin-Cohen.*

Chapter 15

VILLAINS

Rita Presides

OUTSIDE OF HIS CLASSROOM, THE darkened clouds had opened up. It was raining heavily over the entire Bay Area and possibly even more so over San Francisco State, thought Robert Samuels. Inside his classroom, another deluge of a different sort was about to begin. Rita Howard was up tonight and thunder and lightning were about clash in among his students, if Samuels read Rita's set jaw and clenched fists correctly.

"My topic tonight," Rita said, "concerns outlandish charges of treason against a very innocent young woman who was subjected to brutal, discriminatory, and criminal actions by our government."

"Rita," Samuels said, "After listening to your opening statement, I am reminded of an old joke. Stop inferring and just come out and state your case."

"Old is right," Rita said with a determined look on her face. "And this is no joke unless you consider enduring a rigged military case funny."

"I presume you will back up your thesis?"

"I can and I will."

"Then we're all ears."

"Okay, let's begin with this. Iva Toguri was stranded in Japan. Make that trapped in Japan after Pearl Harbor. You already know this. The Japanese authorities considered her an enemy alien. Almost immediately, she was given a choice: either renounce her American citizenship and register as a Japanese citizen, or be subjected to severe, possibly life-threatening consequences.

"Some choice! Iva refused. Score one for her patriotism.

"She requested, as you recall, to be registered as an alien citizen in order to be interned for the duration of the war along with over 10,000 other foreign nationals. The Japanese authorities refused. They based their denial on her gender, Japanese extraction, and the cost to feed and house her. What nonsense! She was, I believe, singled out because she was a Nisei. She was an American. And most of all, she was an all-American gal who wouldn't cave into the brazen demands of her tormentors. She refused to bend to the highhanded actions of her jailers."

"Score two for Iva's patriotic spirit.

Rita was on a roll. No doubt about it. Alone, she probably could have taken Iwo Jima.

"Fix this date in your mind," Rita continued --- August 30, 1945."

"Why?" Stan Mack asked. The 'bombs' were dropped earlier in the month. Aren't those the dates we should be concerned about?"

"Not in Iva's case," Rita said. "Not in her case at all. If I may..."

"On that day, General Douglas MacArthur landed unopposed at Atsugi Airport near Tokyo. The war was over and our American Caesar was about to usher Japan into a new era. Aboard his plane were dozens of civilian and military reporters. The two guys we're interested in were Clark Lee of INS (*International News Service*) and Harry Brundidge of *Cosmopolitan Magazine*. Apparently, on the flight to Japan, they had decided to link resources and get exclusive interviews with General Hideki Togo, Emperor Hirohito, or Tokyo Rose. The first two possibilities would prove impossible. By default, that left Tokyo Rose. And because of this Iva's immediate future would eventually be placed in jeopardy."

"I don't see the relationship," Ron Siegel said. "How could two reporters threaten her? Didn't she just want to return home with her new husband? I don't see a federal case here."

"Hang on to your EVENTS STAFF jacket, Ron," Rita said briskly, "the light is about to shine."

"Their initial efforts to find Tokyo Rose proved fruitless. No one seemed to know who she was. Or, if they did, they weren't talking. Falling back on good old American initiative, they offered a $250 reward to anyone who would put them in touch with the sinister woman. At the time their offer represented a lot of money to the impoverished Japanese, about 3,700 yen or about three year's income. On his own, Brundidge pledged a $2,000 payment for an exclusive interview with Tokyo Rose. That was a literal fortune in those days, about 30,000 yen. He did so without the approval of his editors in New York. With such dollars being thrown around, the two men reasoned, something would come out of the woodwork. And they were right."

"Leslie Nakashima, a Nisei at Radio Tokyo, and a Nisei colleague, Kenkichi Oki, gave Clark and Brundidge Iva's name. They did this even though they knew she wasn't Tokyo Rose. Moreover, they knew at least six other women announcers at the station who might be Tokyo Rose, including Oki's own wife. It appears, based on the evidence I've reviewed, that they were under considerable pressure to name someone and did. The source of this pressure would come out years later.

"Eventually, Clark and Brundidge agreed to meet with Iva even though they knew she probably wasn't Tokyo Rose. In truth, they just needed in the absence of an actual Tokyo Rose, someone who would claim the mantle. They hoped and believed Iva would self-incriminate. If so, they would announce to the world, by way of their journalistic scoop, that they had discovered and interviewed the infamous woman. After that, the American military authorities would decide her fate."

"In retrospect," Iva said in June 1976, "I suppose, if they found someone and got the job over with, they were all satisfied. It was Eeny, Meeny, Miney, and I was Moe."

"The meeting with Iva was set for September 1, 1945. At this meeting, she agreed to sign a contract for the $2,000 if she stated she was the 'one and original Tokyo Rose.' But now Clark and Brundidge had two problems. Unlike the Tokyo Rose of fame, Iva was no sexy Asian beauty. She was short and plain looking, nondescript, and certainly no Mata Hari of the Pacific. The two reporters were now absolutely certain she wasn't Tokyo Rose. The second problem concerned the $2,000 offer. Prior to their meeting and interview with Iva, they had announced to the world that she was Tokyo Rose. This was unfortunate for both Iva and them. Essentially, they had jumped the gun. In reviewing the situation, the editors at *Cosmopolitan* rejected Brundidge's conclusions and story, and flatly refused to pay the $2,000 he had contracted with Iva. Now Brundidge was stuck with the contract and was obligated to pay it unless...

"Eventually, Brundidge took Clark Lee's seventeen pages of notes from the interview with Iva to the 8th Army Counter Intelligence Corps' commander, General Elliot Thorpe, who was strongly urged to arrest Iva. The commander, who was still making a name for himself, accepted Brundidge's statement, 'She's a traitor and here's her confession.' He also accepted the reporter's request for a mass news interview between Iva and over 300 reporters from around the world. The General never understood Brundidge's ulterior motive. By agreeing to meet with the reporters, Iva abrogated the terms of the contract's exclusivity clause, thereby making the $2,000 offer null and void. At the same time, she would place herself on the international 'hot seat.' when she met with reporters from all over the world."

"Iva had no idea what she was getting into?"

"You're so right, Tom. Score one for scurrilous journalism," Rita continued with obvious distaste for the unscrupulous Brundidge. "If there's a hell for scandalous reporting, this guy will be turning over like a pig on a spit. On second thought, maybe that's too good for him."

"Rita, perhaps you're letting your emotions get too far in front of the story," Samuels remarked. "Facts first, emotions secondary."

"You're confusing my passion for emotion. The facts support my claim," Rita burst out, "and that SOB deserves to be skewered from here to New York."

"Thanks for not bringing Texas into this, Rita," Tom Hayakawa said. "I'm headed that way once I leave State."

"Texas?" asked Ron Siegel. "I've never heard of a Japanese-American cowboy punching cows for a living."

"Not cows, the typewriter at a Dallas newspaper," Hayakawa quipped, "if I get past this class and your lack of western lore."

"Easy guys," Samuels interrupted. Then, acting as the Devil's advocate, he turned to Rita and said, "You're acting very much like the judge and jury in this case, Miss Howard."

"And happily, executioner, too, Mr. Samuels," Rita proclaimed for all to hear. "Gleefully, I would have enjoyed placing bamboo shoots under his fingernails for openers."

"Rita, you must be more moderate," Luis Lopez said, realizing even as he spoke, that he was waving a very red blanket in front of an already enraged bull out to gore someone.

"Moderation!" Rita huffed. "Wait until you hear what comes next. If you're still for being moderate, I'll eat my hat."

"Rita," Janet Lee piped in, "I never seen you in a hat."

"I'll buy one, if necessary. Now I'd like to continue the story if there are no more arguments for misplaced clemency in regard to these jerk-reporters."

Inwardly, Samuels was delighted with Rita's rendition. She had the facts. She had the passion. She had the intellectual capacity to bring it all together. My God, he thought, the *Chronicle* should hire her now. He bent an ear toward Rita as she continued.

"As I said a moment ago, Iva had no idea what was going on when she agreed to the mass interview. At this point, she trusted Clark and Brundidge, who encouraged her to think she was a celebrity, a heroine for what she had done during the war, a darling of the American press, and that the folks back home couldn't wait to see her. In so many respects, nothing could have been further from the truth.

"Iva was like a lamb being led to the slaughter. Brundidge and Clark had decided to sacrifice her on an altar of deceit, misinformation, and prejudice in order to preserve their reputations, and to end any legal and or financial obligations to Iva.

"The mass interview took place at the Yokohama Bund Hotel. Seemingly, to all accounts, it was a cordial affair. Questions were asked. Questions were answered. Iva did not dispute Brundidge and Clark. She was indeed Tokyo Rose. When requested to simulate an "Orphan Ann" broadcast for newsreels, she did so. When asked to give interviews to *Yank Magazine* and the *Stars and Stripes*, she did so. When asked for autographs, she happily complied. When requested to pose with reporters and military personnel, she did so like the celebrity she thought she was. Her apparently unforced confession convinced those in attendance that she was Tokyo Rose.

"In addition to meeting with the reporters, she also cheerfully answered all questions put to her by the 8th Army CIC. To both groups, Iva tried to laugh off the suggestion that she had done anything wrong in making the broadcasts. She was puzzled and confused by questions intimating that she gave away or made predictions of troop movements and impending counterattacks. She vigorously denied doing these things. She also refuted accusations that she talked about wives and girlfriends going out with 4-F's. The truth was that she didn't know what a 4-F was until meeting with reporters. Iva even offered her Radio Tokyo scripts to set the record straight. Unknown to her, the government already had them, since all Radio Tokyo broadcasts were taped 24/7 during the war.

"She had no idea how this was playing out in America, where the press' twist on the story marked her as a traitor. What never came out at this mass interview were three important points. First, after an almost six year separation from her family, she wanted desperately to rejoin them. Secondly, while working under immense strain at Radio Tokyo for over two years, she was tired. She was physically exhausted. Third, she had lost a child after a difficult pregnancy only two months earlier. The woman was emotionally drained, but her ordeal was just beginning.

"On October 17, 1945, three CIC officers took Iva to Yokohama to answer still more questions. Iva was told to bring her toothbrush since she might be staying over night. Once at 8th Army HQ she was placed under arrest. No warrant had been issued for her arrest. No charges were filed against her, yet she was jailed. It was almost as if the Army didn't know what to do with her beyond jailing her. Was she an American? Was she Japanese? If American, she would get a cot and bread during her indefinite incarceration. If Japanese, she would receive rice and a futon. The Army decided she was an American.

"A constant stream of curious onlookers came by her cell. She was subjected to constant rowdy name-calling. She was provided with one bucket of water every three-days for bathing and to launder her clothes. Felipe, Iva's husband, was denied a visitor's pass when he tried to see his wife. One of the guards extorted an autograph from her by keeping on the lights in her cell for a week.

"Then the 8th Army did the unthinkable. It was announced publically that Iva was Tokyo Rose and had been arrested for treason. While in jail, she was never told about this. After one month, she was transferred to Sugame Prison in Tokyo, where she was placed in a cell on 'Blue Block.' This part of the prison held diplomats and women who were accused of war crimes. Iva would spend the next eleven and half months in a 6 X 9 cell. In her new home, she was only allowed one 20-minute visit from her husband at the beginning of each month. She was permitted to have a bath every three days.

"While in Sugame Prison, she learned of her mother's death on route to the Gila River Internment Camp in Arizona. She also learned that her family had been released from the relocation camp with the ending of the war, and that they now lived in Chicago. On an almost daily basis and she was interviewed by the FBI or the Army CIC. Neither group chose to believe her statements of innocence even though all the evidence indicated that Tokyo Rose was a composite person and that Iva had done nothing treasonable.

"On October 24, 1946, Iva was told she would be released 'without condition' from Sugama Prison. When she was released, a large gathering of reporters greeted her at the prison gates, including one reporter from Domei, the radio station she had once worked for to survive. To that hour, she had spent a year, a week, and a day in prison under military custody without ever being charged with a crime.

"A platoon of soldiers formed double ranks around Iva as she neared the reporters. They plowed ahead and kept the reporters from questioning her. As she left the prison, Colonel Hardy, the prison commander, gave Iva a bouquet of flowers. Amid flashing flashbulbs, she got into a waiting car, where her husband was waiting for her. At this point, Felipe was now working for an English-language Yokohama newspaper as a linotypist.

"The Army CIC communication stated that:"

> *An extensive investigation to determine whether Iva had committed crimes against the United States proved that the evidence then known did not merit prosecution and therefore, she should be released.*

"The FBI reached the same conclusion. As stated by Nathan T. Elliot:

> *The prosecution for treason was unwarranted. Her show contained nothing whatsoever of propaganda, or troop movements or any apparent attempts to break down the morale of the American forces.*

Continuing, he stated, "Toguri's broadcasts were innocuous and could not be considered giving aid and comfort to the enemy."

"Iva was free, at least for the moment."

Rita stopped, announcing to the class, "Okay, I'm ready to eat my hat at our next meeting after I buy one."

"No need," cried Janet Lee. "I'll help with the bamboo shoots."

"What bastards," Tom Hayakawa said without concern for institutional civility.

"They needed to have their legs broken," Stan Mack said in a voice devoid of pity.

"Start with their fingers," Luis Lopez added. "It's tough to type with torn digits."

"Tar and feather them, and parade them through Tokyo," Philip said scornfully, "and then place them in the village square for all to view."

"Write them a ticket and then drop them into Tokyo Bay," Ron Siegel said. "And make sure large rocks are attached to them. We wouldn't want them to resurface."

I don't believe this, Samuels thought to himself. My students are out for blood. God, I better pass all of them with high grades. No need to get on their bad side. Christ, tar and feather...

"What happened next?" Janet asked.

"For a short time," Rita said, "Iva and Felipe tried to remain below the radar. But this proved impossible. Iva applied for a passport to return home. Her application was rejected. She was told by our Consulate in Tokyo that she lacked identification to document who she was. This, of course, was the original problem that had stranded Iva in Japan in the first place. Consider how outrageous this was. On the one hand, the Consulate claims she is undocumented, while the whole world identifies her as Iva Toguri, the Tokyo Rose of shame. How absurd! Because she was married to Felipe, the Portuguese Consulate offered her a passport, which she declined. She didn't want to go to Portugal. She wanted to return to the USA. Score another one for Iva's love of country."

It was almost break time, and though the restrooms and coffee machines clamored for the class' use, Samuels knew a good thing when he saw it. These future reporters were into it. Why permit bladders and caffeine-withdrawal to disrupt things. He decided to push the class to the edge.

"I agree, Rita, our government doesn't come out smelling like the proverbial rose, but doesn't Iva deserve some responsibility for what happened to her?"

"How can you say that?" Rita asked "Lee and Brundidge deceived her. They lied to her. She trusted them and they sacrificed her for their own ends."

"True enough. But didn't she let her hoped for celebrity status lead her astray? Wasn't she interested in possible royalties from a book or movie?"

"So what?" asked Philip. "Even if she wanted those things, she deserved them. Regardless, she hadn't lied. The two reporters lied."

"But she did claim the title of 'Miss Tokyo Rose,' didn't she?" Samuels asked with a trace of harshness to his voice.

"She did," Rita admitted, "but what should she have done? No one else stepped forward to claim the dreaded title, and she needed the money to survive, and to get back to America. Plus, she felt a legitimate right to be Tokyo Rose, since it was all so harmless in her mind because there was no Tokyo Rose. Anyway, how could she know what was happening back home?"

"What was happening?" Stan Mack asked.

"The *San Francisco Examiner,* a good old-fashioned William Randolph Hearst newspaper, resorted to its 'yellow journalism' past and pronounced Iva guilty of being Tokyo Rose under the byline, *Traitor's Pay.* The paper ran the story even before the facts were complete. In short, the editors tried her in their headlines. You can imagine the public's response."

"Couldn't agree with you more, Rita," Samuels said. "And, of course, there was the movie."

"What movie?" Luis Lopez asked.

"You know about it, don't you Rita?" Samuels asked.

"I do."

Hollywood and Tokyo Rose

"In 1946, Hollywood got into the act. Talk about the exploitation of the public's prejudices and biases. This film, produced by Lew Landers and written by Les Adams, was the equivalent of pouring oil on a fire. To begin with, Tokyo Rose was portrayed as seductive and vicious, a woman who taunted the Marines, a hideous person without conscience, who preyed upon young Americans in the Pacific without remorse. This characterization, though glitzy and purposely contoured to sell tickets at the box office, was, as you already know, the exact opposite who Iva Toguri was in real life. The plot line was more akin to science fiction than historical fact.

"The story unfolds as follows: a group of American prisoners is taken from a POW camp, cleaned up, fed, given new clothes, and presented to the neutral press corps during a broadcast of Tokyo Rose late in the war. Americans B-29's disrupted this attempt to show Japan in a compassionate light as an enlightened people who treated their prisoners humanely. The falling bombs permitted many of the American POW's to escape. One of them plans to kill Tokyo Rose because he believes one of her broadcasts led to the death of a buddy. With the help of a war correspondent, he kidnaps the turncoat disc jockey. He hopes to meet up with an American submarine and bring the wicked woman to stand trial. While trying to rendezvous with the sub, this brave young man is overtaken by the Japanese. He returns to the POW and Tokyo Rose returns to the microphone. In a nutshell that's the story."

"Science fiction would get a bad name from this movie," Stan Mack said. "That wacky story is better suited for fantasyland, if not the waste basket."

"Perhaps," Rita said, "but guess what? It supported and reinforced every stereotype Americans had of Tokyo Rose and the Japanese people. After this film, Iva never had a real chance to pursue a normal life in America, especially after she made one final and fatal mistake."

"Which was?" Samuels asked.

"Unbelievably, Clark Lee and Harry Brundidge visited Iva again with a deal. They promised to get her home to America with her husband if she would do just one thing: certify with her signature that Lee's notes were correct. Though Felipe cautioned against doing this, Iva, still trusting these guys, did so even though she was later quoted as saying, 'Most of this is made up.'

Her trust in Brundidge in particular was misplaced. Unknown to her, he had contracted to publish a ten-part series in American newspapers about her crimes against the country. The first part was entitled *Arrest of Tokyo Rose Nears: She Signs Confession to Sell-Out*. There is no question that he knew it was a lie. Our Justice Department would later use his series to indict Iva once she was back on good old American soil. Brundidge, by the way, died in 1960, but only after continuing his attack on Iva as he did in the *Mercury Magazine* in January 1954 while she was in an American prison. The article was called *America's First Woman Traitor*.

"With her signature in hand, this traitorous two some, waved it before the American public as final "proof" that Iva was, as they had stated, Tokyo Rose. This was the final evidence her enemies in America wanted. With this, they could either keep her stranded in Japan, or, if she returned to the States, have her arrested and placed on trial, one that would surely place her in jail for the rest of her life.

"That's the story to this point," Rita concluded. "Hopefully, I won't have to eat a hat."

"Never fear," Samuels said. "And one more thing, Rita, a really good job."

Chapter 16

MUTTERINGS

DURING THE WEEK BEFORE ROBERT Samuels' next class meeting, a quiet lull settled over San Francisco and a strained, "she is, she isn't," play took place beneath the surface of the outwardly tranquil West Coast metropolis. But if you listened very carefully, you could hear the "mutterings" of a tangled historical mess attempting, however in perfectly, to sort itself out.

"Do you think he's dangerous?" Mrs. Rose Franklin asked the VA psychologist, Dr. Harold Malone. "Would he really hurt someone?"

"I don't think he would, but he might."

"You wouldn't care to be more definitive?"

"The mind is very complicated and my field lacks, all too often, the relative absoluteness of certainty enjoyed by physicists."

"Or until they make their next discovery," she said.

"There is that," he said.

The two were meeting at the VA Hospital to review Michael Simms' case. The chain and ball business at San Francisco State had caught their attention and concern. The 24/7 television coverage for one day had reinforced their need to review his situation.

"Why does he call himself the Warrior?" Mrs. Franklin asked. "Of all the possibilities, why that?"

"Try to see the world from his perspective," the psychologist said. "To compensate for the loss of his legs, he anoints himself with a title suggesting strength and power in our society, the lone man fighting against the forces of evil, waging a lonely struggle on behalf of some greater good. In that sense, he would have stood with the 300 Spartans, the all but defeated soldiers at Valley Forge, or the men at the Alamo."

"Or at Guadalcanal?"

"Wherever, as the lone man, he can make a difference?"

"I don't want him to hurt anyone."

"I don't think he will."

"Your professional opinion, Sir?"

"My gut, Madam."

They paused in their conversation. They needed to. They knew what was coming next, though not a word had been said.

"His letters to Mr. Samuels and his daughter, Rachel, were they not threats?" Mrs. Franklin asked.

"Fortunately, Samuels shared both letters with us after that episode at the college."

"So?" she asked impatiently.

Possibly threats. Or pleas. Or both."

"Pleas?"

"If I read him correctly, he's not only asking Samuels to stop writing about Iva Toguri," he said. "He's also crying out for help."

"And if he concludes none is forthcoming?"

"Then he will threaten and act."

"Act?" she asked.

"Do something just short, I think, of hurting anyone."

"If that fails in his eyes?"

"Professionally speaking, all bets are off."

"I don't understand why he hates this woman so much," Mrs. Franklin said. "All the new evidence coming out suggests her innocence."

"Again, look at it from his perspective. He needs to blame someone for his condition. He knows a Japanese solider shot him. That soldier might have died on Tarawa, or survived the war. But either way, the *Warrior* can't get at him. He can't say, 'look what you did to me.' He can't get closure. He fastens his anger and pain on a visible, easily identifiable target, a woman our government jailed for being Tokyo Rose and epitomizing wartime Japan. For Iva Toguri to receive a pardon, if it were to occur, would be a terrible insult to Simms. For a school to be named after her, would be beyond the pale for the *Warrior*."

"It almost sounds like he needs Toguri, someone against whom he can direct his rage and ..."

"Provide him with a reason for continuing to live," he said finishing her sentence."

"Yes. We need to help him. You know I've been his social worker for a decade now. I've grown to like him even though he can be a handful."

"Like a son?"

"More like a missing brother."

"Either way, I think we shrinks refer to it as transfer."

"You shrinks are probably right," she said.

"In advance of any criminal activity, there's little we can do."

"We sit and wait?"

"Yes."

Once again, silence crept into their conversation, only to be broken by Dr. Malone. "You know, one thing really interests me about this case?"

"And that is?"

"Well, how does a wheelchair-bound, 51-year old vet, who has no real friends beyond, if I may say, us ... How does this guy get to the college with a chain, lock, and handcuffs all by himself?"

"The police report and television coverage said another man helped him."

"Precisely."

"So?"

"It seems, dear lady, that our patient has a friend."

"We're on track, Rachel," Superintendent Andy Anderson said. "School Site 1776 will open February 1, 1977."

"Construction is on schedule?" she asked.

"Actually, if one can believe Harry Greenberg, the liaison for the contractor, yes."

"Any reason to doubt him?"

"To this point, no."

"Good."

"Over the summer, I'll need you to put together a competent staff and get things organized generally," he said.

"Already working on it."

"And?"

"Things are falling into place."

"Excellent."

"Except for one thing," she reminded the Superintendent.

"That again?"

"Sir?"

"Well, you were at the last Board meeting, Rachel. You heard the 'topic of conversation' demanding almost all the Board's time."

"Naming the school."

"What else? Seven Board members and five nominees with community activists stirring the pot, and the even more aggressive folks threatening lawsuits, demonstrations, and boycotts."

"Keep their kids at home?"

"Can you believe it?" he asked.

"We'll try to contain the situation, Sir."

"I'll do what I can at my end."

"Thank you."

"Rachel, one thing concerns me."

"Yes."

"After that craziness at State, please be careful."

"You sound like my father."

Laughing, the Superintendent said, "Well, be careful anyway."

At that, Rachel said, "I will," and to prove it, she opened her purse and pulled out a pepper spray canister. "First line of defense," she said. "And you should know, I ordered a bolt cutter. No way I'm going to let that guy lock himself to my school. No way at all."

— ◦ ◆ ◈ ◦ —

"Thanks for meeting me, Larry."

"Always happy to accommodate a friend. George."

"Great. But aren't you curious as to why I invited you for drinks?"

"You want to know about authentic Chinese cooking?"

"That's good."

"Perhaps we could trade," Larry responded. "I'm interested in authentic Hispanic dishes."

"You're putting me on."

"Yes, I am."

"But perhaps we can still trade, Larry."

"Go on."

"I need your vote, Larry. I need you to vote for Cesar Chavez."

"Guess what, George, I was hoping you would accept my nominee, Dr. Sun Yat-sen."

"My community wouldn't buy it."

"Same with my folks in reverse," Larry countered.

"Stalemate?"

"Seems so," Larry said. "Now what?"

"We bargain, George."

"I'm listening."

The two men eyed each other, half curiously, half suspiciously, and half perversely. In an old-fashion Western film, they would have been at a card table with a mountain of chips, coins, watches, and greenbacks piled up before them as they checked their cards one last time before raising and calling. Looking more closely, it was apparent that only one hand held their cards. The other hand reposed at their side quiet near a holster and *Colt 45*, the judge of last choice easily available to them through open jackets. Those crowding around the table peered at the players, yet were careful to stay out of their line of sight if cooler heads didn't prevail.

As George and Larry spoke, it appeared that their jackets were open. One could almost hear the music to *High Noon* background instead of *Blue Lady*.

"Put your cards on the table," Larry said.

"Right to the point."

"Why waste time?"

"Why, indeed," George said. "Your folks want a new Chinese Center for the kids with a basketball court, enclosed swimming pool, and facilities for seniors. Right?"

"Go on."

"I know people on the City Council. I'll push hard for it. I still have some influence on the Council after three terms."

"Before you lost your last race, George?"

"Sadly, yes."

"Any guarantees?"

"Only that I'll push hard, Larry. Very hard."

"For my vote?"

"Yes."

"I need time to think about your offer."

"Of course, Larry."

"I assume you made an offer to Board member, Nogata?"

"Now why would you say that?" George asked.

Smiling, Larry reached into his jacket and pulled out a ten spot. "On me", he said.

"Ribs. You're taking me to the Rib House on Fillmore?" Matthew Nogata asked the Minister.

"Not just any rib joint. Anyway, it beats that funny uncooked stuff you folks like so much."

"Are we speaking ethnically?"

"We are speaking 'ribs vs. sushi'," the Minister responded. "No contest. Game over."

"You're paying?" Matthew asked.

"I invited. I pay."

"Let's go."

The two men hopped into the Minister Harrison Fork's old, but serviceable Oldsmobile 98 and headed up Fell Street to Fillmore. As they did, they acknowledged the rationale for their meeting.

"Your vote. I could use it," the Minister said.

"As I could your nod."

"Loggerheads?"

"Seems that way," Matthew said.

"Anyway out of this?" the Minister asked.

"Horse trade?"

"What's on the table?"

"Your turn first, what are you offering, Harrison?"

"My Black folks needed School Site 1776 named after Martin. You understand. Community pride. Something more than drugs, gangs, and those lousy stories, all negative stuff that hound our people and stereotypes us as thugs."

"I understand. Again, what are you offering?"

"The Japanese-American community has been pushing for an elementary school focused on the Japanese culture, including language and art, but open to all students."

"Old news," Matthew said.

"True enough. Last year your pet project lost by one vote. Board members were afraid they were instituting a form of reverse segregation."

"As I recall, Minister, you voted against my pet project, as you say."

"That was last year. Next year I'll support you."

"No fear of reverse segregation?"

"Lots. But first things first."

"I vote for King," Matthew said, "and you vote for the elementary school."

"That's the deal."

"You must really want this."

"The community needs it, Matthew."

"I've got to check with some of my supporters."

"Naturally."

The Olds pulled up at the Rib House. Matthew found himself suddenly famished for succulent beef ribs dripping in savory juices, along with baked potatoes prepared with a mystery seasoning that was fantastic. God, he thought, it's great to live in the land of diversity.

School Board member, Lucy Patrissi, had to admit that this was different. She had never been invited to a VFW Post, and here she was about to enter Post 1941 at the invitation of former General Mark Longstreet, the post commander. In preparation for the meeting, she had researched a few facts about the VFW. She knew it never paid to go into a potential den of lions without doing your homework. And Lucy always did her homework.

The VFW, the Veterans of Foreign Wars, was a congressionally chartered war veteran organization by an act of Congress on May 28, 1936. Though chartered by the United States government, the VFW receives no funding from Congress. It is completely supported by charitable donations. Its main purpose is to work on behalf of American veterans by lobbying Congress for better veteran health care and benefits. It also assists veterans with their VA disability claims. Membership totals more than 1.3 million belonging to more than 6,500 posts. As such, it is the largest American organization of combat veterans.

Membership was very regulated according to strict rules, Lucy discovered. A new member must be a US citizen either currently serving in the US military or honorably discharged. Membership also requires overseas military service during a conflict and decoration with an expeditionary medal, a campaign medal or ribbon. Both men and women are admitted into the organization.

"Welcome to our house," General Longstreet said with a widening grin akin to the girth of his waist. "It was good of you to come."

"How could I decline your invitation, especially from such a formidable and distinguished soldier as yourself?"

"Hopefully, you couldn't, Mrs. Patrissi."

"Call me Lucy."

"Reciprocity, then. I'm Mark."

"Longstreet," Lucy said. "Are you related to the gifted Southern general of Civil War fame?"

"Very distant relative."

"Good genes."

"Spoken like a true Yankee."

"Started out in Brooklyn."

"What could be more Yankee?"

Mark, a former Army man, who had seen combat in the last days of WWII before tours of duty in Korea and Vietnam, towered over Lucy. That happens when one is 5 feet-two inches, and the other person is six feet-five. Still robust, Mark was the very essence of a former military officer, straight back, uniform pressed, shoes shined, and straightforward in his speech. They sat down in his spick and span office.

"I suppose you are wondering why an old warhorse like me asks you to come over?" he asked.

"The thought had crossed my mind."

"Easy explanation. Tokyo Rose."

"Iva Toguri?"

"One and not the same."

"I'm not sure I heard you correctly, Mark."

"Until very recently, the VFW, along with the American Legion, had been strongly opposed to Miss Toguri for many different reasons."

"You will elaborate."

"For most of our guys, she was Tokyo Rose based on what the FBI said after Japan was defeated. This view was reinforced by her confession to those newspaper fellows and the trial that took place in San Francisco, when she was found guilty of treasonable actions against the government."

"Please continue."

"Initially, our organization didn't want her to return to the US. When she did, we wanted her jailed. Beyond that, if released, our membership wanted her deported back to Japan. We saw her as persona non grata. You get my drift?"

"Impossible to miss it, Mark," Lucy said with a beguiling smile.

"But...."

"But?" Lucy asked.

"We've changed our minds."

The General's words hung in the air, "We've changed our minds." What, thought Lucy, was this leading up to?

"In the last three years, new information has come forth that called into question our view of Miss Taguri. The VFW now believes that, pending any new information to the contrary, President Ford should pardon her and therefore, return to her all the rights of citizenship. With this in mind, the VFW is lobbying on her behalf."

"Making amends?" Lucy asked.

"Recognizing an injustice."

"She spent a long time in jail."

"Unfortunately."

"You can't bring back those missing years," Lucy said.

"Emotions were running high after the war. You can't imagine how bad it was in the Pacific. The Japanese Imperial Army wouldn't surrender, even when faced with imminent defeat. I saw this firsthand on Okinawa. It was an ugly war without any rules, except one: survive. It was kill or be killed in the worst possible way. It was different with the Germans. At some point, they gave up. The Japanese played by different rules. Anger, bitterness, savagery were outcomes of this conflict. Imagine what it would have been like if we had invaded Japan? The loss of life would have been so great."

"And Toguri was caught in the middle of these emotions?"

"Not Toguri, but Tokyo Rose."

"As you said, unfortunately they became one and the same."

"They did."

"What is it you want, Mark?"

"You mistake me, Lucy. The VFW wants nothing. Rather, we want to give you something."

"And that is?"

"We support naming School Site 1776 after Iva Toguri."

The call from the White House had come quite unexpectedly. "A member of the Ford reelection team would come by tomorrow to discuss a few things. Would that be okay?" Naturally, Ruth Gordon's secretary said it would be fine. What else could one say?

The next day a lovely young woman, newly minted from Georgetown's political science department, and working in her first presidential campaign as an intern, dropped by Ruth's Office. Buzzing with the enthusiasm and vigor of youth and party to the high and powerful, the young thing literally flew into the office. God, to have energy like that again, thought Ruth.

"Hi, I'm Mary Parker."

Mary Parker indeed, thought Ruth. Gads, she's an all-American girl with a name I can pronounce.

"I'm Ruth."

"Glad I caught you on such short notice."

"Actually, the White House nailed me."

"Yes. Of course."

"How can I help you, Miss Parker?"

"Not me personally. Rather, my boss."

"Who is?"

"The President of the United States."

Ruth could tell that Miss Parker loved to say that --- "President of the United States." Heck, who wouldn't? It had such a nice ring to it.

"How can I help your boss?"

"He's caught up in a tight reelection."

"I've noticed."

"Working on getting every vote he can."

"Good plan to get reelected."

"California would help."

"Lots of electoral votes here," Ruth said.

"Lots of Asian votes."

"Only Hawaii has more."

"The President is considering pardoning Iva Toguri."

"Based on the facts or Asian votes?"

"The facts, of course," Miss Parker said.

"Of course."

"I trust you agree with his decision."

"Certainly. And when will this happen?"

"After the election."

"If he wins?" Ruth asked.

"During his first full term."

"If he loses?"

"Well, I assume before he leaves the White House."

"Some time between the second Tuesday in November and mid-January?"

"Presumably," Miss Parker answered.

"What does the President want me to do?"

"Spread the word."

"Particularly to Asians."

"That would be helpful."

"And for this?" Ruth asked.

"The President will be most grateful."

"Gratitude is nice but…"

"Additional federal funding for special school projects is always helpful."

"It is, isn't," Ruth said.

The mutterings of the week ended with **four** phone calls. The first occurred when Larry Chin called Matthew Nogata. The two men, though playing it close to the vest, shared their experiences.

"What did you tell the good Minister, Larry asked.

"I was inscrutable."

"Very Asian of you, Matthew."

"Difficult not to be. What about you, Larry?"

"I was very Asian."

"And?"

"I almost heard the sound of one hand clapping," answered Larry.

"Why did I bother to ask?"

"That occurred to me, too."

"What did it sound like, Larry?"

"What?"

"You know, Matthew, one hand clapping."

"Different."

"I should have known."

George Luna received the second phone call from Reverend Fork. Giving away very little, they talked in hush terms even though no one else was present.

"Did Nogata take your offer, whatever it was?" George asked the Minister.

"I'm sure you made one."

"Perhaps. Difficult for me to read the Asian face. What about you? Did anything come of your offer?"

"Hard to know," the Minister said. "It's very hard to know."

"Too many beans in the pot," George said.

"What is that supposed to mean?"

"Who knows? My mother used to say that when things were too hectic in the house."

"Sounds like your mother was on to something" the Minister replied.

"It does, doesn't it."

Mrs. Ruth Franklin-Cohen made the third call. It was to Lucy Patrissi.

"Tell me everything, Lucy," Ruth said without any preamble. "What was the General like?"

"Very Army like."

"That's it?" Ruth asked.

"The Army will support Iva if Ford pardons her."

"No kidding," Ruth said.

"No kidding is right," Lucy said, "now tell me about the White House, Ruth."

"The President wants Asian votes."

"Who doesn't?"

"He's going to pardon, Iva, I think."

"And he wants you to get the word out," Lucy said.

"Big time. But how did you know?"

"Figures."

"Ruth, what did they offer you?"

"Lucy, how could you think such a thing?"

"Well, what do you think?"

Rachel Samuels had called her father to see how he was doing? This was code in her mind for "covering his backside."

"Doing okay. You?"

"Same."

"Good," Rachel said.

"I take it you're checking up on me?"

"Really, do you think I would do that?"

"Yes."

"You're being watchful?"

"The *Chronicle* has increased security."

"San Francisco State?"

"Ditto."

"Dad, I'm worried."

"Try not to."

"But his threats!"

"Just that, Rachel."

"You're sure."

"Sure."

"You're fibbing."

"Me?"

"You."

"Only a little."

"Meaning?"

"He'll do something."

"But?"

"Something short of physically hurting anyone, Rachel."

"I hope you're right."

"I am."

"Pretty confident."

"I'm a trained observer of human behavior."

"You read too many Robert B. Parker books."

"I do?"

"You do."

"Sounds like you've read a few yourself."

"I have."

"Too bad we don't have Hawk around."

"Or Vinny, Rachel."

"Not even Pearl the Wonder Dog."

"We'll get by."

"I love you, Dad."

"I love you, Rachel."

The week of mutterings ended as it had started, in a tangled historical mess that was still sorting itself out, at least as far as the School Site 1776 was concerned. Time would ultimately determine how it would be untangled.

Chapter 17

JUSTICE ON TRIAL

Stan the Man

"You're ready, Stan?"

"You harbor doubts, Mr. Samuels?"

"Well, our relationship hasn't been actually smooth."

"Glad you noticed," Stan said.

"Hard to miss."

"Anyway, I'm ready to kick judicial backside."

"Just make sure you've got the facts," Samuels said.

"That's the least of my worries."

"Let's do it, then."

The two men had been standing in the hallway near Robert Samuel's classroom. The other members of the grad seminar in journalism were already seated and waiting for things to start. Stan Mack, rather than entering the room, had signaled to Samuels that they needed to talk. They had spoken, short and sweet, and right to the point. For whatever reason, there was a tension between the two. From Samuels' perspective, Stan was carrying something, some anger, just below the surface, and while it did not impede their work or cause problems for the class, it was always present. Hopefully, thought, Samuels, they would get through tonight without a problem. When everyone was seated, Stan entered the room and began.

"My task was to research Iva's second trial," Stan began. "This I have done. To understand what occurred, judiciously speaking, in our own city, I need to set the stage, that is, explain the emotional and prejudiced background against which Iva's fate would be determined. But understand that from the beginning, her trial was the closest thing I know to a 'kangaroo court.' I state that with a touch of anger etched in my voice. Why, you might ask? The simple answer: the Army and the FBI contrived to lynch her and did. Short of a firing squad, they attempted to void her citizenship, place her in jail, and throw away the keys. Not even Judge Roy Bean would have been this callous, or even Bull Connor in Birmingham. She probably could have received a fairer trail from the KKK."

Samuels considered interrupting Stan to slow down the rhetoric and the emotionally tinged images he was presenting, but to what purpose? Sometimes, he thought, it's just better to roll with the flow. Stan would either make a credible case or flounder on rocks he could not navigate.

"Let's begin with Walter Winchell," Stan said, a racist in a three-piece suit and a microphone."

"In the late 1940's, Walter Winchell campaigned against Iva Toguri returning to the US. He was convinced she was either Tokyo Rose herself, or the next closest thing, certainly, symbolic of the evil broadcasts emanating from Radio Tokyo during the war. Once he was certain she would return, he fell to his odious backup position. If she returned, jail her, place her on trial, and find her guilty before putting her in jail. If Winchell had been just another loudmouth, his rants and raves might have come to nothing. But Walter Winchell was much more.

"Every Sunday night, he broadcasted on radio to an expectant audience of over 20,000,000 people. His syndicated newspaper column was in 2,000 American newspapers and in many foreign dailies. Over 50,000,000 people worldwide read his column each day that was a combination of Hollywood gossip, strong rightwing, ultra-conservative political views, and a disgraceful tendency to attack those he didn't like. He was a law and order guy who wrapped himself in Old Glory, while supporting the FBI and his hero, J. Edgar Hoover. He was always careful to cater to the VFW and the American Legion, the country's two largest veteran organizations and ultimately influenced their negative views of Iva. The man had extraordinary influence. He used his position and talents to whip up wartime passions and influence sentiment against

Iva. He even attacked President Truman as being 'soft on traitors.' His outsized power pushed the Los Angeles City Council to pass a resolution opposing Iva's return to the States. And perhaps, worst of all, he succeeded in getting his journalistic colleagues to join in the rant. Sadly, journalists cowered rather than enlightened the public with respect to Iva's real story. At the time, journalists and politicians were gutless in standing up to Winchell and his cronies, all of whom wanted Iva's head.

"Long after the trial, Ramsey Clark, son of US Attorney General Tom C. Clark, who ordered Iva arrested in Japan and brought to San Francisco to stand trial, stated that the working press had failed in its obligation to denounce the prejudiced role of the US government. The younger Clark wasted no words.

"In a desperate effort to develop evidence of guilt, investigators threatened witnesses until they perjured themselves. Exculpation evidence was destroyed. Witnesses from Japan were not permitted to testify and to give evidence favorable to the accused. Statements she (Iva) made there (in Japan) which would benefit her defense were classified secret and she was denied copies. At least one witness committed perjury before the grand jury that permitted the trial to go ahead."

Catching his breath and heaving deeply, Stan stopped talking and waited for his words to sink in. Looking around the room, his students, Samuels thought, looked as if they had been hit with a broadside. Even the normally talkative Rita was still. Then Stan surprised everyone.

"Those ink pushers at the *Examiner* and *LA Times* had really lost their scruples when it came to journalistic ethics. They needed to take this class."

In unison Samuels' students turned and looked at him. For a moment, he didn't know if their behavior portended approval or the rope. Then, and most surprisingly, Stan began clapping. In a moment the other students followed his lead. Samuels, always a bit shy, nodded his acknowledgement even as he turned a little scarlet.

Stan was not through with his surprises. "Mr. Samuels, I don't always agree with you, but I do on one point which you have made crystal clear to us. A reporter has the duty to use his position carefully, to get the facts, to avoid misusing his special place in our society, and to always fight for the truth. Compared to those jokers back in the 40's, you're an absolute saint."

Samuels was stunned by Stan's comments, yet he knew some perspective was needed. "Stan I certainly appreciate your comments. Truly, I do. But let me for a moment ask all of you a question. Had individual reporters acted differently, are you sure more objective stories concerning Iva would have made the front page? A newspaper, I must remind you, includes editors, publishers, owners, and share-holders, all of who have views and possibly conflicts of interest when it comes to reporting the truth. To sell papers, readership must be maintained. Realistically, to make a profit and pay the bills, advertisers are needed and courted. Both can be adversely affected when unpopular 'truths' are banner headlines. Isn't that so, Stan?"

"Mr. Samuels?"

"The *Nashville Tennessean*," Stan. According to your outline, you're covering that next, aren't you?"

Stan nodded and continued.

"In 1948 our old friend, Harry Brundidge, was working for the *Nashville Tennessean*. The publisher was Sillman Evans, who was a close acquaintance of Attorney-General Tom Clark. Evans was also close to John B. Hogan, a former FBI agent and now an attorney for the Department of Justice in the Immigration and Naturalization Service Division. Brundidge urged them to let him return to Japan where he would endeavor to get Iva to sign and certify Clark Lee's notes from his original interview with her. With this done, the FBI would then demand her arrest, and she would be brought to the States for trial. Brundidge's plan was accepted. He went to Japan, and, against Felipe's better judgment Iva, signed and thereby certified that Lee's notes were true and accurate. In doing so, her fate was sealed.

"Parenthetically, they also put pressure on Norman Reyes, now a student attending Vanderbilt University, to be a witness against Iva. His testimony, they concluded, would be unassailable since he had been a colleague at Radio Tokyo. If anyone knew what she did, he would. Shortly thereafter, the Justice Department announced that Iva Toguri would be arrested and forced to stand trial in the 12th District Court in San Francisco. When she was arrested, Iva leaned for the first time why the government was after her. She was presented with a formal warrant charging her with 'treasonable conduct against the US government during World War II.'

"On September 25, 1948, she returned from Japan under heavy FBI guard aboard the troop ship, the *General Hodges*. The ship was filled with returning troops from Japan and Korea. As such, the ship was greeted by cheering crowds when it docked in San Francisco. On the pier, a band played, *California, Here I Come*. Even as the returning soldiers crowded the railing to see the city skyline and look for loved ones on the pier, Iva, an unknown hero but a traitor to many, was quietly escorted off the troopship by government agents. She was finally home."

"Why did she sign Lee's notes?" Rita asked. "How could she trust Brundidge again?"

"Right," cried Ron Siegel, "how could she trust this guy?"

"The answer," Stan said, "is difficult to get at. But it appears she was very depressed from the loss of her child, and weak from the illnesses that had afflicted her over the years. She also wanted to return home and see her family again. She had been away from them for over seven years. But finally and tragically, she accepted Brundidge's promise of safe conduct and no problems once she was back in America. He won her trust because she wanted to believe things would finally be better. To some degree, we've all been in that situation, haven't we? Sometimes we so want to believe even though…"

"I've felt that way," Janet Lee said "about an old boyfriend."

"And I've had that experience with an ex-girlfriend."

"That about covers the romantic exploits of this class," Ron Siegel said with a half-moon smile.

"What about you, Mr. Samuels?" Luis Lopez asked.

"I had a good friend. He died on the *USS Aaron Ward*. Neither he nor I wanted to believe his wounds would…"

"I guess we've all been there," Tom Hayakawa added. "I couldn't believe it when my grandmother was diagnosed with cancer. I kept thinking, believing there would be a magical cure."

"Include me in the group," Philip Aquino said. "I keep thinking I'll pass this class."

That, of course, got a big laugh from the class and permitted Stan to continue in a somewhat happier room. Unfortunately, gloom and doom were to mark his next remarks.

Back Home

"Once Iva returned to San Francisco, she was immediately placed in jail. She remained in custody for nine months awaiting her trial in the city's County Jail without bail. During that period, she earned the nickname, *The Little Nurse,* for the assistance she gave the medical staff and other inmates. She kept busy (and her sanity) by helping out at breakfast and dinner waiting on tables and cleaning up tables afterwards. She also worked as a clerk-typist in the Marshall's Office weekdays from 8:00 am to 9:00 pm when she wasn't doing other things. In her spare time, she embroidered floral designs on the three table cloths in the jail's dining hall.

"And during all the time from her arrest in Japan to the beginning of the trial, Iva lost 30-pounds.

"Iva's attorney was Wayne Mortimer Collins. He was an experienced civil rights attorney from the ACLU with an excellent reputation earned defending the 'average guy.' From the very beginning of the trial to the end, Collins would pound away at the prosecution, declaring that Iva was not being given a fair trial. For example, he stated that the defense 'had uncovered evidence of perjury in the Grand Jury that indicted Iva.' The Judge ruled that information inadmissible on the grounds that the alleged perjurers weren't testifying at the actual trial. All references to the POW's whom Iva had helped in Japan were ruled inadmissible as not being relevant to the question of treason. Inadmissible! Always inadmissible! Only evidence, it seemed, brought by the government was admissible.

"The trial lasted thirteen weeks and, up to that time, was the most expensive in American history, costing more than $750,000. It began on July 5, 1949, a day after Iva's 33rd birthday. The trial was costly because the government flew in witnesses from Japan, all expenses paid, plus a per diem allowance of $10.00 per day. The government seemed to have an unlimited amount of money for the trial. On the other hand, Iva's father paid for her expenses by borrowing from friends and through loans. Talk about an unequal struggle.

"Essentially, the government tried to prove four things. First, Iva had maliciously betrayed the United States during the war. Second, she

155

had urged Americans to lay down their arms. Third, she had voluntarily remained in Japan after Pearl Harbor in order to make radio broadcasts as Radio Tokyo. Fourth, Tokyo Rose was not a myth. It was the radio moniker of Iva Toguri even if the actual Tokyo Rose never existed, and Orphan Ann did. Punishing the living symbol of the Tokyo Rose broadcasts was necessary.

"In listening to the parade of witnesses against Iva, the reporters attending the trial found them less than convincing, so much so that nine out of ten reporters, by their own poll, believed she would be found not guilty. They were convinced she would be acquitted.

"Support for Iva came from an expected but welcomed source. At his own expense, Charles Hughes Cousens flew to San Francisco from Australia. He presented an impassioned plea on Iva's behalf and defense of her behavior while she was at Radio Tokyo. He pointed out that he had chosen Iva, and that she only broadcasted what he wrote, that she was a 'soldier' under his command, and that at no time did she feel any loyalty other than to her own country. He also pointed out that they were under constant threat from their Japanese guards and that they received 'brutal treatment and threats of death.' As he stated, 'We were in the hands of a barbarian enemy.'

"More support for Iva came from Wallace Ince, who was never prosecuted for his role in the Zero Hour. In fact, following the war, he was promoted by the Army to major. He explained how Iva brought food, medicine, and, on one occasion, a blanket at great risk to herself. When asked about his experiences in the POW camps, as well as at Radio Tokyo, he almost broke down, stating, 'It is not easy to speak so matter of fact of Japanese brutality. Men I lived with, worked with, fought with died horribly at the hands of the Japanese.' Though bitter about his treatment by the Japanese, he still wholeheartedly supported Iva.

"Finally, the case went before the jury. After over 80-hours of deliberations, the jury returned with an unexpected declaration. The jury foreman, John Mann, told Judge Michael Roche that no verdict had been reached, that it was a 9 to 3 to convict. The jury, he said, was hopelessly divided. His exact words were, 'We cannot reach a unanimous verdict.'

"The prospect of a hung jury meant that Iva would go free. Collins,

Iva's attorney, was jubilant. His joy soon turned to ashes. The Judge told the jury to go back to work. He instructed them to resume deliberations and bring in a verdict. In doing so, he provided the jury with a very liberal interpretation concerning the definition of treason. He more than insinuated that this was an important case; the trial had been long and expensive, that like all cases it must be disposed of sometime, that there was no reason to believe another trial would not be equally long and expensive, and that they should 'sleep on what he had said.'"

"Talk about setting up the jury," Stan said angrily.

"This is justice?" Philip Aquino asked.

"Stan was right," Ron Siegel said. "This trial was an organized lynch mob."

"She never had a chance," Janet Lee said quietly. "Poor woman."

"And that guy, Ince, "Tom Hayakawa almost yelled out, "instead of facing the music like Cousens and Iva, he gets promoted by the Army."

"Hell of a judicial system," Rita Howard remarked.

"Remind me not to get the FBI on my case," Luis Lopez said flatly.

"All good points," Samuels said. "Time to finish the story, Stan."

"On September 29, 1949, the jury returned with a verdict. Out of the eight counts against Iva, the jury found her guilty of only one, and then so with only the greatest of effort; that 'she did speak into a microphone concerning the loss of ships.' But this would be enough for the prosecution. This verdict would condemn Iva to a federal prison for over seven years. The exact count had read:

> *That on a day during October 1944, the exact date being to the Grand Jurors unknown, said defendant, at Tokyo, Japan, in the broadcast studio of the Broadcasting Corporation of Japan, did speak into the microphone concerning the loss of ships.*

"This count was based on what would later be proved to be perjured testimony by a colleague of Iva's at Radio Tokyo. The Grand Jury had heard:

> *I said to Iva I had a release from the Imperial General HQ giving out results of American ship losses in the Battle of Leyte*

*Gulf, and I asked that she allude to the announcement, making
reference to the losses of American ships in her part of the
broadcast, and she said she would do so. She said, 'Now you
fellows have lost all your ships. Now you really are orphans of
the Pacific. How do you think you will ever get home?*

"Paradoxically, the naval battle alluded to in the Philippines had
proved a tremendous American naval victory. The Battle of Leyte Gulf
ended Japan's reign as a naval power in the Pacific. Naval and Marine
personnel who heard the broadcast could only laugh. They knew better.
Japan had ceased to be an aggressive force. She could defend isolated
islands to the death, as she did on Iwo Jima and at Okinawa, but she
would never again threaten her neighbors.

The Verdict

"With the verdict in hand, the Judge now handed down his
sentence. On October 6, 1949, Iva was sentenced to ten years in prison
at a federal reformatory prison in Alderson, West Virginia. She was
also fined $10,000 and deprived of her citizenship. She was now a
stateless person. When released from prison, she would be deported.
In rendering his penalty, Judge Roche far exceeded the minimum
penalty, which would have been 5-years and a $5,000 fine. On the
other hand, she avoided the death penalty, which had always been
available to him.

"Wayne M. Collins described the verdict and sentence as 'Guilty
without evidence.' An Associated Press reporter, who had followed
the entire trial at ringside, believed that 'any fair-minded group of
Americans would have wondered why there was a trial in the first place.'
The foreman of the jury, John Mann, who had tried to call a hung jury,
later stated, 'I knew she was innocent. I should have stuck to my guns at
the time.' He also said, the 'prosecution never proved her guilt beyond a
reasonable doubt.' Her father simply said of his daughter, 'you were like
a tiger. You never changed your stripes. You stayed American through
and through." A few years later, Judge Roche would reveal that his son

had been a Marine in the South Pacific during the war. The Judge freely admitted he had been biased against Iva from the beginning.

"Iva, who wasn't permitted to testify until September 7, 1949 before an all-white jury, though pale and haggard, still showed outward calm and was confident she would be okay, since she had done nothing wrong in her own mind. How wrong her assessment proved to be.

Stan stopped his presentation, but added, "I have one more thing to share with you. Ten years ago when interviewed, she stated the following, which you need to hear."

The trial? Well, it covered thirteen weeks, and there was just a multitude of witnesses who appeared whom I'd never seen before, never heard of before, and yet they professed to have known me. They testified that they saw the broadcasts, heard the broadcasts, which was impossible because the Allied POW's were under guard, and they couldn't have gotten into the studio. But they all testified that they heard me say those things, and they saw me actually perform. So many witnesses were brought over here. I suppose, after the war, they were asked to come and given so much per-diem and three meals a day, a trip to the US that a lot of people just jumped at the chance. It didn't make any difference what sort of witness they would make.

Stan stopped with that, collected his notes, and closed the book on this episode in Iva Toguri's life. The grad students remained in their chairs. To a person they felt like someone had kicked them in the face, and they weren't too far off in thinking this. History, at times, could be very stubborn and very forceful. In time they filed out, idealistic young people, who had to come to grips with the shadier side of the human condition. In doing, they were preparing themselves, as Samuels knew, for a career in journalism and in the long run, they would be better reporters because of this experience.

The last to leave were Stan and Samuels. As they did, Samuels said, "You earned your stripes tonight, Stan."

"It was personal."

"Personal? I don't understand."

"In the 1920's, my grandfather was beaten to death in rural Mississippi for talking to a white woman. Nothing more. Just talk. But it didn't matter. They never gave him a chance to explain. The mob just beat the life out of him. The local sheriff and judge covered everything up. Life went on minus one 'nigger.' That's the way I felt about Iva as I researched the trial and her conviction. Life would go on minus one 'Nip.' Nothing but ugliness."

There was nothing Samuels could say. Together the two men, the teacher and the student, walked out into the night...

Chapter 18

JAIL TIME

Alderson Federal Prison

"WEST VIRGINIA, HERE I COME, was never the state song of the Mountaineer State," Luis Lopez said in his opening remarks to his fellow grad students a week later. "Yet, West Virginia was where an innocent woman from California was sentenced by Judge Roche who laid down her penalties for being Tokyo Rose. Located in Alderson, a small rural town about 275-miles southwest of Washington D.C., this Federal Reformatory would be Iva Toguri's home for more than the next six years."

Unlike previous presentations, Robert Samuels thought, no one in his grad class tonight thundered with impatient questions. Where was Rita Howard claiming, "The jail was so close to Washington D.C. Why didn't the Judge just have Iva chained to the Washington Monument? If the government wanted to make a point, do so where everyone can see what happens to traitors." Nor did Tom Hayakawa say in his own quiet way, "I guess Alcatraz was unavailable." Nothing was heard from the usually talkative Philip Aquino. Samuels had expected him to say, "Some 'Big House!'" As for Stan Mack, not even this refugee from the "land of Dixie" made any comment alluding to tall trees and strong ropes. As for Mr. EVENTS STAFF, not a peep was heard from Ron Siegel. He was, thought Samuels, probably tabulating the day's parking tickets he had written. As for Janet Lee, no words were spoken. Her sad face conveyed all that needed to be said.

161

Indeed, Samuels' young, aspiring journalists seemed unduly subdued, as if Stan Mack's rendition last week had knocked the wind out of their sails. It wasn't that they were inattentive. Nor were they bored. Rather, it seemed like they were still recovering from being hit in the stomach, still digesting and acknowledging the unacceptable in the interval between class meetings: their federal government they wanted to believe in had been senselessly "out of control" in prosecuting the woman called Tokyo Rose. For his students, Samuels reasoned, the prosecution was really persecution.

Iva had not been tried; she had been, as Stan had suggested, lynched. In an earlier day, she would have been burned at the stake. All that his students once believed about the fairness and decency of America justice was cast adrift. If Iva were stateless, they were rudderless. If Iva were innocent of treason, they were, Samuels concluded, guilty of not knowing their own history, certainly as it applied to Tokyo Rose, and they felt uncomfortable knowing this. If Iva were to be incarcerated, they, too, were in a jail of doubt and misgivings about the unbridled use of power by government. If Iva's freedom were terminated, so was their now shaky belief in a justice system seemingly more responsive to prejudice and passion than the rule of law.

But what could he do, Samuels thought, to alter the landscape of their painful introduction to the complicated and messy world of life as it is, not necessarily as we would like it to be? There was, he thought, little he could do to alleviate the concerns of his charges. Their adjustment to the realities of life, which every reporter faced daily, would take place at a rate he could not abridge. Nor did he have any right to do so. Their metamorphosis would occur individually and internally. They would simply have to endure until, if at the end of the story, the President signed a full pardon for Iva. Only then would redemption be possible, and government would stand again as a bright and shining hope for all its citizens. Already, he knew, good people were battling the past, confronting the present, and struggling to absolve Iva of crimes never committed. Time, hopefully, was on his side, and his students', and Iva's.

With that in mind, Samuels said, "Please continue, Luis."

"Iva was sent to Alderson Federal Prison Camp (FPC), where she would be known as prisoner 9380-W. The small facility located in the Alleghenies with a prison population of about 300 at the time was first opened in 1927. Oddly enough, the idea of a federal prison for woman was initially supported by two of America's first ladies of unquestionable contrasting political persuasions. Florence Harding was a Republican blueblood, a 'Daughter of the American Revolution,' with distinctly conservative views mirroring the ex-President, her husband, Warren Harding. Eleanor Roosevelt was "the Wife of FDR, the monarch of Hyde Park. She was a Democrat with decidedly strong liberal political views. Both women, however, felt that prisons for women needed to be reformed. Alderson, a minimal security facility was needed for women in an effort to alter behavior rather than merely punish it. Due to their efforts, Alderson was the first federal prison for women in the United States.

"Unlike most prisons, this facility, composed of over a 150 acres of greenery and lovely sloping hills, had no fences or barbed wire. There were no guard towers to scar the landscape. It was an open prison, so to speak. The inmates, most of whom had been convicted of non-violent crimes, were locked into a prison without the presence of gun touting guards and mean searchlights cutting through the night. Each inmate slept in a bunk bed in one of two large dormitories. All of them had daily schedules and were expected to work as part of their stay. Alderson was referred to as *Camp Cupcake* by local residents, the media, and those opposed to prison reform in this manner. For Iva, it was just a way station before she would be reunited with her family.

"Among those who served time at Alderson was Katherine Kelly, the wife of the notorious George "Machine Gun" Kelly. With the exception of one other woman, most of the inmates were from the mountains of Tennessee and the Carolinas, who were in prison for assisting others who were "moonshiners" during Prohibition. They were charged with federal liquor tax law violations.

The exception to the rule was Mildred Gillers-Sisk who, if the facts are true, often played chess with Iva. Ironically, Gillers, as she preferred to be called, was also in Alderson for treason. Though relatively unknown by that name, she was better recognized by another, *Axis Sally*, an American woman who had broadcasted German propaganda from Berlin. In many respects, she was Iva's counterpart. One could only speculate what the two women discussed while playing chess or sharing a meal.

The Unknown Conversation

"Well, it was fun while it lasted," Axis Sally *said.*

"Fun?" Tokyo Rose *asked.*

"Sure, all the attention?"

"I didn't need it."

"Don't kid me, kid. Every girl likes to be on top of the heap."

"I didn't."

"Well, I have to admit it," Axis Sally *continued, "The government sure hit you harder than me. You must have really pushed someone's nose out of joint."*

"I did nothing wrong."

"That's what I told the military officers in Berlin when they arrested me. It didn't work."

"All I did was read prepared scripts," Tokyo Rose *countered. "I never said anything against my country."*

"Good for you of pure heart," the older woman said." *I told the Feds the same thing. I just read what the Nazis gave me to broadcast."*

"The Nazis were beasts," Tokyo Rose *said definitely.*

"And the Emperor's boys were Boy Scouts?"

"Berlin wanted to control all of Europe."

"And Nippon wanted to control the Pacific basin. Just what's the difference?"

"There's something I don't understand," Tokyo Rose *said, changing the subject slightly. "You gave Berlin a voice for the most oppressive regime in history, for thugs who created death camps and practiced the 'final solution' to ethnically and racially cleanse Europe and the world's undesirable, Jews, Russians, Poles, gypsies, and homosexuals. Yet, no one seems to be that mad at you. Why is that?"*

"Easy, dear. Bad as they were, the Germans were Caucasians. They were Christians of a particular sort. They played by at least some rules. They would give up when the jig was up. Of course, they preferred surrendering to the Americans as opposed to the Russians. But most importantly, the Germans

always declared war before attacking. They might gut Poland, trounce the Low Countries, and fire away at London with V-2's, but they always announced their intentions unlike your friends who bombed Pearl Harbor in a sneak attack."

"They weren't my friends," Tokyo Rose shot back. "But what about the attack on Russia? There was no declaration of war."

"True enough, but along a 3,000 mile front, there didn't need to be. Both sides knew what was coming. With over a million soldiers facing each other, it was only a matter of when, not if."

"Still, you don't seem to raise the same passions as I. The public doesn't denounce and hate you," Tokyo Rose said. "The media, especially this person Walter Winchell, isn't out to get you with the same venom"

"That's because I smile a lot, dress fashionably, and cross my legs when the male reporters seek interviews."

"It can't be that simple."

"Try styling your hair and putting on a little lipstick. Act a little sexy, and see what happens," Axis Sally said with obvious flair. "And eat something. You're far too skinny and tired looking for their cameras."

"No other reason for the hatred?" Tokyo Rose asked.

"One other."

"What?"

"You're Japanese."

"Japanese-American!" Tokyo Rose said with pride.

"Have it your way, kid. Your move."

"Did they really talk to each other?" Janet Lee asked, for once beating Rita Howard to the punch. "Did they really say those things?"

"They met. That's for certain. They played chess. No real question about that. They ate together. As to what they said while playing …"

"You made it up, Luis," Rita said.

"Not completely."

"What do you mean, not completely?" Ron Siegel asked.

"I improvised."

"Improvised?" asked Tom Hayakawa.

"Sure. I checked the historical record and assumed they might say certain things to each other," Luis pointed out.

"Sounds more like you checked out the hysterical record," Stan Mack said with a twinkle in his eye.

"I feel the same way," Philip Aquino said. "What do you think, Mr. Samuels? This is a class to prepare us for journalism, not fiction writing."

"Might be more money in fiction if you hit it off big," Rita Howard said before Samuels could answer. "I always wanted to try my hand at it."

"They could have said those things," Janet Lee added. "You know, girls talk during jail time."

"As I think about it, maybe Luis is on to something," Ron Siegel said. "Perhaps a little creative play can juice up the story. You know, keep the reader's attention."

"Just as long as the reader knows what you're doing," Stan Mack said brooking no counter argument.

"Agreed," said Tom Hayakawa.

Almost as an aside, "Philip Aquino repeated his earlier question. "What do you think, Mr. Samuels?"

"I think," he said, "you've covered the topic. Not much I could really add. So let's get on with it, Luis."

"Initially, Iva met with open hostility from the staff and other inmates. In time she was seen as a model prisoner. The reasons for this change are pretty straightforward. Though unfairly in prison, she was somehow always cheerful and helpful. With regard to her dorm room, it was always spotless, the floor always shining, and everything in its place. In the prison's handicraft program, Iva made leather goods and bookends, which took 1st and 2nd place in the 1952 West Virginia State Fair. Beyond these things, the staff appreciated in time her fine intellect. She had tested out at 130 on the renowned Wechsler Intelligence Scale. In other words, she was one smart lady.

"She impressed everyone with the quality and quantity of her work in the prison that included working as a supply clerk, assisting the medical officer, operating the X-ray machine, functioning as a lab assistant, and taking EKG's. Though denied a medical degree because of the war, Iva finally entered the field through the backdoor, so to speak. The only black mark on her record referring to a disciplinary action against her occurred on June 12, 1953. What was her offense? In the absence of the dental officer, she extracted an inmates tooth without authorization or supervision. Once a villain, always a villain, I guess.

"Iva would end up spending six years and two months at Alderson. She was visited periodically by her family, mainly her father, Jun. Sadly, Iva received no visits from her husband, Felipe d'Aquino. The FBI arrested him and forced him to return to Japan immediately following his testimony on behalf of his wife. He was forbidden to reenter the United States. In Hawaii, FBI agents boarded his ship and required him to sign a document barring him from returning to America. Had he not, he was threatened with a jail sentence.

"At this point, Iva couldn't leave the United States. If she did, she wouldn't be permitted to return. Her husband couldn't renter the country without risking a jail sentence. For all intents and purposes, they were separated from each other, and would remain so the rest of their lives.

"But the government could not keep them from corresponding with each other, which they did once per month until shortly before she was released from Alderson. As Felipe said, 'He wanted to keep up her morale.' The enforced separation, however, all but destroyed their marriage.

"Every year Iva appealed for a parole, and every year it was denied thanks to the continuous public resistance of Walter Winchell, the FBI, and the Justice Department. Some of the objections to her early release came from expected sources. Always on the attack, Walter Winchell railed against her and goaded the government, saying. 'Japnazis who radiorated for the Japanese in Tokyo but faced no punishment for the treachery.' Apparently, her sentence to Alderson was insufficient for him. Equally evident was his purposeful creative word use to convey his inflammatory views. James O'Neill, the National Commander of the American Legion objected to her initial return to the United States and pursued the same view over the years, stating, 'It is unthinkable that she should be afforded a haven by the government whose extinction she sought during the war.'

Surprising Criticism

"One unexpected source of opposition came from Japanese-Americans themselves."

"I don't believe it," Janet Lee interrupted. "Why would the Japanese community be against Iva?"

"As always, the historical setting was far more complicated than it appeared on the surface," Samuels stated. "That's right, isn't it Luis?"

"No question, Sir. I'll get to that business now."

The *Pacific Citizen*, a Nisei Newspaper, originally objected to Iva returning to the United States and maintained a less than low-keyed resentment of her during the San Francisco trial and for a period while she was in jail. It was a complicated matter. On the one hand, Japanese-Americans, especially the second generation, wanted to be considered loyal Americans who deserved the respect of their fellow citizens. On the other hand, it was very painful to see a member of their community treated in a high-handed manner. An editorial in the *Pacific Citizen* after the war summed up the problem.

There are thousands of loyal Japanese-Americans who proved their loyalty to the country during the war, both in the army and in the civilian war effort, and there is no reason why one person who pulled the despicable tricks, which Tokyo Rose did on her broadcasts to our men should taint the reputation of all the Japanese here.

"On an individual basis, the evolution of views and feelings toward Iva by the Nisei generation was typified by Grant Ichikawa. In 1941, though a graduate of the University of California, Berkeley, he was still rounded up and forced to relocate in a government camp following Pearl Harbor. As with other Nisei, he did so literally at gunpoint. The wholesale incarceration of Japanese-Americans, who were American citizens, had a devastating effect on him. As he stated, 'I lost all self respect since I was now considered an enemy alien.' Eventually, he took advantage of an opportunity to serve in the military. He was eager to prove his loyalty to the country. In time, he was stationed in Australia.

"There, as he recalled, 'some of the Caucasian soldiers regularly listened to Tokyo Rose and enjoyed listening to the soft American music. In my mind, it was an enemy broadcast, and therefore, I would not attempt to listen to it. I just did not want to do anything that would question my loyalty. Since I understood that they broadcasted in flawless English, I only assumed they must have been Japanese-Americans working for the enemy. I felt that they were traitors.'"

"When Iva was convicted of treason, Ichikawa was glad. However, as time went on and newer information was made public, he began to change his mind. He reached the conclusion that Iva was not Tokyo Rose and that she had been made a scapegoat by the government. What happened to Iva reminded him of his own past experience when General DeWitt manufactured a threat in order to clear the West Coast of all Japanese-Americans. Just as he had remained loyal to the country, he came to feel that way about Iva. In time, he spoke out on behalf of his fellow Nisei.

"One way or another, all things come to an end. So it was for Iva's stay in West Virginia. On January 28, 1956, she walked out of Alderson Prison a free woman, at least for a few minutes before a federal official handed her a deportation notice ordering her back to Japan. The deportation notice came from the INS at the insistence of the Justice Department and the FBI. To ward off deportation, Iva spent the next two years secluded in self-inflicted house arrest. For the next two years, as her benefactor fought one round after another with the government, Iva lived in the home of Wayne Mortimer Collins. In this home, at least, she had a caring, loving family fighting for her rights. By 1975, the fight was won.

"Iva Toguri would not be deported to Japan."

As the class departed following Luis' report, Samuels had the distinct feeling that the tide was turning, both for Iva and his students. And, he knew, a little hope was good for the soul.

Chapter 19

BREAK IN

5:00 a.m. – San Francisco – A Few Days Later

T HE RENTED WHITE VAN SKIRTED the freeway, taking instead the slick city streets, which were always wet from the evening fog and the morning dew. From the lower Mission, the van headed in a northern direction, first crossing Market Street before heading toward the Marina. There was little traffic this early in the morning beyond the ubiquitous Muni buses and Yellow Cabs hustling weary night shift folks home, or taking barely awake souls to work. Where possible, yet always according to a pre-set plan, the van avoided steep hills, always a challenge in San Francisco and especially in the Marina District. Passing across famous Lombard Street, the van approached the corner of Beach and Webster. There it stopped in front of a construction site, which had once been home to the Franciscan Beer Brewery. A school bond issue and two large wrecking balls had banged the brewery into history to make way for a new high school.

The van's lights turned off, and a moment later a tall, blond-headed young man exited the driver's side with a heavy bag and a small flashlight. His name, as later police reports would show, was Scott Foster, an out-of-work junior at Cal Berkeley, who needed a quick $3,000 to complete his education. The nameless man who had found him and offered the money to drive the van's occupant had been the Santa Claus of all time. It was a huge amount of money, too much for Scott to turn down. It would pay off his bills and provide him with an opportunity to take his girl to a really nice steak house where real linen was used, and competent waiters hurried to meet your every need. It would be a nice change from the fast food joints he usually frequented.

Already Scott had successfully done one job at State for his unknown benefactor. This morning he was doing another, planned, he hoped, as meticulously as the first. There was, of course, some risk involved. There always was when you broke the law. But a financially desperate Scott needed the dough. He would take the risk. Anyway, it wasn't as if he were breaking into the Bank of America. Hell, this was a school construction site. Nothing would be stolen, and he would be well clear of the place before the police arrived. Easy money.

Scott turned on the flashlight, careful to keep it pointing toward the ground and walked toward the portable cyclone fencing that encircled the construction site's perimeter. He headed directly for the heavily locked front gate. There, he shut off his flashlight and reached into his bag. He brought out the mother of all bolt cutters and a pair of strong workingman's gloves. These he put on and then checked his situation. The few floodlights cast their faint glow more on the heavy equipment and piles of construction materials inside the fencing than on the gate itself, which remained in half shadows. Mistake number one by the security company protecting the site, thought the young man. So far, things were going as Santa Claus said they would.

Beyond the equipment and building supplies was the new school. No longer was it an architectural dream of Norton and Norton, Inc., nor a figment of thin, bluish construction plans. It was real. Cement pads had been poured. Block walls had been erected with considerable rebar steel in them out of a healthy respect for the seismic possibilities of a city situated on the northern end of the San Andreas Fault. Lots of steel would in theory keep the kids safe when the tectonic plates rumbled and the land trembled again. The roof of most of the buildings had been topped off, and the classrooms were taking shape, more than 90% completed at this point. The Main Office was done; the tiled floors laid, interior walls painted, and furniture and file cabinets moved in, plus telephones installed and up and running. The room was close to operational. All it needed were the secretaries, who would add the human touch: framed photographs of their kids on desks, fresh cut flowers in vases, and secret drawers where unthinkable, if not sinful chocolate delights, were secretively stored away for late afternoon bursts of energy, or so one was led to believe.

School Site 1776 was becoming a reality.

The new school would be finished, if the work schedule were maintained at the present rate, two months ahead of schedule. Already the gym and cafeteria were completed, as was the baseball diamond. A grassy meadow was planted, and shoots of grass were poking their way into the light. Asphalt had been poured. Dirt was covered. Soon the symbolic school bell would be rung.

Scott wasn't interested in the school's future, only his own, and the job at hand. A strong metallic crunching sound met his ears as the oversized bolt cutters did their job. The cable-lock snapped, and the gate squeaked open to his gentle but insistent pressure. As he was about to replace the bolt cutters, he heard a noise. Feet were crunching toward him. This was not an unexpected event. He had been told a uniformed, elderly rent-a-cop from *Deluxe Protection Agency* would be at the site armed only with a radio and a heavy flashlight. Sure enough, out of the shadows, an old guy appeared, yelling, "Hey, what are you doing?" Scott found the question amusing. What was he supposed to say? "Sir, I'm breaking into the school with a friend. Please calm down and give me a few minutes to complete my job. I promise you, I won't take anything."

"Stop what you're doing," the guard yelled as he approached Scott. "Stop now, or I'll call the police." When the man was about three feet from him, Scott lunged toward him and sprayed him with a heavy dose of pepper spray. He caught the guard right in the face. Eyes watering, the old guy took a misstep and tripped over a pile of re-bar material. The poor fellow dropped his flashlight and radio as he pitched forward and fell heavily to the ground. In doing so, he unfortunately banged his head into a unused cement pier used as foundation for 6 X6 wooden blocks. There was a sickening whack, and old guy was out. Scott checked his pulse. Happily there was one, alive, banged up, but not dead. Killing someone was not part of the deal. No way. Now, had it been the professor at Cal who had given him a C+ in Philosophy 310, well that was quite another thing. Scott quickly dragged the still unconscious guard into an unfinished classroom, where he tied and gagged him with rope and cloth brought for that very purpose. As he did so, he thought, thank God the guard didn't have a watchdog. But then his Bank of Santa had said there would be no bared teeth on four legs. Once more, he had been right.

Scott returned to the van and drove it through the cyclone-gate, lights turned off, and parked it in the shadows between a tool shed and a classroom. Once in, he returned to the gate, closed it, and linked the cable-lock together with a short piece of rope. To all appearances, no one passing by would think anything was amiss. Then he went back to the van and stored his "bag of tricks" before sliding open the side door of the van.

Inside the van, sitting quietly in his wheelchair that was secured to the floor, was the *Warrior*, a slight smile on his face.

"We're in?" the Warrior asked.

"In and secured," Scott responded.

"Step two?"

"Now."

Scott pulled a ramp out of the van and connected it to the open door before reentering. He unclamped the wheelchair and slowly pushed the *Warrior* out of the van. He then pushed the wheelchair into the Main Office. He went back to the van and brought out three one-gallon containers, a heavy 15-foot length of chain with a lock, and pair of handcuffs that any police officer would envy. It took him two trips to bring every-thing to the Main Office. Once there, he handcuffed the *Warrior* to his wheelchair, and then chained him to a plumbing fixture in the office bathroom. Before proceeding, he said, "Ready?"

"More than ready."

"Okay. Cover your eyes."

Scott opened the first of the three one-gallon containers. He walked over to the *Warrior* and slowly poured a very red, wet sticky liquid over him. The smelly blood that was really animal blood, streamed down the Warrior's head, neck and shoulders before pooling in his lap. Next, Scott poured the other containers over the desks, typewriters, and the newly laid carpet. In a moment, the room was transformed into a grotesque parody of some B-movie horror film devoid of a script, but with plenty of gore. But, as Scott knew, this wasn't a horror flick. Looking at his gory handiwork, Scott was appalled by what he had done to earn his keep. Sitting amid this bloody scene, the *Warrior* looked as if he had been struck squarely by a Jap mortar and left for dead.

"You okay?" Scott asked the *Warrior.*

"Never better."

"I'll put up the sign."

"Do it, kid."

Taking a sheet of paper out of his pocket, which he then unfolded, Scott carefully placed the diminutive sign on the Warrior's lap. It simply read, **"Thanks, Tokyo Rose."**

"Time to go," he said to the Warrior.

"Scram. You've done your job."

Leaving the empty gallon containers and his bloody client, Scott retreated to the van after first reopening the gate. He drove through, stopped, exited the van, and relocked it. Again to all appearances the gate was secured. Entering the van again, he drove off, his mission accomplished. As he did so, he never saw the live video recording cameras that had been quietly installed late yesterday without notice, three days ahead of schedule.

Breaking the law was always risky.

Rachel Samuels and the Superintendent of Schools, Andy Anderson, arrived at School Site 1776 at 6:30 a.m. They arrived in separate vehicles at promptly half-past as the Friend had known and planned tightly for. They had set up their appointment the day before.

The two school people left their cars parked in front of the cyclone fence and hurried to the gate. Even as the Superintendent pulled out his key to open the gate, he knew something was wrong.

"Rachel, the chain's been cut."

"Sir?"

"Someone went to a lot of trouble to make the gate appear secure," he said. Here, look at the cable for yourself."

The Superintendent was right. Rachel could easily see that immediately. Almost as quickly, she looked around. Except for their cars, there was no other vehicle present in front of the construction side.

"Someone broke in," Rachel said directly. "And it looks like they're gone. Perhaps we should call the police."

"Yes, but let's look around first."

"Is that wise?"

"If the intruders have left, why not?" he asked. "There shouldn't be any problems."

Together they headed toward the Main Office. As they passed an almost completed classroom, they heard a low groan.

"What was that?" Rachel asked.

"Sounded like someone groaning," her boss answered.

"There it is again," Rachel said. "It's coming from inside this classroom."

Cautiously, they entered the room and almost immediately, though the early morning light was dim, found the night guard tied and gagged, and groaning quite loudly now. Quickly, they pulled out the gag and untied the poor guy, who muttered something then grabbed for his head.

"Damn that hurts," he said.

"What happened?" Rachel asked.

"Break-in."

The guard took the next few minutes to massage his head and to relate what little he could tell.

"That's it?" Rachel asked.

"Not much to tell," the guard said. "Everything happened so fast."

"What could they have wanted?" the Superintendent asked. "Why trespass a school construction site?"

"Not just any site," Rachel reminded him. "School Site 1776."

"But why?"

"Maybe we should look around," the guard said. "Start with the Main Office. If someone came to steal office equipment, that's the logical place to go."

"Lead on," Rachel said none too cheerfully.

The three entered the Main Office and even in the morning light saw a sight they wouldn't soon forget. Sitting in the middle of the blood splattered and severely damaged room was the Warrior, a curtain of crimson hue coloring his personage. He appeared to have ascended from hell on a fiery chariot with only his eyes not blanketed by blood.

"Good morning," the *Warrior* said. "Right on time as I expected."

For a moment no one said anything. The guard, still massaging the back of his head, said, "That wasn't the guy who sprayed me."

"Quite true," the *Warrior* said.

"Who?" Rachel asked.

"Does it really matter?" the *Warrior* asked almost too politely. "I'd ask you to sit, but as you can see the furniture is a bit scrambled."

Losing it, the Superintendent said, "Scrambled! You nutcase, you've ruined costly furniture and equipment."

"Ruined is a harsh word Dr. Andy Anderson. I prefer anointed. I spilled blood on everything as a sacrifice to end the sacrilege."

"You're certifiable, you son-of-a-bitch."

"No, that's not the case; at least I don't think so. No, I emulated the Berrigan Brothers, and no one considers them certifiable. You know, the Catholic duo."

"The 'who?' the guard asked.

"Two priests," Rachel said. "Philip and David, I think, and seven other Catholic lay people."

"Ah, someone does know recent history."

"They poured animal blood on Selective Service files," Rachel continued.

"Why?" the guard asked. "Aren't those government records?"

"Slowly the sun dawns," the *Warrior* said.

"It was their way of protesting the Vietnam War."

"Some way," the guard said. "Hell, I went to Korea and didn't complain."

"It was in Catonsville, Maryland, wasn't it?" Rachel asked.

"May 17, 1968," the Warrior said.

Suddenly, Rachel's heart leaped in her chest. "May 17th!" she yelled. "That's today."

"Eight years ago," the Warrior added, "almost to the minute."

"Bloody fools," the Superintendent said.

"Blood, yes," the Warrior said. "Fools, no."

"He's right," Rachel said. "Christ's blood is holy. The use of blood in sacrifice is significant to Christians. By pouring animal blood on the files of potential draftees, the two Catholic priests and seven other members of the church sanctified their actions. They were protesting evil. They were acting out of righteousness."

"You're got to be kidding!" the Superintendent shouted. "This jerk is acting out of righteousness?"

"In his mind, he is, aren't you, Michael Simms," Rachel said, "and very Irish and Catholic."

"Raising your voice and cursing won't get you any place, Superintendent," the *Warrior* said as if he hadn't heard Rachel. "I should know. I tried that with phone calls and letters, and, well, it didn't work for me."

"You're going to jail for this," the Superintendent said.

"So?" asked the *Warrior.*

"I'm calling the police," the guard interrupted.

"Don't bother," the Warrior said. "They were called once your cars arrived. How, you ask? Easy. I'm not acting alone. Got that? San Francisco's finest will be here shortly."

"'You're gone bonkers," Andy Anderson said in a high-pitched voice. "You must have a hundred screws loose."

<hr/>

"You called the police?" Rachel asked. "That's exactly what the *Catonsville Nine* did. They called the police and waited to be arrested."

"That's screwy," the guard said.

"Not if you want to be arrested," Rachel pointed out.

"But why?" the perplexed guard asked.

"To go before a judge," Rachel said. "Of course, that's what he wants. Don't you see it? He wants to take his case against Tokyo Rose to a jury in order to make it public. He needs to go to jail to achieve his purpose."

"To achieve what?" Andy Anderson asked.

"To stop this school from being named after Iva Toguri."

"Very good," Miss Samuels," the *Warrior* said "and almost correct.

I don't want the school named after Tokyo Rose, who Iva just happens to be."

"There are questions about that, Michael," Rachel said.

"Yes. Questions your father has raised in the *Chronicle*."

"But if he's right all this is unnecessary."

"He's not."

"How can you be so sure?"

Stripping away a small now blood stained blanket covering his lap, the *Warrior* said unmitigated anger, "Because Tokyo Rose did this to me."

What could Rachel say? Michael Simms wanted to blame someone for his loss. No amount of arguing would change his mind. He interrupted her thoughts.

"Did I forget to mention I also called *KRON*. They'll be here, too. They love this stuff. They'll be here with cameras whirling and that cute little reporter asking inane questions. By tonight, we'll all be on the evening news."

"Mr. Michael Simms, what is it you really want?" Rachel asked.

Instead of answering Rachel, the *Warrior* just held up his sign. At that moment, they all heard sirens filling the morning sky. The *Warrior* smiled.

The plan was working.

The first police cruisers arrived right on time as planned by the Friend. Exactly at 7:00 a.m. The officers quickly created a secure perimeter around the construction site. No work would be done today. Hopefully, there were good movies in the theaters and lots of bowling lanes open. If it were fishing season, it would have helped. The police were fast. They kept the construction workers out, but not fast enough to keep the KRON van from barreling into the area and two cameramen, plus a shapely reporter, leaped from it. As hoped by the *Warrior*, the station's rising star, Marie Preston, notebook in hand, was ready to plunge into the story.

All was going well according to the Warrior's schedule.

The Police Commander was a man by the name of Carl Richardson. Strongly built and very professional in his bearing, Richardson, an African-American, was escorted by two officers into the Main Office.

They quickly took in the scene, but not its meaning. A moment later the press and television folks arrived. The Main Office was getting crowded.

"What a mess," the Commander said. "Jesus what happened here."

"She'll tell you, Sir," the *Warrior* said, pointing to Rachel.

Rachel did, explaining to the incredulous group what was taking place at the school construction site. She also explained the "why" for the "what." Her every word was captured on film. With a bit of editing, Marie Preston had a great evening story. No doubt about it.

The Commander, a no nonsense sort of guy, turned a stern look on the *Warrior.*

"Look, Mister, the Commander said, " I'm not really sure what this is all about, but here's what's going to happen. In a minute, one of my guys is going to cut you loose from the plumbing. Then we're going to hose you down. After that, a police ambulance will take you to San Francisco General. Got it?"

"Got it, Sir."

"Good. I don't want any trouble with you once we remove the handcuffs."

"You won't have any."

"Later, it will be up to the D.A. to decide what will happen."

"You're not arresting me?"

"Like I said, the D.A. will make that determination based on a review of the facts and any complaint by the School District."

"Well, I fully expect them, too. Just look around. There must be thousands of dollars worth of damage here. A complaint must be filed on behalf of the good taxpayers of the city."

"As I said, up to them."

Though difficult, a fire hose was brought into the Main Office and a rather clumsy effort was made to wash the blood off the Warrior. The results were less than desired. To the cameras flashing and running, the Warrior was pushed out of the school and to a waiting ambulance. As this happened, he held up his sign, reminding everybody that this was about Tokyo Rose. At the ambulance, three sturdy paramedics hoisted the *Warrior* into a van; then with a wailing siren, he was off, soon to be lost in the morning traffic.

Second Thoughts

As he left, Andy Anderson turned to Rachel and said, "I'll get the Board to file enough complaints to put this guy away for an eternity."

"Isn't that what he wants?" Rachel asked. "A jury trial? Public exposure? A chance to air his grievances?"

"So what! We'll get him out of our hair."

"I'm not so sure," Rachel responded. "For many, he's going to be a sympathetic soul, an older vet in a wheelchair jammed by an unfeeling Board of Education."

"Well?"

"Not a good deal. The Board will deflect the charges, pointing out it acted on the basis of what the Superintendent recommended."

"I'll take the heat."

"Yes."

"There's another problem beyond public relations," Rachel said.

"Such as?"

"An arrest and court trial will undoubtedly stir our multicultural pot, probably creating tensions between Asians and the white community. Once that starts, it's difficult to do school business."

"Is that what this guy wants?"

"Anything to detract the Board from naming the school after Toguri."

"What's my other option?"

Rachel told him.

That afternoon the Superintendent held an emergency meeting with the Board of Education. He explained what happened and made two recommendations. After thirty minutes of heated debate behind closed doors, the Board agreed to the recommendations. An hour later, the President of the Board called the Office of the D.A. An agreement was reached.

The Evening News on *KRON* carried the story. Marie Preston summed up the Board's position.

The Board has decided not to press charges against Mr. Simms. He is obviously a disturbed World War II vet who needs our fullest understanding and sympathy. He was terribly wounded in the war. He lost both legs at the knee. He has lived alone for many years and holds strong emotional views regarding naming any school after a proven traitor, who is in his mind Tokyo Rose. As such, criminal charges and a possible jail sentence do not seem in the best interest of Mr. Simms. Instead, the Board recommended and the D.A. agreed to mandatory counseling at the VA Hospital and a restraining order to keep Mr. Simms off school property. As to naming School Site 1776, the Board will consider every credible name placed before it by the community.

Following the news, Rachel called her father and explained all that had occurred. He was thankful she was okay and delighted in the strategy she had strongly recommended to the Superintendent.

"You're a born politician, Rachel."

"Thanks, Dad."

In his home, Thomas Williams was not happy at all. He had been forced to vote yes with Board members to the strategy proposed by Andy Anderson. To do otherwise might have compromised his situation. His effort to get a public trial for Michael Simms, but really to put Iva Toguri on trial again, had failed. He knew Simms would dig into himself and keep his Friend out of things. If forced, he would deny any accusations put forth by Simms, twisting the vet's views on the basis of misunderstandings and misplaced emotions. Hopefully, that wouldn't happen. What he need now was a new plan. In the back of his mind one was already forming.

The next day the security tapes from the cameras at School Site 1776 were checked by technicians to make sure the equipment was working. The equipment exceeded every expectation. Later that same day, the head technician called the head of security. An hour later he contacted the SFPD. An hour later, a full written report was sent to Police Commander, Carl Richardson, whose only remark after reading it was, "I'll be."

Chapter 20

AXIS SALLY

Events Staff Man

IN LATE MAY, ROBERT SAMUELS met with his graduate journalism class to begin, as he saw it, the last part of the semester, and for his students, the first part of their professional lives in the world of print news. His feelings, of course, were mixed. On the one hand, he was delighted with the research work of his students, especially since their "digging into the past" had certainly helped him with his series on Iva Toguri. There was no question about that. He knew in his journalistic heart that any newspaper that picked up one of his students would be the better for it. On the other hand, he hated to see them go. The truth of it was that he had grown quite fond of all of them. They had made him laugh, cry, and think. They had pushed him in ways he hadn't thought possible. And that included his chosen foil for the semester, young Ron Siegel, whom he still teased on occasion.

"Well, Ron, the floor is yours tonight," Samuels said, "much like the Faculty Parking Lot."

"I'll try to be equally efficient here as I trust I am there."

"No criminal activity gets by you, Ron."

"Rules are important. Without them, we…"

"Return to paradise."

"I was thinking more along the lines of anarchy," Ron said with confidence. "And we wouldn't want that."

Samuels had to admit it. The young man could give it as well take it. He was the kind of tough kid the Japanese suicide bombers hadn't counted on when they attacked *the Aaron Ward.*

"You're so right, Ron. "The law demands enforcement. Enforcement demands evidence. Evidence demands an investigation. And an investigation only occurs when there has been a violation of law, even if trivial, don't you agree?"

"I do, Sir, whether a parking ticket or a 'wicked witch' in Berlin."

Nice move, kid, Samuels thought to himself, from Frisco to Berlin without one mention of *Crisco.* Time to give him his head.

"Ron, as I said, the floor in yours tonight."

Taking off his EVENTS STAFF jacket, Ron began. "When Luis shared with us a possible conversation between the alleged *Tokyo Rose* and the apparently less controversial *Axis Sally* while they were at Alderson, I wanted to jump up and yell, 'not fair, not fair at all.' But that would have been the wrong time to do so. But tonight is not, so I shout, 'not fair, not fair.' Naturally, the question you should be asking yourself, and I trust you are, is, what's not fair? That answer, as I shall show you is this. The hatred against Iva Toguri was misplaced. There was no Tokyo Rose and Iva certainly didn't spread propaganda. You know that already. All we need now is for the public to fully grasp this, and just maybe a pardon will be forthcoming. But there was an *Axis Sally,* and she did spread propaganda of the worst type throughout the war. With this in mind, our story starts on May 11, 1944, a short month before D-Day and a typical day for our "Berlin baddie."

D-Day Propaganda

"On that day, Axis Sally, or if you will, Mildred Sisk Gillars, broadcasted the most infamous radio show of World War II. It was the show that would eventually get her convicted of treason and sent to Alderson. The show was about a radio play entitled *Vision of Invasion.* It was beamed to American and British troops in England preparing for the invasion of 'Fortress Europa.' It was also beamed to the home folks in America. Understand, it wasn't the usual stuff: news, music, Nazi propaganda. It was something more. In her role, Gillars played an

American mother who dreamed that her soldier son, a member of the invasion forces, died aboard a burning ship in an attempt to cross the English Channel.

"The play had a very realistic sound track. Sound effects simulating the moans and cries of the wounded as they were raked with gunfire from the beaches gave the play the sense of a documentary. Over the battle action sound effects, an announcer's voice said, "the D of Day stands for doom, disaster, death, and Dunkirk. The purpose of the broadcast was to prevent the invasion by frightening the Americans with grisly predictions of staggering casualties.

"Though the show had little impact on Allied troops, it did play harshly in American homes. Propaganda it certainly was, but there was an element of truth to it. The invasion of France would be costly in life. The Germans were waiting. The Germans were prepared. The Germans would fight. The Allies would invade. That was beyond question. American and British sons would perish at sea, or on the beaches, or in the air. That, too, was a given. *Vision of Invasion* broke the heart of future Gold Star Mothers even in advance of those terrible telegrams from the War Department --- 'We regret to inform you.'

"By comparison, Iva Toguri never did anything like or similar to what Mildred Gillars was broadcasting to the enemy. *No Vision of Invasion* was ever written by Charles Cousens or read by Iva. More to the contrary, as we know, Iva and her little band of warriors attempted successfully to undermine Radio Tokyo. Mildred Gillars did quite the opposite.

"The woman who played the mother went by many names. Originally, she was Mildred Elizabeth Sisk when she was born in Portland, Maine, on November 30, 1900. She became Mildred Gillars after her divorced mother was remarried to a dentist, Dr. Robert Bruce Gillars. During the war years, she referred to herself as *'Midge at the Mick,'* but the GI's in the European theater dubbed her as simply *Axis Sally*. The name stuck. The name of her show was *'Home Sweet Home.'* The show usually aired sometime between 8 P.M. and 2 A.M. each day. The broadcasts were heard all over Europe, the Mediterranean, North America, and the United States from December 11, 1941 through May 6, 1945.

"Unlike the many Nisei candidates who might have been Tokyo Rose, there was only one unquestioned nominee for Axis Sally, and that was Gillars. Again, unlike Iva Toguri, Mildred Gillars was not trying to undermine the Nazi propagandistic efforts. Unlike Iva, who never exploited the American POW's, Mildred could and did. But unlike Tokyo Rose, who engendered such public contempt and hatred on a visceral level, Axis Sally, though disliked, never did. Both were stranded in a foreign country when war came, but only one was a real traitor by the standards of the 1940's, and, I might add, my own."

I've got to give the kid credit, thought Samuels. He sure knows how to run with the ball.

"Again, unlike Iva, Mildred had a sultry, sexy voice that came across the radio loud and clear. Unlike her counterpart in the Pacific, Mildred seemed to enjoy teasing the GI's about their wives and sweethearts back in the States. As an example: 'Hi fellows, I'm afraid you're yearning plenty for someone else. But I just wonder if she isn't running around with the 4-F's way back home.' When signing off, she added salt to the wound, declaring, 'I've got a heavy date waiting for me.'

"Pretending to be a representative of the International Red Cross, Mildred Gillars would visit POW camps and hospitals holding captured Americans in particular. From them she would gather information, names, serial numbers and hometowns. After that, she would carefully insert this information into her program that suggested concern for the GI's she would mention. It went something like this. 'The poor doctors don't…. I don't know… only time will tell, you see.' The effect on the American population was significant. Families worried about their sons, especially those mentioned on the radio.

"As in the case of Iva, the broadcasts from Berlin were recorded at a secret listening post in Silver Hill, Maryland. The listening post was manned and operated by the Federal Communications Commission. The recordings were eventually used against both of them in federal courts after the war. But unlike Iva's trial, Mildred Gillars was able to use her taped shows in a fruitless defense of her activities.

The following is typical of what was taped.

Good morning, Yankees. This is Axis Sally with the tunes that you like to hear and a warm welcome from radio Berlin. I note that the 451ˢᵗ is en route this morning to Linz where you will receive a warm welcome. And, by the way, Sgt. Robert Smith, you remember Bill Jones, the guy with the flashy convertible who always had an eye for your wife, Annabelle; well, they have been seen together frequently over the past few months and last year he moved in with her. Let's take a break here and listen to some Glen Miller."

"She was a piece of work," Rita Howard said none too politely. "That babe was really out of line."

"Christ, Iva never said anything like that," Philip Aquino said with a harshness to his voice.

"What's the story on her?" Tom Hayakawa asked. "As an American citizen, how did she end up on Radio Berlin working for the Nazis?"

Ron obliged and shared more. "If she is to be believed, love was the cause of everything?"

"I don't believe it," Janet Lee said loudly.

"The jury that later weighed the case against her didn't believe it either," Ron said. The story began in an American college."

"Not UCLA?" Stan Mack asked. "That would be too great a coincidence."

"No, not UCLA," Ron said. "How about Ohio Wesleyan University?"

"Never heard of it," Philip Aquino said.

"You have now, and you're about to learn more," Ron responded.

Background

"Mildred Gillars graduated from high school in Conneaut, Ohio, in 1917, the same year that Woodrow Wilson took the country into war against Germany. Ohio Wesleyan was located in a small town of Delaware. Gillars majored in the dramatic arts and had dreams of becoming a major star. Despite really excelling in her drama studies and speech, she never graduated from Ohio Wesleyan. I was unable to determine why she didn't. Anyway, she moved to New York City to continue her drama lessons while taking a series of menial jobs to support herself. Apparently, she did work with touring stock companies and in vaudeville, but no big break came her way. She was capable and smart, but not a star.

"With financial assistance from her grandmother, she enrolled at Hunter's College where in 1925 she met Max Otto Kolschwitz. He was a German immigrant professor and, by all accounts, a dynamic teacher with a persuasive personality. He was also a naturalized American citizen. Gillars had a heated, very passionate affair with the charismatic professor until she found out he was married.

"She didn't see the romantic womanizer again until 1932 when she went to Europe to continue her drama studies. There she encountered him again in Berlin. He was handling propaganda on Radio Berlin for the emerging German Nationalist Party we called the Nazis. Unable to become a famous actress in America, she went to "good old Otto." He encouraged her to work with him as a broadcaster. She took the bait and his bed. She was in love once more. As to Otto's wife, I could not determine if she was still around. Nevertheless, Gillars was enticed by the exposure she was sure the new job would provide her. In making that assumption, she was correct.

"Dear Otto became Radio Berlin's program director and, in time, Gillars' supervisor. Gillars worked as a DJ playing music and reading on-air anti-Semitic rants. One such statement said:

> *It's a disgrace to the American public that they don't wake to the fact of what Franklin D. Roosevelt is doing to the Gentiles of your country and my country.*

"The job proved very lucrative for her, and she was now receiving all the attention and recognition she always desired. At Radio Berlin, her official title was *Station Mistress of Ceremonies*. Gillars had finally made it big-time. She was a star.

"During her later trial in an American Federal Court, her defense attorneys tried to point out that Max Otto Koischwitz had an undue influence on Gillars. She backed this claim up, stating that her immediate superior had a Svengali-like influence over her. She tried to convince the jury she was not responsible for her actions. Her lover, she maintained, had strong emotional power over her. She referred to him as a "man of destiny." She did not mention that he had renounced his American citizenship in 1932 and returned to Germany to become a high official in the Nazi radio service. In short, it was all Otto's fault that made her make the broadcasts for Hitler's government. On the surface, this seemed a bald-faced lie. On the stand, she learned of Otto's death, and burst into tears. For her detractors, it was her greatest performance.

"The chief prosecutor, John M. Kelly, Jr., countered her arguments, pointing out that after being hired by Radio Berlin, she had signed an oath of allegiance to Hitler's Germany. In doing so, Gillars had forsaken her country. A steady stream of witnesses attested to her impersonation of a worker for the International Red Cross, who had persuaded captured American solders to record messages to their families and relatives in the States. Naturally, they were never told that Nazi propaganda would be inserted between the GI's messages. This testimony was enough to sway the jury.

"Her trial ended on March 8, 1949 after six hectic weeks, and was sent to a jury of seven men and five women. The jury acquitted her of seven of the eight counts pressed by the government in its indictment. She was, however, found guilty on count No. 10, involving the Nazi broadcast of the play *Vision of Invasion*. On March 26th, Judge Edward M. Curran pronounced sentence: 10 to 30 years in prison, a large $10,000 fine, and eligibility for parole in 10 years. She was sent to the Federal Women's Reformatory in Alderson. There she would end up playing chess with our friend Iva.

On June 10, 1961, at exactly 6:25 A,M. she walked out of Alderson, newly paroled. She was greeted by reporters and bursting flashbulbs. They were there to cover her early release. Ever the actress, according to *the Charleston Daily Mail*, she strode out of the prison with a flourish. She was a free woman.

"No Walter Winchell hammered at her, demanding that she be deported to East Germany, where the Russians, now masters of half of Germany, would be her ungracious host. However, no VFW or American Legion commander railed against her. No surging cry of anger emerged from the public at the behest of right-of-center newspapers. No demonstrations occurred in front of her home. She simply walked out of prison into relative obscurity. Unusual as it may sound, her first job upon release was to live in a convent in Columbus, Ohio, where she taught Roman Catholic schoolgirls. Hopefully, she pointed out to them the pitfalls of falling in love with visiting professors. Scrub that. That's an intended editorial, but not one you should take to the bank. After working for the good Catholics, she reenrolled again at Ohio Wesleyan University. She finally completed her bachelor's degree in speech in 1973, three years ago. She now lives in Columbus. Anybody want to visit her?"

No one in the class did. As Ron had said, "it's so unfair, so unfair." They now accepted this contention unequivocally. Compared to what Iva had gone through to support America during the war while in hostile Tokyo, Gillars was complicit in broadcasts to harm America. Ron had done a splendid job, mixing historical fact, excellent interpretation, and, under the circumstances, just enough satire to liven up the content. The kid deserved a hearty "well done." Samuels would make sure he got it.

Only one question remained, thought Samuels: why the difference in treatment? The question continued to haunt him. Was it as simple as Gillars had stated to Iva at Alderson: "You are a Japanese-American; I'm not." If that were the core point, than next week's presentation might settle the issue once and for all, at least in his class.

Chapter 21

PLANS AND DECISIONS

Stormy Weather

MAY BROUGHT AN UNEXPECTED STORM, which swept southward from Alaska and eventually slammed into San Francisco. For three days, dark clouds hung over the city like an armada of Spanish galleons peppering the streets with a continuous shower and icy temperatures. Umbrellas and raincoats were hastily retrieved from their winter hibernation and once again drafted into use. Sturdy hats and warm gloves kept one's head and hands dry and warm, while even the word *galoshes* came back into common usage. People had to get to work and did.

The first responders were having a field day. The "city's finest" were kept busy keeping the peace between drivers of fender benders. The amusing oddity of the fire department responding to fire alarms in a howling storm was not lost on most people. While banks remained open and the Post Office carried on, the public schools closed and children remained at home, baby-sat by the "boob tube." Old folks claimed they hadn't seen anything like it in years, if that.

Those who give advice suggested that, if possible, it was best to stay at home, warmed by PG&E and a hot bowl of clam chowder soup with a large chunk of sourdough French bread coated with butter. Add a little wine, or a jigger of brandy to your coffee, and life was more than tolerable, regardless of Mother Nature's tantrums. Political intrigue and deal-making, of course, continued, as might be expected.

In a small café off Castro Street near Market, George Luna kept a breakfast appointment with the Reverend Harrison Fork. After breakfast:

"Reverend, I can't give you my vote," Luna said.

"I'm disappointed, George."

"My folks feel that King already has a street named after him, a shopping center, and one city building. Cesar Chavez, on the other hand, has nothing, not one thing."

"There is some talk about naming a street after him."

"Only talk to this point, Reverend."

"Looks like we're canceling each other out, George."

"It does, doesn't it?"

Across town at *Fosters*, a great place for pancakes and sausage, Larry Chin and Matthew Nogata were talking.

"Larry, I can't back Dr. Sun Yat-sen."

"I don't understand."

"My community is being territorial or provincial. You can decide. They want me to vote for an American if Toguri isn't pardoned, anyone but Dr. Sun Yat-Sen. is

---

At the *Bagel House* on the Great Highway fronting the Pacific Ocean, Jews and Gentiles alike, whether agnostics or theists, gathered in the morning rainfall at this little hole-in-the-wall eatery that made the best bagels in town.

Into this happy little spot, Mrs. Ruth Franklin and Mrs. Lucy Patrissi had come for an early morning talk.

"I can't vote for Joe, Lucy, if Iva gets a pardon."

"If she doesn't?"

"Then we'll talk, Ruth."

Secluded in his bunker and involved in his own intrigue, Michael Simms picked up the phone. He had been expecting a call from the Friend and was not disappointed.

"Michael, its me."

"I screwed up."

"Calm down, Michael."

"No courtroom in which to speak my piece."

"They cut a deal."

"Who?"

"The Board and the DA."

"How? Why?"

"That woman, Rachel Samuels, she convinced that jellyfish of a superintendent to back off."

"What?"

"She recommended no criminal charges."

"And?"

"Without charges, Michael, the police had no reason to arrest you."

"Why did she do that?"

"She didn't want you to speak out against Tokyo Rose."

"We missed our opportunity."

"Only in court. Michael. You still had some television exposure. Your message got out. Lots of sympathy for you, and your cause."

"Not like before a jury."

"True."

"They'll name the school after Toguri."

"Not necessarily. No candidate has a majority. Things are up in the air."

"And when they fall?"

"We'll hope for a safe landing."

"What can I do?"

"I'm working on a new plan, Michael. Hang tight."

"That's all I do."

At the VA Hospital, Mrs. Ruth Franklin and Dr. Harold Malone were talking in subdued tones in the hospital cafeteria, where the institutional breakfast fare was just that, fair. A half-eaten bear claw and an untouched cinnamon bun were before them. Apparently, their appetites were on strike.

"Well, here we are, Ruth."

"Yes, Harold, we are here."

They had spent so much time together recently discussing Michael Simms' case that an informal relationship had formed.

"I like your plan."

"I hope it works, Harold."

They had discussed and debated a strategy for dealing with Simms. The referred to it as "the plan."

"It's our best shot, Ruth."

"If we can get them together, it has a chance, Harold."

"The plan depended on any number of variables, most of which are out of our control.

"You wrote to her?"

"Oh, yes."

"And?"

"No response yet. Harold."

"If she doesn't?"

"I'll call."

"Do you think we have a fighting chance, Ruth?"

"Thanks to that administrator, yes. Her recommendation to avoid criminal charges was smart."

"I agree. That Miss Samuels is an extraordinary lady. And she's in on our strategy?"

"Harold, up to her administrative ears."

"Good. We'll need all the help we can get."

"She's a good one to have on our side, Harold.

At the Board of Education Rachel was deep in thought, that is checking out the latest report from the contractors when the Superintendent dropped by her office. This was something he seldom did.

"Ah, Rachel, here you are," Andy Anderson said. "Hard at work, are you?"

"At least, I hope, working hard."

"Good turn of words. Anything I should know, Rachel?"

"The damage has been cleared. New equipment has been installed."

"The cost?"

"Less than we expected, Sir. Way less."

"How can that be?"

"The lead contractor did the repair work with no charge beyond the damaged materials and labor. No profit for him. Looks like Board member Williams urged his friend Greenberg to help us out. Pointed out that it was good PR."

"And that there would be other contracts?"

"Very true, Sir."

"And the equipment?"

"Installed at cost. No one is making a profit on this tragedy."

"That is good news, Rachel."

Saving money was always good news to the Superintendent. Whatever his faults, he strove to keep the District on an even financial keel. Today, however, he had other things to discuss.

"Your recommendation proved excellent, Rachel. My heartfelt thanks."

"Hopefully, the VA can finally help Simms."

"Whatever happens from now on, we know we made an effort to keep the police and the DA out of the picture. Next time around, of course, that won't be possible. Too much water under the bridge."

"Hopefully, a next time won't happen, Sir."

"If we just had a way to deal with Simms," the Superintendent said. "If we had a way to change his thinking."

Rachel smiled inwardly at her boss' comment, saying, "Perhaps something will turn up."

The Proposition

Professor Jonas Morgan sailed into Samuels' office at the *Chronicle*, that same morning all cloth unfurled to the wind, and the riggings set against even the most hostile seas.

"Ahoy there, mate," he bellowed like his hero, Horatio Hornblower. "How goes it?"

"What a delightful surprise," Samuels answered. "Nice to see you docked at my pier."

"I was in the area and needed to make landfall."

"Pirates after you, Sir?"

"Only the tyrannical bean counters, Morgan said. "But that's another story. I'm here to tell you in person."

"Tell me what?" Samuels asked.

"The gods have decided that, if you want it, of course, a fulltime position might be possible for you next year, beginning in the fall. I was chosen to be the bearer of this news."

Fulltime, Samuels thought. How would that be possible? He already had a fulltime position. Yet, the possibility was did entice him. Still…

"I'm grateful, Sir, I really am."

"But?" asked Morgan.

"I couldn't handle two full jobs at once."

"Perhaps you could leave this port for another anchorage?"

"This is the harbor I know and love."

"Well, you're the captain of your own soul," Morgan countered. "You've plenty of time to decide."

"Which amounts to what?"

"At the end of the semester, the gods need an answer," Morgan said.

"I'll need to check with my quartermaster."

"Naturally. Check with Mrs. Samuels."

"And my crew?"

"Rascals, they are, but talk with your offspring, if you must."

"Anything else on your mind, Sir?"

"No, not really beyond telling you what a great job you've done this semester with the grad class. You really got them into "digging for treasure.""

"Right. I pleased too. All hands seem to be bending their backs to the oars."

"That they are, by God. Drake would have loved them against the Armada."

"And Halsey at Midway?"

"Without a doubt," Samuels said.

"Hopefully, there will be no more scraps with this pirate, Simms."

"Depends, Sir, on how the wind blows."

"Aye, it does at that."

After three days, the storm abated, and the sun once more shimmered in the Bay Area sky, and, as it always did, fired slivers of sunlight through the caverns of skyscrapers piercing upward to the heavens. In the neighborhood parks, kids and dogs, each content to be in the outdoors again, joyfully scampered around yelling and barking in sheer delight. Older folks, no longer cooped up, once more took to the still glistening streets to do their chores. Tourists emerged from hotels and headed for Golden Gate Park and the Golden Gate Bridge. Fisherman's Wharf and Chinatown were again on the radar of visitors to the city. Even college students returned to class to close out the spring semester, and, in the case of some, to march in the graduation exercises to, it might be added, the lasting appreciation of their parents and their depleted bank accounts. Life in the city was returning to normal.

Bill Kurtis
https://www.independent.org/aboutus/person_detail.asp?id=1121

Husband and Wife
https://i2.wp.com/michelduchaine.com/wp-content/uploads/2014/04/
felipe_daquino_greets_iva_on_day_of_her_release_from_sagumo.jpg

Fred Korematsu
https://www.kgou.org/post/
korematsu-v-united-states-decided-foundation-fraud

Major Cousins
http://www.psywarrior.com/TokyoRose.html

President Ford Pardon's Iva
https://en.m.wikipedia.org/wiki/Gerald_Ford

blication by Readers'
shall be turned over to

(sgd) Iva
Signed __Ikuko Toguri (Tokyo Rose)

Signed (sgd) Harry T. Brundidge

The Infamous Contract

Walter Winchell
https://www.britannica.com/biography/Walter-Winchell

Chapter 22

FRED KOREMATSU

Far too Close

TOM HAYAKAWA WAS AT THE podium shuffling his notes and preparing to do his presentation. He had, if he were honest with himself, mixed feelings about his topic. On one side of the ledger, things seemed to be working out for the subject of the class' research, Iva Toguri. But the ledger had two sides. On the other side, the woman, who had been accused of being Tokyo Rose, had gone through a lot, and since he, Tom Hayakawa, was a Japanese-American, she was family, at least an ethnic-ally and culturally. They were tied together by an invisible bond of history and shared pain. What had happened to her had also happened to him, though in a slightly different context. On an intellectual level, scholarship and a commitment to historicity provided some immunity to the halting feelings of anger and sadness that he experienced when speaking of Iva and those terrible things that his family had experienced. It was, therefore, very difficult for him to remain aloof and distant from what he was about to share with his colleagues. So very difficult…

"All of us," Tom said quietly, "are beginning to understand by now that there was an environment of racism that provided the backdrop to permit and justify the unwarranted legal attacks on Iva. Tonight, I'm going to explore that backdrop as dispassionately as possible, though I must add, not entirely. The racial attitudes and practices Iva encountered, I must say with great sadness, were also experienced by others, including my family. So be forewarned. While we, as journalism students, seek objectivity in our reporting, the sum of what we are always influences our view of the world. It cannot be avoided. I could not avoid it in preparing for tonight. The trick, I believe, is to be aware of this human frailty and to minimize its effect on our analytical approach to discerning the truth. Keeping that in mind, "I'll begin by asking you a question."

"Not too hard a one," Stan Mack said.

"Hard enough," Tom responded.

"Shoot," said Rita Howard. "I'm ready."

"Okay," Tom said with a casual smile, "who was Clyde Sarah?"

"I wasn't ready for that one," Rita said under her breath."

"Sound like the name of a shampoo," Janet Lee added.

"More like the name of a good wine," Philip Aquino broached. "Perhaps a Port."

"I know," Ron Siegel said with his usual confidence.

"Yes," Tom said.

"It's the name of a line of clothing for women, Ron said. "You know, like the "Clyde Sarah bra." Right?"

"Wrong," Tom answered.

"Okay, we give up," Luis Lopez volunteered. "Who is, or was Clyde Sarah?"

"He was a young 21-year old guy who underwent plastic surgery on his eyelids in an unsuccessful attempt to pass as the product of a mixed marriage, half Spanish, half Hawaiian."

"Okay, I'll bite, Rita said. "Why would he do that?"

"He was evading the law," Tom answered.

"The law or a law?" Janet asked.

"Both."

"We're hooked," Stan Mack said, "so tell us."

"Clyde Sarah was born on January 30, 1916. His given name was Fred Toyosaburo Korematsu. He was the third of four sons to Japanese parents who immigrated into the United States in 1905. His family lived in Oakland, California and ran a nursery in nearby San Leandro. He attended public schools and was on the swim and tennis teams at Castlemont High School. He planned to go on to college after graduation. Regretfully, that was not to be his lot. Pearl Harbor ended that dream.

"Immediately following that attack, Korematsu marched down to an Army recruiting station near his home to sign up. His country had been attacked, and he wanted to do his part, as did millions of other young men. But unlike others, he was told, "We have orders not to accept you." Fearful of traitors and sabotage, the Army wanted nothing to do with Nisei. Ingrained in the policy was a history of prejudice and discrimination against Asians that had muddled California's history since the "Gold Rush." For Korematsu, this was not the first time he had experienced the hot sting of bigotry. He had first felt it when his girlfriend confessed that her parents 'felt that people of Japanese descent were inferior and unfit to mix with white people.' Many of her friends couldn't understand how the Japanese could even fly airplanes. "Weren't the Japanese slanted-eyed, many thought? Didn't they have large, buckteeth and silly wide-mouth grins? Didn't they live in paper houses and eat uncooked food?" Of course, the contradiction in thinking was overwhelming. If the Japanese couldn't fly airplanes, how had Pearl Harbor happened?

"A short time later, Korematsu was rejected by the US Navy when he tried to enlist. but this time for a more respectable reason. He had stomach ulcers. In any event, he trained to be a welder in order to help in the war industries springing up in the Bay Area. For a time, he worked at a shipyard. On the day he was fired, he was told that, 'since he was Japanese, he was not allowed to work there among the other men.' He found a new job, but was fired when the boss returned from an extended vacation and found there was a 'Jap' working at his business.

"To be a Japanese-American in 1941 was a curse. Astonishment turned into anger after "December 7th". Defeat in Hawaiian waters turned into rampant discrimination. Already existing racial prejudice turned into government policy.

Prejudicial Policy

"As you already know, shortly after Pearl Harbor and America's forced entry into World War II, President Franklin D. Roosevelt issues very unnecessarily, as events later showed, Executive Order 9066. This federal edict authorized the Secretary of War and his military commanders to require all Japanese-Americans, regardless of their citizenship status to be removed from designated "military areas" and placed in internment camps. For many in California in particular, including my family, the American dream closed shut with that "order." On March 27, 1942, General John L. DeWitt, commander of the Western Defense Area, prohibited Japanese-Americans from leaving the "limits of Area No 1" in preparation for their eventual evacuation to detention camps.

"Fred Korematsu decided to evade evacuation. He was prepared to move to either Nevada or a Midwest state. To do so in safety, he underwent the surgery in question. If he were not considered an Anglo, he, at least, would not be Japanese. His disguise did not last long. On May 3, 1942, General DeWitt ordered Japanese-Americans to report on May 9 to assembly centers as a prelude to being removed to relocation camps. Korematsu refused and went into hiding. Twenty-one days later, he was arrested in San Leandro after being recognized as a 'Jap.' He was placed in a San Francisco jail.

"At this point, I should add that my parents and extended family reported to the assembly points as demanded by the Army. Eventually, my family was sent to the Manzanar Relocation Camp near Lone Pine, California. My older brother and sister were born in the camp. I missed it by a few years. My family was given only a few days really to liquidate their small grocery store, which really meant selling it for almost nothing. Talk about a fire sale. With only a few dollars and their suitcases, they boarded trains that took them to the high desert east of the Sierra Nevada Mountains. They spent almost four years at Manzanar Relocation Center."

"While in jail, Korematsu was visited by the director of the American Civil Liberties Union in northern California. The director was Ernest Besig, who would later be called the "father of American civil liberties.""

Besig wanted to test the legality of the Japanese American internment. To do so, he needed a test case. Korematsu agreed to challenge the constitutionality of the law. He was assigned a civil rights attorney. It was none other than Wayne M. Collins, who had defended Iva Toguri. Korematsu felt that:

> *People should have a fair trial and a chance to defend their loyalty at court in a democratic way, because in this situation, people were placed in imprisonment without any fair trial.*

"On June 12. 1942, Korematsu was given a trial date and his $5,000 bail was paid by Ernest Besig. He was then released. At this point, it appeared that the system was working. However, the moment Korematsu stepped outside of the courtroom, he was again arrested. He was tried and convicted in a federal court on September 8, 1942 for a violation of Public Law No. 503, which criminalized any violation of military orders issued under the authority of Executive Order 9066. He was placed on five years probation. He was taken to the Tanforan Assembly Center, which was an old racetrack just south of San Francisco. From there, he and his family were transported to the Central Utah War Relocation Center in Topaz, Utah. There he was placed in another horse stall with one light bulb. He remarked later of this place," 'jail was better than this.'

"Korematsu paid a price for challenging the government beyond jail time and being forced into a relocation camp. At Topez, many Japanese-Americans didn't want to associate with him fearing that they would also be seen as troublemakers. Many saw him as a threat to their effort to be seen as loyal to America. Things got so bad for him that he was placed in the back of the camp as his own request."

The Court Rules

"Through a number of appeals, his case reached the United States Supreme Court, which rendered a 6-3 decision against him on December 18, 1944. The majority opinion authored by Justice Hugo

Black held that compulsory exclusion, though constitutionally suspect, is justified during circumstances of a military emergency.

"Justice Black continued:

All legal restrictions, which curtail the civil rights of a single racial group are immediately suspect. Courts must subject them to the most rigid scrutiny.

"Black stated that Korematsu had not been discriminated against because of his ethnicity. He did not challenge the military claim that 'Japanese-Americans living on the West Coast constituted a threat to National Security.'

"A majority of the Court found that the military necessity justified the exclusion order. They agreed with Black that Korematsu was not excluded from the Military Area because of hostility to him or his race. He was excluded because we were at war with the Japanese Empire, because the properly constituted military authorities feared an invasion of the West Coast and felt constrained to take proper security measures, because they decided that the military urgency of the situation demanded that all citizens of Japanese ancestry be segregated from the West Coast temporarily, and, finally, because Congress, reposing its confidence in this time of war in our military leaders, as inevitably it must, determined that they should have the power to justify this."

"Crazy," Janet Lee said angrily, adding "what about Germans and Italians?"

"And what about the Japanese-Americans living in Hawaii?" asked Luis Lopez. "I understand they were not placed in camps. Is that true?"

"I believe so," Tom said.

"That's nuts," Philip Aquino said. "If they're a threat in California, why weren't they a threat in Hawaii?"

"I agree," Stan Mack voiced. "Even more of a threat, I would think since Hawaii is a lot closer to Japan than the Bay Area."

"It was out and out racism," Rita Howard said. "No way you can get by that. From what I understand, the war merely gave a lot of people the opportunity to acquire land and businesses owned by the Japanese. No more Japanese, no more competition."

"I assume there were dissenting opinions," Robert Samuels said quietly. "This might be a good time to share them, Tom."

"There were and I will. But first… I find the whole episode ugly, a stain upon our history and the rationale behind the treatment of Iva Toguri and my family. I just wanted that on the record. Because of that, I am more than predisposed to accept the views offered by dissenting judges."

"Acknowledged and recorded," Samuels said. "Now, as to the minority view, what was it?"

"Justice Frank Murphy provided a vehement dissent. The Supreme Court Justice stated, that the exclusion of the Japanese falls into the abyss of racism.' Continuing, he pointed out that this nation was fighting the racial policies of Nazi Germany, a government and policy that we had pledged to destroy. He pointed out the differences in the way Japanese-Americans were treated in comparison to people of Italian or German ancestry. He concluded that this was 'evidence of racial prejudice, rather than an emergency alone' that led to the exclusion order which Korematsu was of convicted of violating.

"In a passionate closing paragraph, Justice Murphy said:

> *I dissent, therefore, from this legalization of racism. Racial discrimination in any form and in any degree has no justifiable part whatever in our democratic way of life. It is unattractive in any setting, but it is utterly revolting among a free people who have embraced the principles set forth in the Constitution of the United States.*

"He ended by arguing eloquently for fairness. All Americans, he said, are "entitled to all the rights and freedoms guaranteed by the Constitution."

"Justice Robert Jackson spelled out his dissent in a straightforward fashion. First, Fred Korematsu was born in the U.S, therefore, the Constitution makes him a citizen by nativity.

Second, no claim has been made that he was disloyal to this country.

Third, except for the matter before the Court, no suggestion has been made that he is anything but law-abiding.

Fourth, he has been convicted of act not commonly considered a crime.

Fifth, he has been convicted of being present in the state whereof he is a citizen, near the place where he was born, and where he has spent most of his life.

Sixth, the military orders that made his actions a crime forbade him to remain and forbade him from leaving the area noted.

Seventh, the only way he could "avoid committing a crime was to surrender himself to the military authorities."

Eighth, that meant submission to custody, examination, and transportation out of the territory.

Ninth, to do so meant that he would be confined in detention camps.

Tenth, the only difference between his treatment and that of German or Italian-Americans was that he was born of a different 'racial stock.'

Eleventh, in this sense guilt was made personal and inheritable since he was born to Japanese parents as to whom he had no choice, and belonged to a race from which there is no way to resign.

"Justice Jackson ended his dissent by pointing out the danger of excess military policy during a crisis. We should all consider his words carefully in light of what happened to Fred Korematsu and Iva Toguri.

The existence of a military power resting on force, so vagrant, so centralized, so necessarily heedless of the individual, is an inherent threat to liberty.

By the time Tom Hayakawa finished, class time was almost over. Though he would have enjoyed discussing the Korematsu Case further, Samuels was tired, as were his students. It was time to call it an evening. Going against his own best interests, Samuels said, "If there are no questions, we'll call it a night."

"One question," Rita Howard said.

"Yes, Rita?"

"What happened to Korematsu after the war?"

"Tom, do you want to answer the question?"

"After his release from camp, he moved eastward to Salt Lake City, Utah. There he ran into lingering racism. He found a job repairing water tanks in Salt Lake City. In time, he discovered he was only being paid half as much as white workers. He demanded to be paid the same.

Rather than paying his fair wage, his boss threatened to call the police and have him arrested for being Japanese. He was forced to quit his job, and, this time he moved to Detroit, where his younger brother lived. He worked in Detroit as a draftsman. In Detroit, he met a Caucasian woman and was married in 1947, where mixed marriages were legal at the time. Later he moved backed to Oakland where he resides today."

"That's it?" Janet Lee asked.

"There is one more thing," Tom said.

"What's that?" asked Ron Siegel.

"He's still waiting for judicial review of his case. Like Iva and my family, he wants redemption. He wants his conviction overturned. He wants the injustices of the past ended."

Chapter 23

INJUSTICE CHALLENGED

Graduation

LATE JUNE CAME TO SAN Francisco and with it the annual influx of tourists from all over the world. The port city still had its admirers. The onset of summer also saw the semester end at San Francisco State, and with it, Robert Samuels' journalism class. For him, the end was bitter sweet. He had never enjoyed a class so much. Final course grades were given, along with very personal letters of recommendation for each student. His students had been the best crop ever of eager, young people preparing for jobs in the profession. As befitting the moment, a class party was held at a local pizza place where toasts were made to thank Samuels for a great course. Attempts at speechmaking increased in direct proportion to the beer consumed. Some of them actually pushed a subject against a verb and made sense to the listeners. Finally, a present was given to Samuels. a beautiful bracelet with an engraving: *"Let the Truth Reign."* Samuels was pleased with the gift and quickly put it on to the applause of his students. Moments later the waitress appeared with a cake, which she placed on the table. The cake's history was short and memorable. Rita Howard had smuggled it into the *Pizza Joint* prior to the gathering, white cake filled with raspberry filling and icy, vanilla frosting coating its surface. It was a swell party, one that Samuels would always remember.

As a group, they made a commitment to attend the final School Board meeting, which would announce the name for School Site 1776.

If permitted, they would speak out in favor of Iva. Prior to that, they would send summaries of their research to the White House in order to support Iva Toguri's bid for a pardon. To a person, they felt an inner satisfaction in supporting an underdog's effort to right the world. It was the happiest moment in their young lives. Though the semester might be over, their interest in the story continued unabated. Out of respect for their diligent work and with the agreement of his editors, these summaries, at Samuels' insistence, would also be printed in the *Chronicle*. His students, overjoyed with the prospect, finally had a byline.

Late June also coincided with a tough decision for Samuels. Though very much enticed by Jonas Morgan's offer, Samuels made the decision to remain a full-time reporter at the *Chronicle*. He would teach one class per semester, but not more. Though Morgan fired one volley after another, Samuels steered clear of becoming a full-time teacher at State. Naturally, Morgan's finally words on the subject still rang in his ears. "You are being bloody difficult, Samuels, but don't worry, I'll have my harpoon out for you next year. You can bloody well believe that." Samuels did.

As to Samuels' series on Iva Toguri, the last article on her was written. It had opened:

> *I believe that Iva Toguri deserves redemption. She did not violate any law, nor did she transgress against the people of the United States. Her over eight years in prisons more than atoned for any sins suggested by her critics. It is time, I think, to absolve her of the charge of traitor. It is time to clear her name and to restore her citizenship.*

Iva, Samuels had continued, now lived a quiet life since her release from jail and the two-year struggle to avoid deportation. She lived in Chicago and helped with the family business. She keeps a low profile and shuns publicity. Until very recently, she avoided the media like a plague. Who can blame her? After her experiences with Harry Brundidge and Clark Lee, and the hammering she took from Walter Winchell, she saw reporters as dangerous and treacherous. Still, she was determined to recover her lost citizenship, which she had fought so hard to keep while stranded in Japan. Thankfully, she was no longer fighting alone. She had allies. Paradoxically, a new generation of reporters is leading the charge to expiate the charges against her. Three media-types emerged, Samuels explained, who feel Iva was wronged.

BILL KURTIS

"I first met Kurtis in the 1961 when he was a news anchor for WBBM TV in Chicago. I watched his ascension in the media world. Today Kurtis hosts the A&E show, *Investigative Reports*. While in Chicago, as Kurtis told me, he became interested in the story of Tokyo Rose and Iva's relationship to the myth. After a cursory review of her case, Kurtis took a keen interest in Iva. He made a number of efforts to interview her. Initially, she rebuffed all of them. Again, who could, of course, blame her? She was frightened that her words would be twisted and distorted as they had in the past by reporters. She was--- with good reason --- incredibly wary of media attention. Yet, she wanted to clear her name. She needed the media on her side to do that. In time, she came to trust Kurtis and finally granted an interview.

"The interview took place on November 4, 1969, almost seven years ago. His interview entitled, *The Story of Tokyo Rose*, was a thirty-minute documentary featuring a long interview with Iva. CBS broadcasted the show. This was the first time that Iva had an opportunity to tell her side of the story as it happened. For the first time, she was able to explain what happened without attorneys and reporters misrepresenting what she said. At the time, many found the show interesting, but not necessarily convincing in terms of overturning her conviction and loss of citizenship. Kurtis, however, was enchanted by Iva and said this about her:

> *I was struck by the epic spectacles of her life, being labeled one of the most infamous enemies in the Pacific Theater of World War II, yet believing that she was innocent, indeed a patriot in the grandest sense. As I immersed myself in her life and the story, I came to believe that she was not only innocent but one of the strongest people I had ever met.*

"Kurtis was the first media person to actually hear her whole story and he came to sympathize with her position. The inevitable conclusion he reached after his interview was that:

> *Iva Toguri had been imprisoned and stripped of her citizenship largely by certain members of the media.*

RON YATES

"Ron Yates was a colleague in the newspaper business. We had met at various conferences and even worked some of the same stories, most recently the Watergate Scandal, which destroyed Richard Nixon's presidency. At the time, he was the working for the *Chicago Tribune*. In the "Windy City," he picked up Iva's story. In reviewing the records available, he found the prosecution's case very shallow.

In the aftermath of his review of the case, he wrote:

> *The evidence and the trial itself didn't seem to be done in the right way. If you take it out of the context of the time, three years after the war, 1948, there was a lot of hatred toward the Japanese. A lot of people had lost sons and fathers. You could kind of get some sense about why she was being persecuted. But even so, even when you allow for the temper of the time, there seemed to be something wrong.*

Yates decided to find out what was really behind her conviction. A transfer to the Bureau Office in Tokyo, where he was the Bureau Chief, provided him with that opportunity.

In time, Yates came to know many of the people who had worked with Iva at Radio Tokyo. In particular, he met Kenkichi Oki and George Mitsushio, two Japanese-Americans who were her superiors during the war and privy to the wartime broadcasts. Their testimony was largely responsible for Iva's conviction. After developing a relationship with them, the two men shared a shocking confession. As Yates later wrote about the meeting in mid 1976, the following interview took place with the two men over drinks at a local Tokyo bar.

"Did you work with Iva Toguri on the Zero Hour?" Yates asked.
The two men nodded almost in unison.

"What's the real story behind Iva Toguri?"

"What do you mean?" Oki responded.

"I mean, the evidence against her seems to be flimsy, so contrived,"
I said.

Oki and Mitushio looked at one another and for an instant a mutual,
unspoken covenant was established between them. They would finally
tell the truth.

Oki cleared his throat "She didn't do anything wrong," he said. He
looked at Mitushio, who nodded and said,

"That's right, Iva is innocent."

Yates, as he admitted in retelling the story, was shocked at what
he was hearing. This was new information by two men who were
Iva's contemporaries. For the first time, they were sharing long hidden
secrets. Yates continued:

"I'm not sure I understand," I said. "It was your testimony that
convicted her, wasn't it?"

"That's right," Oki said. "But we didn't exactly tell the truth."

"You mean you lied, perjured yourselves?"

Following a long silence, Mitsushio spoke. "We had to do it," he
said. "We were told by the occupation police and the FBI that if we
didn't cooperate, Uncle Sam might arrange a trial for us too."

Right then and there, Yates wrote, the two men most responsible for
Iva Toguri being convicted of treason admitted that they had committed
perjury. They went on to explain that they had been coached by the
FBI and the Department of Justice, that they had been told what to say,
that they had heard Iva make a treasonable broadcast, and that they had
heard her allude to the infamous line about the "loss of ships."

The two men had lied at the trial when they claimed she made a
treasonous broadcast after the US Naval victory in the Leyte Gulf of
the Philippines in October 1944. Through tears of guilt and shame,
they finally admitted that Toguri had done nothing treasonous. Of
course, the question that kept Yates' attention riveted on the two men
concerned, "How could they do this to this woman who hadn't done
anything wrong?" But looking back at the times, "these two men were

terrified of the FBI and the CIC." The irony of the situation was not lost on Yates. Two Niesi, California-born Japanese-Americans, pressured by American officials, had destroyed the life of a fellow citizen in order to protect their own skins.

Oki's final words totally cleared Iva:

> *She never said those words... I can say that now," Oki told me. "Iva never said anything like that. She never did anything wrong. She never uttered a treasonous word, not once. Heck, she wouldn't even work on Sundays or on American holiday.*

Yates had a story. He knew that the FBI and the Justice Department would spin whatever he wrote so as to deflect any involvement with perjury as it related to Iva's case. He knew the myth of Tokyo Rose, still powerful in the minds of many, would challenge whatever he wrote. Still, he decided to write what he knew. His story appeared in the *Chicago Tribune* and was picked up by over 500 newspapers worldwide, as well as the leading wire services at about the time Samuels' class ended. The case against Iva was finally beginning to unravel. Not long after his story was published, Yates received a phone call from the Ford White House seeking more information about the two men and their confession. Yates complied.

In summing up his story, Yates wrote:

> *It's a wonderful story. A beautiful story... It's a love story with everything you could possibly want. It has survival, an indomitable spirit; a woman who was born on the 4th of July, and who graduated from UCLA with everything in front of her. She does her duty and gets caught up in World War II like a whole lot of other people did and winds up suffering the rest of her life.*

Yates later admitted he had to write the story. "Poor Iva," he wrote, "she's getting old. This story is never going to get told until I tell it myself. I've got files on her, files and files, from when we have talked. It's just a shame. It (the story) ought to be put together."

Yates also reflected on his own efforts:

I feel especially gratified that I played some part in righting the wrong done to Iva because it was journalists who got her into trouble in the first place. And after so many years, it was a few journalists who finally did the right thing for Iva.

MORLEY SAFER

On June 24, 1976 just two weeks before the San Francisco Board of Education would meet to decide on a name for School Site 1776, the television news show, *60-Minutes*, aired a broadcast based on the work of Yates and Kurtis, plus the staff of the show. Morley Safer, one of the show's personalities, moderated the segment. It began with an interview with George Guysi.

Guysi was the counter–intelligence officer in charge of investigating Iva shortly after the war ended. He determined that Iva had done nothing wrong. He found that in fact she had been wronged herself. This was in 1948. "It would be accurate to state that the United States government abandoned her in Japan," Guysi told *60-Minutes*:

She was picked out by Major Cousens when he was told to create a disc jockey program. The next thing that happened to her was the Radio Tokyo personnel coming down to her, and telling her to go down and read a script and be auditioned. She wasn't asked if she wanted to do it. She was told to do it. And she did.

Based on his investigation, Guysi told *60-Minutes*, after an exhaustive review of Iva's actions, the CIC came up with nothing against her. As Guysi stated:

There was no evidence, and subject denies, that she ever referred to herself, or was referred to, on the Zero Hour program, as Tokyo Rose. There is no evidence that she ever broadcast greeting to units by name and location, or predicted military

> *movements or attacks indicating access to secret military*
> *information and plans, as the Tokyo Rose of rumor and legend*
> *is said to have done.*

Also interviewed was John Mann, the foreman in the San Francisco trial. He stated, He always thought Iva was innocent, but he had given into the pressure of the other jurors and the judge by voting guilty on one count of conviction." He described his vote as the "worst thing" he had ever done on a jury.

The *60-Minutes Show* was seen by millions, including Robert Samuels' students, the San Francisco School Board, and officials at the White House. The past, it seemed, was no longer dragging its feet. "Let the Truth Reign" was now more than an inscription on Samuels' bracelet."

Chapter 24   THE DREAM

The Night Before the Board Meeting

ROBERT SAMUELS WENT TO SLEEP convinced that Iva would get a fair hearing the next day. Usually a quick-to-sleep guy, Samuels tossed and turned. It was as if he were sleeping on pins and needles with halftime collegiate bands marching through his mind, percussion instruments banging away and trumpets blaring. Then, exhausted by the frantic football festivities, he finally fell into an uncomfortable sleep, and began to dream.

Samuels was in a large, vacant room, dimly lit. His gaze fell upon a loathsome, snake-like creature sitting in the shadows. He recognized Harry Brundidge, the rotten, reptilian reporter who had made Iva's life so painful.

"Mr. Samuels, we meet at long last. I'd extend my hand as a token of peace, but I'm quite convinced you'd bite it off."

"All the way to the elbow."

"And, if you did so, what would you gain?"

"The sweet sound of you screaming."

"You do want a pound of flesh. Well, before you start chewing, perhaps you should hear my side of the story. Another chair awaits you."

Listen to Brundidge's side of the story, Samuels thought, would be like asking the Fuhrer to justify the death camps. Still, he sat down.

"I'm listening."

"I gained a bit of notoriety covering the war for *Cosmopolitan*

Magazine. With MacArthur's gang, I landed in Japan with other reporters. All of us were looking for a scoop. You know, the story that makes a career. This was my big chance. I needed an interview with the Emperor. Not possible. Okay, what about the Prime Minister, Tojo? I couldn't get near him. By default, that left Tokyo Rose. I bet the house on her. I needed an interview."

"There's a difference between a scoop and scurrilous reporting. You knew Iva wasn't Tokyo Rose."

"Sure. But so what? She signed the interview contract and grabbed the two grand with two greedy hands. She signed a confession. No one held a gun to her head."

"You manipulated her."

"Oh?"

"You promised her celebrity status at home, royalty rights from books, possibly even a movie."

"I implied. I didn't promise."

"She bought your line."

"She wasn't as shy and demure as she seems now, Samuels."

"You lied to her."

"The FBI and the Justice Department didn't see it that way."

"Not after the vitriolic stuff you wrote."

"A little hype."

"You bastard."

"Sticks and stones… What's the matter with you? Iva broadcasted propaganda on Radio Tokyo. She was no angel."

"She was forced."

"A matter of debate, Mr. Pulitzer Prize winner."

This wasn't going well. Samuels understood that. A few more minutes with Brundidge and he's kill the SOB. A different tact was needed.

"Why did you do it, Harry?"

"Iva was a Jap. She worked for the wrong side and lost."

"Harry, why?"

"I needed the story and she cooperated with the Japs."

"She never really admitted to being Tokyo Rose. You know that.

She was desperate to get home to see her family. She had just lost a child. She had spent four years living under the threat of death."

"The guys on Iwo Jima and Okinawa wanted to go home too. Iva didn't own the market on desperation. They had families. They had homes. They had memories."

Samuels rose from his chair and advanced on Brundidge who seemed to sink into himself, but didn't back off.

"Going to beat my brains out, Samuels?"

"Don't push it."

"I'm not the one with tight fists."

"Brundidge, you knew people were committing perjury at the San Francisco trial, lying through their teeth."

"What did you want me to do, Mr. High and Mighty? Tell the truth?"

"Yes."

"You're so naïve. The FBI and the Military Police wanted information. The word was passed to the Nisei who worked at Radio Tokyo. Cooperate or find yourself in hot water with the military police. They cooperated to protect themselves."

"You could have blown the whistle."

"I wasn't about to take on the Feds. I was no hero."

"You wanted the story, no matter what."

"I never said I was an angel."

"But even after Iva went to jail, you kept after her, always attacking her. When she was released from Alderson Prison, you pushed for deportation. You fought any effort to permit her husband to come to the US. You never let go. Why?"

"How could I stop? She wouldn't. She kept pleading her innocence. That damn attorney from the ACLA, Mortimer Collins, kept filing petitions and appeals. They wouldn't stop."

"She was trying to restore her name. She wanted to regain her citizenship."

"And what about me? Samuels, she wanted the public to see what I wrote as a pack of lies."

"Which is what you did/"

"Open to debate. Did I load the dice? Yeah, not as much as you might think… Did I shuffle the cards to give myself a good hand, of course, but only enough to get Iva interested."

"You perjured yourself."

"Not true, I never testified against her. You know that."

"That's because the government wouldn't let you testify for the defense."

"That's because the Justice Department had two Nisei Nips testifying under oat. They didn't need me."

"You feel no remorse, Harry?"

"None at all."

"How can you be so callous?"

For a moment it was quiet, then the dam burst.

"How can you pretend to be so innocent, Samuels? The county wanted a scapegoat. Blame me if you wish, but don't forget the millions who read my stuff, or what Walter Winchell wrote. I wasn't in this alone. I bet you even thought she was a traitor in '45. I didn't begin the vendetta against Iva. That began with the Jap atrocities in the Pacific."

"You still knew the truth."

"Here's the truth. Postwar America remembered Pearl Harbor, the Death March, the Marines dying in the jungles. There's no meatball on my backside, no 'rising sun.' You want to take a swing at me, go ahead. But remember, you were no hero during Iva's trial. I don't remember you demonstrating on her behalf in front of the Courthouse. No, you came along years later when it was safer, when you could be a big hero, a knight in white armor protecting a poor misjudged princess. When the public wanted blood, you were AWOL. Some hero. You watched Iva go down the judicial drain without even a whimper. You're a fraud, Samuels."

Brundidge's indictment stuck in Samuel's throat. The dastardly reporter raised uncomfortable questions. No getting away from that.

"Time for me to depart, Samuels."

It was over. Samuels understood that. Brundidge was convinced he acted in the best interests of America. Iva was a traitor in his mind and deserved her punishment. She conspired with the enemy. He was beyond either self-introspection or self-incrimination.

"Still want to smack me. Well, get on with it while you have a chance. I'm ready to take the Southern Pacific Express."

It was no good. Brundidge would never be hauled up in front of his peers to be judged for his actions. He would escape any verdict of condemnation. Almost as much as his actions themselves, this realization disturbed Samuels.

"Thinking it over, Samuels?"

"You brought distain to our profession, Harry."

"You never crossed the line? Everything you penned for the *Chronicle* met the highest ethical standards? Everything? Virtue clung to every story you submitted?"

"Harry, go."

"I am. Don't invite me again."

A few moments later, Samuels woke up, his body in a sweat, his mind whirling with troubling questions. He couldn't get back to sleep. Giving in to the inevitable, he went into the kitchen to brew a cup of coffee. Tomorrow would be a long day.

Chapter 25

THE BOARD MEETING

Democracy at Work

PURSUANT TO ESTABLISHED PRACTICE, THE meeting of the San Francisco School Board was scheduled three weeks in advance in order to alert all interested parties as to the date and major focus of the meeting. The 7:00 p.m. meeting was scheduled for Tuesday, June 3, 1976. All those who wished to speak before the Board had to register at least three days in advance. Understandably, there was no dearth of potential speakers, given the topic under discussion, the naming of School Site 1776. One of the least known names on the speaker's list was a W.M. Collins, Attorney at Law. Given the community interest in the topic, the Board agreed to move to a larger room in the 555 Franklin Building, which housed the San Francisco Department of Education. Seating was doubled, than tripled by moving into Room 100, which was really a small auditorium that held, if squeezed a bit, 1500 people. Attention was also paid to having additional school police and SFPD officers present in make sure things didn't get out of hand.

Absolutely clear skies and a giant pumpkin-like moon greeted people as they filed into the Room SF-100. The Board, already present with aides, sat at desks on a riser, which gave its members a clear view of the crowd. Microphones were hooked up to each member in addition to two stand-up mikes, which would be used by speakers. These were placed on either side of the auditorium, where coincidently law enforcement personnel were strategically placed. The agenda for the meeting had been printed and was distributed to all who entered the room.

Acting on established guidelines, the Board's current President would gavel the meeting into order and moderate the evening's expected heated debate and discussion. The current leader of the Board, as only historical irony would have it, was Thomas Williams.

From his perch on the riser, Williams took in all before him. He swiveled his head slightly to the left and right to glance at his colleagues. They were all, as he expected, present and accounted for this particular gathering. No one was playing hooky tonight to catch a Giant game.

Mrs. Ruth Franklin-Cohen sat furthest from him on the left, dressed warmly for the evening with her trademark red woolen scarf around her neck. Next to her was the erect figure of Reverend Harrison Fork, his baldhead shining in the glow of the room's lights. As always, his white collar, heavily starched, stood out against his otherwise severe black suit. On his right hand was a large class ring from Moorhead College in Atlanta. It, too, sparkled in the light. The Reverend knew his people liked to see the ring.

Seated by Fork was Matthew Nogata in a light brown sport coat that contrasted nicely with his dark-colored trousers and tie of an equal hue. He looked like a businessman doing the business of his Japanese community. Tonight, however, the usually very calm Nogata seemed a tad nervous. To his right, Williams saw Mrs. Lucy Patrissi. As always, she was nicely dressed, very fashionably in a kind of lacy black dress with a light jacket. It must be the Italian in her, thought Williams. At Board meetings Lucy always looked like she was prepared to step out into a star-lit night in Naples.

Past her, Williams spied George Luna. As usual, his dress for Board meetings was a little over the top in an attempt to tap into his community's culture. A colorful, western-style shirt under a leather jacket covered his torso. Below, a pair of Levis and shining black boots held the rest of him together. He wore no tie. He had placed his cowboy hat at off to one side, but clearly where all could see it. George really knew how to work his constituency. Furthest from him on the right was Larry Chin, who wore his usual conservative gray suit with a black tie against his white shirt. Larry, Williams knew, had other more flamboyant clothes, but not for Board meetings. Larry's Chinese community liked him to fit quietly into the background rather than to dominate it.

As for Williams, he was dressed in a newly bought blue suit from the *Emporium*. A red power tie and a white shirt all but shouted the American flag and patriotism. One half expected an eagle to fly unfettered from his attire. Attached to his lapel he had pinned a small American flag for the TV close-up shots that would inevitably come. After all, he was President of the Board. Certainly, no fashion critic could criticize Williams for being too flashy. On the other hand, the right-of-center folks he represented were not against a little dignified chauvinism.

Looking out at the gathering audience, Williams saw Michael Simms in his wheelchair near a microphone. Seated next to him on an aisle a seat was Scott Foster, the young CAL student he had hired to help the Warrior around, first at State, then at School Site 1776. Williams was surprised that the police had not contacted Scott about either incident, especially after the Board President learned that a newly installed camera at 1776 had filmed the white van and its occupants. The absence of any police inquiry seemed to go along with the Board's vote support of the Superintendent's desire to avoid filing charges against the Warrior. Perhaps there was another shoe, Williams wondered, that might fall after tonight's events. Be that as it may, the Man and the Warrior would make one last effort to scuttle any attempt to name the school after Iva Toguri.

Off to his left in the front row was Superintendent, Andy Anderson, and the new principal of School Site 1776, Rachel Samuels. They were huddled closely and speaking softly. Sitting directly behind them were three students, who Williams didn't recognize.

"Rachel," Anderson said, "we've got a packed house tonight."

"Anybody who is somebody," Rachel said evenly.

"Lot's of police on hand."

"To protect the Board," Rachel said with a hint of a smirk.

"I guess," Anderson responded with a touch of laughter in his voice.

"Things will be fine," Rachel said, to alleviate her boss' anxiety.

"Good. Hopefully, no surprises."

"At least not nasty ones, Sir."

Williams saw the disagreeable, Robert Samuels, the journalist who had made life very miserable for the Man and the *Warrior* with his string of very supportive articles in the *Chronicle* about Iva Toguri. Samuels had all but anointed her an American hero, and, even absent of a full presidential pardon, an individual to be strongly considered for the new school's name. Samuels was sitting near all but one of his former journalism students, and next to two men. One Williams recognized as Jonas Morgan, the Chair of the Media Center at San Francisco State. The other he didn't know but had made quiet inquires about. Apparently, he was an attorney, Wayne Merrill Collins. The name was vaguely familiar. The three were in a robust talk.

"This harbor certainly has attracted every kind of vessel," Morgan said as he swept one large hand in a half-circle.

"The fleet is in," Samuels said calmly.

"And manned for broadsides," Morgan said.

"Cutlasses and swords sharpened for the Board, I think," Samuels added. "And for any one else crossing their bow."

"Many a ship will be boarded before this night is out, Samuels."

"Lets hope our mates do well in what is sure to be hand-to-hand combat," Samuels said.

"Do you two also talk this way," the young attorney asked. "I feel like I'm sitting with escapees from Blackbeard."

"Talk what way, Mr. Collins?" Morgan said. "Do they make conversation differently in your realm?"

"See. That's what I mean," Collins said.

"Aye," said Samuels, "we navigate according to a different compass. But, we're mighty glad to have you aboard, Sir."

"For a few legal salvos?" Collins asked with a knowing glint in his eyes.

"That's the spirit," Samuels said.

"Are you scoundrels keeping something from me?" Morgan asked.

The truth was that Collins and Samuels were privy to a plan hatched by three allies in a small conspiracy to set history right and, perhaps, to save at least a few souls in the process. For this particular engagement, Morgan was out of the loop.

For the first time Williams noticed Dr. Harold Malone, the VA psychologist who worked with the *Warrior*. Sitting next to him was Mrs. Rose Franklin, the Social Worker whose caseload included Michael Simms. They, too, were huddled closely in conversation.

"Harold, *Operation Restore*... It's on, isn't it?" Mrs. Franklin asked, though she knew the answer.

"Ruth, she's on her way. Try not to be so nervous."

"Young Collins arranged it?"

"He's the only one she truly trusts," Dr. Malone said. "He shared Samuels' articles with her. That seems to have helped, too."

"She lived with his young Collins' family for two years, didn't she?"

"Yes."

"It's too bad the older Collins can't be here tonight, Harold."

"Mortality claims all of us."

"Well, it would have made his day," Mrs. Franklin responded. "and he would have loved to meet the spark behind all of this."

"That gal, Rachel Samuels?"

"None other, Harold. Once we explained our idea, she ran with it."

"Kill two birds with one shot, wasn't that the way she explained it?"

"Save a soul and name a school, that's the way she presented the plan."

"Well, Ruth, we'll see, won't we?"

"Our little conspiracy has to work."

"Young Collins, Samuels, the new principal, and us, conspirators all, God help us," Dr. Malone said woefully.

"Now, who's nervous?" Mrs. Franklin asked. "With a name like *Operation Restore*, how can we fail?"

Of course, Williams couldn't see everyone. In the back of the room was a cluster of *Chronicle* reporters and their boss, AA, Abraham Adams. Irish Mike was there, too. Though not exactly a sporting event, he had wiggled his way to 555 Franklin Street because tonight's Board meeting might be the closest thing to a heavyweight-boxing match in recent years for the good folks of San Francisco. GG and DDD were there, too. Gloria Graham could smell gossipy stuff a mile away and this meeting reeked of it. Dolly "Daisy" Davenport, though into entertainment, expanded her definition of the term enough to encompass the Board antics and crowd demonstrations to waggle an "okay" to be here. OP wouldn't miss it for the world. No matter the outcome, Oliver Pine would stir the pot with an on-the-spot editorial. As for Charles Winston III, CW to his friends, finances always lurked in a shadowy world behind all Board decisions. The financial section of the paper would not be left out of this one.

Harry Greenberg was in the back of the room. He never missed an important Board meeting, especially where future construction plans were discussed or the repair of school buildings and properties was being reviewed. While the company he consulted for didn't get every contract, it got its fair share and then some thanks to his old friend who was now the Board President. While tonight's meeting didn't list anything directly on the agenda concerning his more pedestrian interests, it still behooved him to be present. You never knew how Board meetings might go. One had to hustle in this world. Harry knew how to hustle.

Having fully surveyed the crowd, Board President Thomas Williams raised his gavel and prepared to begin the most important Board meeting of his tenure. It was exactly 7:00 P.M.

At almost that exact moment, Flight 555 from Chicago landed on runway J-122. The big American 747 was half an hour late due to heavier than expected jet winds and three storms over the prairie states. So much turbulence was unusual for this time of the year, almost as if the winds of time were pushing back against the jumbo passenger plane, attempting to stall it from some appointed reckoning. After a rather bumpy landing, the plane cruised nicely to its gate, where the "first class" passengers exited first and went immediately to the baggage claim carrousel. There, of course, airport logistics and individual status collided, and they waited, as did others, for their baggage to appear. Waiting for one passenger in particular was a young man wearing an EVENTS STAFF red jacket.

Chapter 26

CONFRONTATION

Parliamentary Procedures

THE SCHOOL BOARD MEETING WAS in session. So far, Thomas Williams thought, it had proceeded along predictable lines. The minutes of the last meeting had been read and approved. Old business had been dealt with. New business was quickly tackled and all motions put aside for the next scheduled meeting. People in the crowded room didn't want to hear about the pending and revised athletic budget for the district's schools, nor were they concerned about a school bus purchase, or the need to meet still another federal edict alluding to special education programs. No, the citizens gathered here tonight had other things on their minds, as did the overflow folks in an adjacent room, where they could plainly hear but not see what was going on. Though not as good as the real thing, it was better than asking people to leave the premises.

Under new business, Williams announced, "It's time to take up our main task tonight. That is, the Board needs to consider various names for School Site 1776 and then vote. To assist the Board in this important endeavor, members of the community are urged to present their views. A speaker's list has been established for this purpose. Everyone in the audience is reminded that appropriate decorum will be appreciated and necessary in order for us to conduct our business. Unruly outbursts and profanity will not be tolerated. If necessary, the police officers present will remove those who cannot abide by these requirements."

The speakers spoke one at a time, providing first their name and place of residence. As is true of any public forum, the views shared spread across the entire spectrum of possibilities. One obviously leftist-leaning Marxist wearing a worn Lenin-type cap and sporting a goatee reminiscent of the Bolshevik leader, argued for naming the school "Commune #1." Scrub one possibility thought Williams. A rather prim older woman wearing a hat and gloves and a flowing, almost floor-length dress, suggested the school be named after the California state flower, the *Golden Poppy.* "Poppy High," she said, "had a nice ring to it." The younger set in the audience gave her an enthusiastic applause. Between these speakers, it seemed, the creative mind of humanity was hard at work. "Alcatraz High" one speaker noted would take advantage of the island tourist attraction. Remembering their own school experience, many older folks felt the name had a certain ring to it, if not truthfulness. "Zoo High" had one supporter and a few laughs from the crowd, as did the nomination for "Earthquake Central High." And so it went until it was time for the *Warrior* to speak.

Michael Simms was dressed appropriately for the meetings, a heavy, dark blue sweater over a white *Arrow* dress shirt and light blue slacks bundled and tied just below the knees. He was groomed for the occasion. A three-day beard was gone, and a recent haircut provided a clean-cut look. Across Simms' lap was a small quilt depicting the American flag in its full glory. The young CAL student, Scott Foster, lowered the microphone to assist his charge.

Michael Simms

"My name is Michael Simms. I live at 150 Howard Street. I am here tonight to speak against naming the school after Iva Toguri, one of the names being considered by the Board."

Simms spoke quietly and calmly, as he had been advised to do so by the Man. This was not a night for outbursts.

"At the onset, I must make a confession," Simms continued. "I posted a very harsh, threatening letter to Mr. Robert Samuels at the *Chronicle* in an attempt to stop him from writing supportive articles about a woman who claimed to be Tokyo Rose. I also spoke to him on the phone. At no time did I ever contemplate harming either Mr. Samuels or anyone. More than most, I know from personal experience the consequences of violence. I was just trying to get his attention in, I admit, a rather absurd way."

Good, thought the Man. He's sticking to the script. It was a nice touch when he lowered his eyes to his legless body as he said "consequences of violence." No one in the audience could help but feel sympathy for the wheelchair-bound man speaking.

"I am also the person who caused the disturbance at San Francisco State College, when I tried to discourage Mr. Samuels' class from continuing their research projects concerning Iva Toguri. I, unfortunately, am also the person who invaded School Site 1776 and had blood poured over myself in the newly constructed Main Office. I was responsible for blood being splattered over all the new and expensive equipment and furniture in the room. I also take responsibility for informing the police and awaiting their arrival chained to a pipe in the office. I also notified *KRON*, particularly Miss Marie Preston, in hopes that my story would be covered by the local news station. Admittedly, this was a rather clumsy way to get attention. However, I was desperate. I wanted people to know how I felt about Iva Toguri. I took the name of 'the *Warrior*' in order to give myself a certain notoriety in the vain hope it would help me gain public attention. I needed the television coverage and a trial in order to make myself heard. As things turned out, I got only limited coverage and no trial."

As he spoke, the large audience was riveted to his words. It was not very often that a handicapped person confessed his misdeeds before his fellow citizens. Intuitively, they knew far more was yet to be said. With their attention focused on Simms, they never saw the back door to the auditorium quietly open and two people slip into the room, a young man and an older woman. From his perch on the riser, however, Thomas Williams did. Inwardly, the shock of recognition tore through his body screaming, "How could this be?" It took all his control to maintain his calm dispassionate bureaucratic demeanor.

"I need to share with you," Simms said, "why I did these things. In 1943, I was just 18-years old. I had joined the Marines a year earlier after lying about my age. I was big for my age and strong. The recruiter, I'm sure, looked the other way. The country was at war. It needed young men, and I wanted to get into the war. I wanted to fight. I wanted to be a Marine. I got my wish. In November 1943, I was on a troop ship plodding through the Pacific to rendezvous with a larger naval task force. I…"

Simms' voice cracked at that moment and his eyes moistened, and after a deep breath he continued.

"I… We listened to the radio the night before the invasion of a piece of rock the generals said we needed to take. The rock was called Tarawa. As I was saying, the night before we were listening to the radio, to Tokyo Rose, to a broadcast from what was called Radio Tokyo. We liked the music and the slapstick comedy, even some of the news, but not the propaganda, which we took with a grain of salt. That night a woman announcer warned us that 4,500 highly trained and prepared Imperial Japanese soldiers were prepared to defend Tarawa to the death. I was barely out of high school. I just laughed at her attempt to frighten us. The battle was supposed to take a day at the most. That's what the planners said. The planners were wrong. It lasted three days, November 20 through the 23rd, 1943. Before it was over with, 950 sailors and Marines were killed. Over 2,100 were wounded. All but a handful of Japanese soldiers survived."

Many in the audience recognized the name Tarawa and recoiled from the memory of newsreel accounts, a bloody horror in the Pacific. Others, younger in their memories, listened intently. They were getting a history lesson.

"I never made it to the beach. I was cut down while wading in over the razor sharp coral reefs surrounding the island. Cut down… A poor choice of words… I was cut in half by machine gun fire. A brave navy medic pulled me ashore, tied two tourniquets, and pumped me full of morphine. I passed out. The next thing I knew I was on a hospital ship off shore, the *USS Mercy*. At least some of me was on the ship. I left my legs on that damn beach."

Tears were flowing down Simms' cheeks as he spoke. Not the tears of an actor playing for the audience's feelings. Not the tears of pretense to manipulate viewers. No. These were real, salty reminders of a 51-year old man recalling the worst day of his youth. No one in the auditorium was immune from what they were hearing. A few *Gold Star* mothers in the audience heard their own sons speaking and remembered their own heartache.

"The doctors did their best to save me, to save most of me, what they could of me, and the psychologists tried to help me to adjust. They all did their best. But it wasn't enough. Every night I relive the attack. Every night I have bullets tear through me. Every night I flounder on the coral reef and taste the salty water and my own blood. And every night I hear that woman's voice, Tokyo Rose, warning me to stay off that island. I came to hate her voice, her name, her warning. She represented all the pain I was going through, all the sleepless nights and pain I'm still going through."

Thomas Williams watched the audience intently. The crowd was bonding with Simms. Things were going as he had planned.

"When I heard that School Site 1776 might be named after Iva Toguri, the Nisei who claimed to be Tokyo Rose, I lost it. How could we name a school after an American who was a traitor? How could we dishonor all those dead and wounded Marines, my buddies who had to listen to her voice before every invasion, including later over 4900 killed at Iwo Jima and more than 16,000 wounded for that stinking piece of sulfur-smelling real estate? How could we ask our children to attend a school named after a woman who had blood on her hands?"

No doubt about it, Williams reflected. Simms' very real life war story and questions were resonating with the audience. He had touched a nerve. Where previous attempts to bring attention to Iva Toguri's treacherous acts had failed, the *Warrior's* words were finally getting through.

"It's true," Simms said, "that no one person was Tokyo Rose. The weight of evidence supports that conclusion. I may have been rash in my actions at the college and the school site, but I'm not stupid. I read Robert Samuels' stuff and grudgingly I must admit that, if there ever was a Tokyo Rose, more than one woman filled the bill. I also, like many of you, saw the *60-Minute Special on Tokyo Rose* and was taken aback by the admission of perjury on the part of her colleagues at Radio Tokyo. Without question, Iva Toguri was not, by herself, Tokyo Rose her own post-war confession to the contrary. But that misses the heart of the matter."

Excellent, reasoned Williams. As planned, Simms was taking a conciliatory stance. No sense badgering a person who now held the sympathy of many.

"Multiple Tokyo Roses," Simms said in a shaky voice, "does not and cannot end Iva Toguri's culpability. Regardless of the heavy pressure put upon her by Japanese authorities, she still worked for Radio Tokyo and involved herself in a show, the *Zero Hour*, which broadcasted propaganda throughout the Pacific Theatre. To our knowledge, she never refused to work for the Japanese. She could have risked it. Yes, she would have put her life on the line. No doubt about that. But that's exactly what the Marines did every time they hit the beach against an entrenched enemy who would not surrender."

Stopping for a moment to let his words sink in, Simms continued. "Our guys didn't have the luxury of saying 'No!' They simply followed orders. Iva Tagouri followed the wrong orders, no matter her rationalizations and justifications. By her own admission, she read what was placed in front of her, whether written by her Australian associate or the Japanese script writers. To that extent, she was and is symbolic of the mythical Tokyo Rose. She cannot escape the verdict of history. Mindful of this, I ask the Board to avoid naming any school after her."

For a moment, there was absolute silence in the auditorium, then a few people applauded, and then a cascade of applause and cheering reverberated throughout the room as those in attendance rose and then broke into a spontaneous rendering of *God Bless America*. In the back of the auditorium an older woman, diminutive in size, also stood, and through her own tears joined in the singing.

For the Man this was a moment of triumph. Certainly, the Board would never go against this crowd. The *Warrior* had finally won.

Other speakers followed Simms, but it was clear, however, that, if the crowd knew what it was against, it had yet to decide what it was for. To that extent, the divided Board, which had reached no consensus prior to the meet, still was split in enough ways to make even the most bored seismographer happy. Only one more speaker remained and then the Board would vote.

Wayne Merrill Collins

"My name is Wayne Merrill Collins. My residence is Sacramento, where I practice law. I am here to speak on behalf of Iva Toguri, not as a proponent to name School Site 1776 after her, but merely to set the historical record straight. To begin with, I lived with Iva Toguri for two years."

Collins' words hung in the air like the incendiary bombs they were meant to be. The tall, young attorney had chosen his words carefully in order to gain the fullest attention of the audience.

"Before you reach the wrong idea about me, please understand that I was a teenager at the time and had no say in the matter."

Bingo! More word-bombs exploding in mid-air.

"My father knew all about my relationship with Iva, as did my mother. They encouraged me to foster it."

Bingo. Double bingo! Triple bingo. Everyone in the audience waited for the next installment in what appeared to be a rather juicy love story.

"My father, Wayne Mortimer Collins, was a civil rights attorney working for the ACLU, the American Civil Liberties Union, and had been the lead defense attorney at Iva's trial in 1949 here in San Francisco. Unfortunately, my father was unable to stop a conviction. Iva Toguri went to jail. Upon her release, my father again fought for her, this time to keep her from being deported to Japan. During the two-year struggle, she lived with my parents, our family, before the Immigration Service finally ended legal proceedings against her."

Most probably the crowd was relieved by this revelation and, if you will, explanation. No Tokyo Rose had seduced an American teen under the very noses of his parents. On the other hand, those who enjoyed the soaps were let down.

"There is much I could say about Iva Toguri with respect to what has been already been said here so eloquently tonight by Mr. Simms. And what I would say might have some weight with you. But I would still be speaking on behalf of her. It would be better, I think, for this woman to speak to you herself. With that in mind, I grant my speaking time to Mrs. Iva Toguri under Section 122, sub-section C of the Board's bylaws that permits me to do so."

You could have heard a pin drop in the auditorium. Collins had dropped the equivalent of an atomic bomb on the unsuspecting audience and the bewildered Board of Education. The Board members quickly huddled and equally fast returned to their seats. Board President Thomas Williams, though not in agreement with his colleagues, spoke for all of them. "The Board grants Mr. Collins' wish. Iva Toguri may speak, if she is present."

"She is, Mr. President," Collins said directly.

Iva Toguri, accompanied by Ron Siegel, walked down the long aisles arm-in-arm to a microphone. There they stopped not ten feet from Michael Simms. Compared to Siegel, a tall young man in the bloom of life, Iva seemed even smaller than she was. She also seemed older than her 60 years. On the basis of physical looks, her appearance did not suggest in any manner the sultry siren of Tokyo Rose mythology.

As they passed Samuels and his former students, Ron Siegel gave his former teacher a quick wink. To himself, Samuels said, well done, son. Two other people watched the procession with anticipation. Dr. Harold Malone squeezed Mrs. Ruth Franklin's hand. As for Rachel Samuels, she simply glowed inwardly. What she had initially thought impossible, the idea to bring Iva to San Francisco had happened thanks to the efforts of many good people.

"My name is Iva Toguri Aquino. I currently live in Chicago, Illinois, where I work in the family store, *Toguri Mercantile,* located near the corner of Clark and Belmont in an industrial section of the city. I work behind the counter helping customers purchase rice crackers and tea, and other grocery items. If necessary, I speak to them in Japanese, a language I learned in Japan during World War II. At the invitation of Mr. Collins and others he represents, I am here tonight with only one purpose in mind. If I can, I hope to appease the pain that has followed Mr. Simms all these years."

Before the crowd could react, and certainly before the Board President could rule her out of order on some technicality, she turned to Michael Simms.

"Mr. Simms, we have each suffered incalculable loss. You, rifle in hand, lost your legs defending America on a lonely beach. I lost my family and freedom defending our country behind a microphone at

Radio Tokyo. Each of us was transformed by Pearl Harbor. For you, the attack required a call to duty. On the opposite end of the world, I was stranded in the heart of the enemy where I, too, answered the call to the extent I could. You challenged the foe from the outside. I did so from the inside. And each of us paid a high price for our willingness to defend America."

The words, almost poetic in nature, rang in the auditorium, a painful reminder of the bond existing between the antagonists before Iva continued.

"You answered America's call during a desperate time against a foe who seemed truly alien to you, and it is understandable that my name and face could only remind you of the past. Simms, an Irish name, and Toguri, obviously Japanese: two names, two cultures, two languages, yet each connected by their undying love of this country, and again we each paid so dearly for this love. If I could, I would give you back your legs. If you could, you would, I believe, give back to me my dead infant child and estranged husband, and my family that was so unfairly forced into a relocation camp during the war, not-to-mention the eight years I spent in jail on the basis of perjured testimony.

"But we cannot undo the past. We are bound together, I think, by a human tragedy. You suffered at the hands of a determined enemy, the Japanese solider. I suffered at the hands of an enemy equally determined to destroy me, our own government. Each of us has had to persevere against all odds in order to survive. Each of us bears the scars of that effort.

"Michael Simms, I ask you to forgive me for the transgressions you attribute to me. I want you to remember me as a person who made mistakes, but never uttered a word against our country. I want you to remember me as a person who never lied to the FBI and the Intelligence people. I always told the truth. I remained loyal to America during the war.

"Michael Simms, you can either sit in a room, as you now do, and feel sorry for yourself or you can go outside and look ahead. I have always tried to look ahead. I've tried to forget the past and live with an eye to the future, trying to make a new life for myself while I forget the old one. I believe in what I did. I tried to sabotage the enemy's propaganda. I have no regrets for doing that. You did what you could. You should have no regrets. I don't hate anyone for what happened. You shouldn't hate anyone either. It's time for us to make peace."

$\backsim$ *Chapter 27* $\backsim$

THE VOTE

Casting Votes

"I BELIEVE IT'S TIME FOR THE Board of Education to vote," Thomas Williams said, "pointing out that the last speaker had certainly made her views known." And indeed Iva Toguri had. Now seated a scant ten chairs from Michael Simms, she, along with all others in the auditorium waited for the Board to vote. In her case, however, it was with a heavy heart. Her thoughts were still on the wounded Michael Simms, not the vote for a school's name. Simms reminded her so much of the POW's she once smuggled food and medicine to under the ever-present eyes of Japanese bayonets. She wondered what was going through his mind.

"Each Board member will nominate and/or vote for a candidate," Williams said. "If so inclined, each member can also explain his or her vote."

Michael Simms heard the words, but now for some reason he could not explain, he felt distant from the impending vote. It wasn't that it had lost meaning. He was still interested in the outcome and certainly he didn't want the stigma of Tokyo Rose attached to School Site 1776. No, it was something else. His avowed enemy had struck at the heart of his distress. It was true. He acknowledged that he was still hanging onto the past. Hate had crept into his mind and taken up residence. And he had been unwilling to evict the toxic homesteader. As she had said, he had been unwilling to move on. He looked over at her and their eyes met.

Thomas Williams now polled the Board.

Mrs. Lucy Patrissi, how do you vote?"

"I vote with great joy for our city's greatest ballplayer, Joe DiMaggio."

"Comments?" Williams asked.

"His achievements on and off the field speak for themselves," she responded with obvious Italian pride."

"Reverend Harrison Fork, how do you vote?"

"My vote is for Martin Luther King, Jr."

"Comment?"

"None necessary, Mr. President. His life speaks for itself, the great speech on the Washington Mall, Letters from a Birmingham Jail, the Civil Rights Act of 1965, and sadly, his untimely death."

"As you said, Reverend, no comment was necessary."

"Mr. Matthew Nogata, how do you vote?"

"More than ever, I submit the name of and vote for Iva Toguri."

"Comment?"

"Unnecessary at this juncture."

"Mr. George Luna, how do you vote?"

"With pride I put forth a favorite son, Cesar Chavez."

"Comment?"

"His story, I think, is well known."

"Mrs. Ruth Franklin-Cohen, how do you vote?"

"I vote for Iva Toguri."

"Comment?"

"We honor America by honoring this faithful, patriotic woman, who, as her father told her, 'never changed her stripes.'"

"Mr. Larry Chin, how do you vote?"

"Initially, I was going to cast my vote for Dr. Sun Yat-sen. I am, however, changing my vote to Iva Toguri."

"Comment?"

"Her story should be known by our school children. Perhaps naming a school after her will do this in some small way."

"As President of the Board, I have decided to abstain at this time. The first vote reads:"

Iva Toguri	3
Martin Luther King, Jr.	1
Cesar Chavez	1
Joe DiMaggio	1
Abstentions	1

Williams was delighted. The Board was deadlocked. No majority candidate had emerged. In time, the three dissenting votes in opposition to Iva would become four, especially if he swung his abstention to the new majority. Things were looking good.

"Since no nominee has the required majority vote," Williams said flatly, "a second vote will be necessary."

"That may not be necessary, Mr. President."

"To whom am I addressing and why not?"

Compromise

To Robert Samuels' everlasting pride, he saw his daughter, Rachel, standing at the microphone ready to alter and reshape history.

"My name is Rachel Samuels. I am the future principal of School Site 1776. I am also the daughter of a reasonably well-known writer for the *Chronicle*, Robert Samuels, with whom many of you are well acquainted. With the concurrence of the School Superintendent Andy Anderson, I wish to place before the Board a realistic compromise, which might just break this ballot stalemate if votes remain unchanged."

Williams, taken aback by this sudden turn of events, was unsure what to do. What might this proposal do to foul up his carefully laid plans? How would the Board react if he ruled her interjection "New Business" and therefore out of order, at least procedurally? And what about the crowd? How would blocking her offer to compromise play with those seated before him? Better, he concluded, to let her speak.

"You say the Superintendent supports this compromise?" Williams asked.

"Indeed, I do," Andy Anderson said, with hardly disguised joy.

"The floor is yours," Miss Samuels."

Rachel glanced around the room taking in first her father, his ex-students, the VA psychologist and social worker she had quickly grown to like, and, of course, Iva Toguri and Michael Simms. Finally, her gaze rested on Wayne Merrill Collins, who nodded slightly in her direction. It had been this legal scholar who had planted the final seed she now hoped to plant and harvest.

"Members of the Board of Education and guests, I have given considerable time and energy to the naming of School Site 1776. Always before me was the specter of possible ethnic and racial discord given the emotions swirling around this issue, if this situation weren't handled appropriately. Keeping this in mind, I consulted with a number of people, including historians, lawyers, politicians, parents, and last of all, a group generally left out of such discussions, the future students of the school. Standing with me today are three students who represent the interim Student Government of School Site 1776.

They have made an interesting recommendation, which I feel deserves the Board's strong consideration. All three are in leadership classes at this time and will transfer to the new school in the fall. All will be seniors next semester. All have outstanding scholastic and citizenship records, including considerable community service projects under their belts. They represent, I think, the best and brightest of our efforts to educate the next generation. Permit me to introduce them."

The three students stepped forth. "The tall redhead," Rachel said, "and a bit of a string bean, but a fine forward on his school's basketball team, is Sean Murray. The young lady next to him is Michelle Lee, an outstanding tennis player with an out-of-the-world grade point average. The last in this cast is my nerdy buddy, who plays a wild chess game, and has already been accepted to MIT, Joel Smith. Take it away students."

The Students Speak

Sean Murray was indeed tall, a gaunt 6 foot 7 inches of youthful energy still growing into his height. He got right down to business.

"Miss Samuels is right. Adults too often forget students in making decisions. The outcome is predictable. Those who are affected by adult priorities and choices have little stake in the final product. That mistake should not be made in naming School Site 1776. To that end, the Board should give every consideration to the name we put forth, which resulted from talking to many future students of School Site 1776. All ethnic and racial groups affected were included in our effort to find out what students thought. A special "thanks" should be given to Miss Samuels who made this possible through her continuous support. Michelle Lee will explain how we arrived at our name for the new school."

"We considered every name before the Board tonight. Without question, they were all worthy nominees, and any school would be proud to be named after any one of them. As in the case of the Board, we were unable to arrive at a name a majority of students would support. However, unlike the Board, we looked at what made each nominee a great candidate. We arrived at one overriding conclusion. All of them believed in freedom.

"For *Dr. Sun Yat-sen*, this meant freedom from foreign imperialism and a callous dynasty that cared little for its subjects. For *Martin Luther King*, freedom meant the end of discrimination and prejudice in order to live in a multiracial, multicultural society where each person was treated fairly under the law. For *Joe DiMaggio* it meant a ballplayer should be paid what he's worth and not blackballed because he demanded a raise. Economic freedom cannot be divorced from personal freedom. *Cesar Chavez* advocated for those working in the fields, tilling our land and harvesting our crops. They deserved no less, he argued, than the man on the assembly line at General Motors or Ford. Fair wages for hard work was his mantra and call to freedom from extortion by unscrupulous large farmers. As to *Iva Toguri*, her story is the story of the struggle for freedom that you now know so well. All of these candidates marched to the great bell of freedom."

Sean Murray gave way to the nerdy kid, Joel Smith.

"In Algebra, we're always looking to solve for X," Joel said in a somewhat tinny voice. We did the same with the problem of naming the new school. What was X? What was the elusive quality that linked all these names? What was the spirit that animated them in their lives? The answer always came back to one element, freedom. It was the *elan vital* of their nature. With this in mind, we hit upon a plan and name. Dissecting the building plans we noticed that there were five major buildings under construction at School Site 1776. This simplified everything. We propose that the new school be named **Freedom High School** and that each of the five major building on campus be named after each one of the nominees."

Turning quickly to Michelle and Sean, Joel said, "The Chart please." On cue, the two students unveiled a large bulletin board, which they carried to the riser where they placed it on a chair for all to see. Printed in large, bold letters was their plan. The *KRON* television cameras zoomed in on the chart.

FREEDOM HIGH SCHOOL

A	Building	English	-	Martin Luther King, Jr.
B	Building	Mathematics	-	Cesar Chavez
C	Building	Social Sciences	-	Iva Toguri
D	Building	Sciences	-	Dr. Sun Yat-sen
E	Building	P.E. Department	-	Joe DiMaggio

"We confess a certain arbitrariness to our choices of names and buildings," Michelle said, "and certainly the Board could make changes if it felt necessary."

The Board President glanced at his colleagues. Each in turn nodded a quiet vote of approval. The students had given them a way out of the political morass that clung to them. They were not about to lose this God-given exit even if provided by babes in arms. Williams picked up on this quickly. He realized it would make no sense going against his colleagues. He could, however, extend the student presentation and possibly eliminate Iva Toguri's name from even one building. It was worth a try.

"Perhaps you would explain," Williams said to the students, "how each name was attached to the departments named."

Rachel Samuels smelled a three-day old fish, and was happy that the students were prepared for this eventuality. "Board President, the students will happily comply with your request."

"Building A will house the English Department," Sean said, "and what better name than Martin Luther King, who attacked prejudice with the English language."

The Mathematics Department will be in B Building. Rightfully, Cesar Chavez added up the pay for agricultural workers," Michelle said, "and compared them to corporate farm profits. She found the numbers favoring one compared to the other. There was an equity question."

"Building C will be the home of the Social Sciences and especially the government classes," Joel said. "Who knows more about both the positive and sinister sides of government than Iva Toguri?"

"Dr. Sun Yat-sen is the perfect name for D Building and the Sciences," Michelle said. "Science, some would argue, began in China and scholars know that the Confucian philosophy incorporates a logic predating the scientific method."

"As for the P.E. Department," Sean said, "that was easy. We think 'Jolting 'Joe' would have loved our new baseball diamond."

The students, their faces glowing, concluded their remarks. They had, they knew, presented their plan well and defended their choices with zeal. They had, they reasoned, made a compelling compromise. Even the reluctant Williams, if asked directly, would have to acknowledge this. Now, however, the students and the audience would have to wait the Board's final decision.

Conciliation

As Williams was about to poll the Board, history, always fickle, once more jostled with human events and turned a simple vote on its head. Moving down the aisle toward the riser was the *Warrior* and pushing Michael Simms' wheelchair was Iva Toguri. Suddenly and dramatically, everyone's attention in the auditorium, it seemed, including *KRON's* electric eye, was focused on this unlikely pair as they approached the Board. They stopped at the riser and nodded to Rachel's three students to join them, which they did. For a moment they spontaneously clutched each other's hands, two generations now tied together by the vagaries of life's unpredictable turns. Then Michael Simms held up his Americana quilt exposing his lifeless legs and, speaking directly to the Board, said, "It's time for your vote. It's also time to move on."

Epilogue

Jimmy Carter won the 1960 presidential election. It was an extraordinarily close race. On January 19, 1977, which was his last day in office, President Gerald Ford accepted the findings of his Attorney-General, Edward Levi and signed a full pardon for Iva Toguri. In receiving this pardon, Iva Toguri became the only person ever convicted of treason against the United States who was pardoned. In receiving her pardon, Iva Toguri's citizenship was restored.

The decision to pardon her was unanimously approved by both houses of the California Legislature, the same political body, which had agreed with the federal government in 1941-42 to forcibly relocate her family outside of the state.

In September 2005, at a luncheon in Chicago, the World War II Veterans Committee presented its *Edward J. Herlihy Citizenship Award* to an 89-years old Japanese-American woman named Iva Toguri. The award was named after a famous broadcaster whose narration of the wartime Universal newsreels won him the nickname, *The Voice of World War II*. The recipient was also a broadcaster who had an even more famous nickname: Tokyo Rose.

In presenting the award the following statement was read:

> *The Edward J. Herlihy Citizenship Award for 2005 is presented to Iva Toguri in recognition of her courage, patriotism, and loyalty to American ideals, who steadfastly maintained them despite enormous costs to herself.*

Iva's acceptance speech was appropriate for the poignant moment:

I know that for so many years, I wanted to honor my father, and my family. They believed in me through all the things that happened to me. I thank all of the World War II veterans and the World War II Veterans Committee for making this the most meaningful day in my life.

Iva Toguri died on September 26, 2006. She was 90-years old.

———————————— ◆◈◆ ————————————

Felipe d'Aquino and Iva divorced in 1980. It was no longer possible to keep their marriage together. She could not leave the United States and he could not enter the country. He died in November 1996, 43-years after his forced separation from Iva. He was 75-years old at the time of his death. Iva never stopped loving him.

———————————— ◆◈◆ ————————————

In 1984, Judge Marilyn Hall Patel overturned Fred Korematsu's original conviction. Her decision was based partially on the research of Professor Jeffrey Irons of the University of California San Diego who unearthed documentation indicating that the FBI had withheld information from the courts proving beyond question that there was no Japanese-American threat on the West Coast and that the relocation camps were unneeded.

In 1998, at the White House, President Bill Clinton honored Fred Korematsu with the Presidential Medal of Freedom, the highest civilian honor any American can ever hope to receive.

Fred Korematsu summed up his experiences with the government, stating:

I'll never forget my government treating me like this. And I really hope that this will never happen to anybody else because of the way they look if they look like the enemy of our country.

Fred Korematsu died on March 30, 2005 at the age of 86.

———————————— ◆◈◆ ————————————

Mildred Sisk-Gillar converted to Catholicism while serving her sentence for treason. Upon release, she went to live at Our Lady of Bethlehem Convent in Columbus, Ohio. She taught German and French at St. Joseph Academy under the auspices of the Church. In 1973 she returned to Ohio Wesleyan University to complete her degree in Speech.

She died on June 25, 1988 at the age of 87.

A modest proposal to create a national monument to Iva Toguri has been made by her friends and family. "It would be in the form of a tableau in the style of Norman Rockwell rendering. On one side, a scene in Studio #3 at Radio Tokyo, circa 1944, Iva sits on the right side of the table, a turntable behind and to the right of her, reading into a microphone. Normando Reyes sits opposite her at a microphone, waiting for his cue. Charles Cousens stand beside and behind her, following along in his script. Ted Ince is visible through the control room window in the background, a Japanese officer listening in on headphones beside him. Armed guards bracket the scene.

On the other side, a group of Marines gather in and around a tent in the jungle, listening to a shortwave radio with obvious good spirits. In the foreground, one Marine gestures as if inviting the visitor to join in. Iva's 14 August 1944 and 20 September 1945 recordings play back from the radio when visitors approach within hearing distance.

The dedication would read:

> To the loyalty and courage of Iva Toguri (d'Aquino) AKA 'Orphan Ann' --- she never changed her stripes!'"

The memorial would be placed at 7th and Mission in San Francisco, the site of the Courthouse in which she was convicted her of treason so long ago.

Two last points are worth noting. First, historians agree that the Tokyo Rose broadcasts did little to diminish American and allied morale in the Pacific Campaign. Quite to the contrary, servicemen enjoyed the recordings of popular American music. In some ways it was all entertainment to them.

Second, a charge of disloyalty has a sinister ring to it. All too often it ruins the reputation of an accused individual regardless of any innocence later proven. The story of Tokyo Rose illustrates this and cautions us in the leveling of this charge.

Printed in the United States
by Baker & Taylor Publisher Services